Marty Waved the Nine-shot and Plinked One Off into the Ceiling...

"Do something!" Zalman's girlfriend Marie shrieked in terror. "He's got a gun!"

"I see he's got a gun, doll!" Zalman said, wondering how the hell he was going to get out of this impossible situation.

Marty rose from his table and ceremoniously cocked his silver sequin top hat at a debonair angle on his head. "Now, everybody dies!" he shrieked as he walked toward the stage. "You're doomed! Doomed!" He stood in the center of the stage in front of Lydia, who was still squirming madly in the ties that bound her. "Now! At last Lydia will be my queen!"

Marty turned and took a final step toward the Princess of Prestidigitation, waving the automatic over his head like a banner of victory, but as he took that one last step toward his helpless victim, there was a sudden whoosh in the air over Zalman's head.

Zalman looked up and saw the monkey come swinging out of the flies above the stage, chattering fiercely like the tiny terror he was. He was still wearing his Tarzan suit. And as he flew through the air he made a tremendous leap...

⊲ S0-DJM-438

Books by Gabrielle Kraft

Bullshot
Screwdriver
Let's Rob Roy

Published by POCKET BOOKS

Let's Rob Roy

Gabrielle Kraft

POCKET BOOKS

New York   London   Toronto   Sydney   Tokyo

An *Original* Publication of POCKET BOOKS

POCKET BOOKS, a division of Simon & Schuster Inc.
1230 Avenue of the Americas, New York, NY 10020

ISBN: 0-671-66940-0

First Pocket Books printing October 1989

10 9 8 7 6 5 4 3 2 1

POCKET and colophon are trademarks of
Simon & Schuster Inc.

Printed in the U.S.A.

JERRY ZALMAN WAS A VERY GRUMPY LAWYER.

First of all, the traffic on the San Diego Freeway North was miserable. Okay, okay, it wasn't as miserable as it was going to get on Monday morning, say, around eight-thirty when ten million hung-over, pissed-off, sweating Angelenos crawled out of their condos, jammed their mirrored sunglasses over their bloodshot eyes, and hit the bricks on their way to work, but it was miserable all the same. Everybody was put-putting along at a mere sixty-five, and Jerry Zalman didn't like it. In front of him, a brand-new red Peterbilt glinting with chrome spit a hot cloud of leaden exhaust in Zalman's face. Next to him, a Bev Hills matron was giving her acrylic claws a coat of Lavender Flash with one hand and steering her beige BMW with the other forearm. Behind him, a covey of silver-studded road warriors tooled along in formation, revving the engines of their gigantic Harleys and sniffing the breeze. Just another Sunday afternoon on the San Diego Freeway. Suddenly, for no reason, traffic squealed to a dead stop. What now? Zalman thought. He stuck his head out the window and saw a big green semi loaded with pink and red Tupperware jackknifed on the Southbound. Tupperware, everywhere.

Zalman sighed, put the Mercedes in neutral, pulled out his cigar case, and decided to relax, maybe do a little deep breathing in hopes of lowering his blood pressure. It hadn't been a swell Sunday—that was the second thing he was grumpy about. Usually, what Jerry Zalman liked to do on a Sunday morning was relax in bed for a while, read the *New York Times*, take a swim, go out for some deli, catch a late-afternoon double feature in Westwood Village. Later, some Chinese food, a stroll through the darkened streets of Beverly Hills holding hands with the adorable Miss Marie Thrasher, and so to bed. Perfection on a stick, Zalman thought, sighing again as his Sunday skittered away from him like crumpled newspaper down Sunset Boulevard at midnight.

Instead, what he'd done was, he got up too early because Marie hadn't packed yet and drove her over to her house in Studio City while she had a panic attack about what she was going to take to her cousin Sally Wishniak's wedding in Eugene, Oregon. No deli, no *New York Times*, no movie, no Chinese food, and definitely no hand-holding.

Then, for an encore, they'd driven hysterically out to LAX, not exactly a paradisiacal garden of Allah. Just what a guy needed on a warm Sunday evening, a swell trip to the airport, a parking space fifty miles away from the terminal, hauling Marie's so-called carry-on bags to three different gates as the airline gleefully altered its schedule to suit some maniacal plans of its own. The worst. Positively.

Zalman didn't like it. He hated the traffic, he hated blowing a Sunday, he hated the airport, and he especially hated hauling heavy bags around gum-encrusted terminals. Besides which, he hated the whole idea of being alone. Alone without Marie. It was the first time Zalman and Marie had been apart since they'd met a few months ago over the dead body of one Sticky Al Hix, a professional lowlife and geek of the first water. And ever since that fatal moment, Zalman, Marie, and Rutherford, Marie's sniveling, drooling, cowardly Doberman, had been an item. Zalman had tried his best to talk her out of the fun-filled trip to Oregon, and even though Marie had tried *her* best to weasel out of it, she'd eventually bowed to family pressure. So, because Marie was a stand-up lady if ever there was one, she was now winging her way north to Oregon and the heaving bosom of the family Wishniak.

And that meant that Zalman and Rutherford, who was sitting next to him on the passenger seat poking his dark, elegant snout out the window, were on their own for a week, and Zalman was grumpy about it.

The car phone rang. Zalman, who was not only a Beverly Hills lawyer but a very successful one, was instantly on the alert. Sunday was always a bad time; most of your big-time, divorce-with-bodily-injury, if-I-ever-see-that-bitch-again-so-help-me-I'll . . . came down on Sunday when the rest of the world was thinking about maybe buzzing out for a pizza, then snapping up their Dr. Denton's and jumping into their trundle beds to watch "Sunday Night at the Movies." For lawyers in Beverly Hills, lots of bad things happened on Sunday evening.

"Hi!" It was Marie.

"Your plane didn't take off," Zalman groaned, wondering how the hell he was going to get off the freeway, then back onto the freeway and out to the airport to collect her anytime before the ball in Times Square ticked 2000.

"It did! It did! But they've got this deal on the plane where you can make phone calls in flight, so I figured, hey, why not call you! I'm up in the air and you're in your car and I thought this was a great chance to be trendy! Huh? What do you think?" she asked expectantly. "I mean, are we or are we not in the fashion forefront? I don't know about you, snooks, but I'm having champagne wishes and caviar dreams right this very second. The call probably costs a fortune, but I couldn't miss the opportunity," she said with a laugh.

Zalman smiled and chucked Rutherford under the chin. If it weren't for the fact that he'd been married twice and at thirty-five he figured he'd like to quit winners, he'd ask Marie to marry him. Ask her again, that is. The fact that she'd already refused to marry him—twice—on the grounds that she didn't feel like screwing up a perfectly good love affair was simply another point in her favor. Other points in her favor included her auburn hair, her adorable face, her cute figure, her smart mouth, and her height. Zalman was five foot four and a half, though he always lied and claimed he was five foot five, and Marie was a good two inches shorter than he was. Once again, perfection on a stick. "Are you sure you want to go to Eugene?" he asked as he rumpled Rutherford's ears. Rutherford began to lick the dashboard of the Mercedes in case there was some leftover Mighty Dog lurking there.

"Well, it's too late now, isn't it?" Marie said with her usual practicality. "Look, Jerry darling, face up to reality. Nobody wants to leave L.A. . . . We all think something earthshaking might happen while we're gone. I mean, imagine the horror if Southwestern cuisine suddenly falls out of favor or somebody imports some snacks from Mars and I'm not there to see it. Tragedy time, yeah? It's like when we were kids and didn't want to go to bed 'cause the folks were having a party and somebody was playing boogie-woogie on the piano and there was laughter and tinkling ice, but you had to stay in your room because you were only eleven and too young to have any fun. See? That's how I feel about leaving L.A. But my favorite cousin, Sally, is getting married, foolish girl, so I gotta be a bridesmaid or whatever the hell it is. I think I have to wear something in lime green tulle," she moaned.

"Thank God I don't have to see it." Zalman laughed, blowing cigar smoke out the window. The sophisticated Angelenos around him were tired of rubbernecking at the jackknifed semi and traffic was picking up again, back to the normal eighty-five, so he pulled out into the fast lane. "But look, babe, it's only gonna be a few lifetimes, right? Trust me, I'll be waiting for you when you get home. Make sure you get plenty of pictures of yourself in the lime green outfit. I bet you'll look just like a Jell-O mold," he added sentimentally.

"Thanks, Jerry," Marie said sarcastically. "Thanks a lot. That's just the sort of loving support I need right now. Saaaay, I've got a knockout idea! Why don't you join me? You can meet my whole family! C'mon, it'll be a real thrill for you, hon! Uncle Lester's going to be there. You know, lots of people think Uncle Lester looks just like Leatherface in *The Texas Chain Saw Massacre,* but to me the resemblance is too minor to mention. But I'd just love to know what you think, Jerry. You know how I value your opinion."

"No thanks," Zalman said, laughing. "I've had plenty of experience with your Dad, and one lunatic in the Thrasher family is enough. Besides, I've got a heavy schedule this week. E. Y. Knotte is coming in, we gotta go over some papers on the restaurants. He's opening a new Shrimpkin Gourmet in Guam. And I've got to look out for your interest in World O' Yip, my sweet; you don't want to go broke, do you?"

"Go ahead, Jerry," Marie giggled, "make me a fortune. I love it. But are you sure you don't want to meet the rest of my family? You'd have oodles of fun. *Ooo*-dles. I pinky swear it."

"I can live without it," Zalman told her, shivering secretly at the thought of meeting any more Thrashers. Captain Arnold Thrasher, Marie's gigantic father, was a cop, and he and Zalman went back a long, long way. All the way back to Zalman's brief days of starry-eyed idealism and political zeal at the tail end of the unlamented sixties. It was a period Zalman didn't like to think about because, in general, the past made him nervous.

Jerry Zalman was a firm believer in maintaining a positive mental attitude. He'd engineered his professional life straight down the middle of the track he'd picked out when he was just a pisher struggling to make it out of law school alive, and though he'd had a few false starts—an abortive episode with the D.A.'s office, a tedious interlude with a square downtown law firm—he'd kept on trucking, and now he had everything he wanted. A great law practice that wasn't boring, a beautiful girlfriend with a crazy sense of humor, nice house, beautifully restored Mercedes, dough . . . It was all a matter of keeping events in perspective, retaining a degree of control even in the midst of complete hysteria, a firm hand on the throttle and your eye on the main chance. Jerry Zalman was a guy who had a purpose, a guy who had a plan for a happy life all worked out, and he intended to stick to it. So, when thoughts of his misbegotten past on the picket line or one of his divorces floated to the surface, Zalman put his foot on the neck of those unpleasant memories and pushed 'em right back down into the swamp. Only recently, he'd had to deal with his ex-wife Tracee. . . . Zalman shivered and shook the memory of those insane few days out of his mind.

"I'll call you when I get there," Marie said. "Looks like the steward is bringing around some hors d'oeuvres. Oh!

Lovely gelatinous bacon wrapped around grapes! What a lucky girl am I! Jerry, you were right—now that I can afford to fly first-class, it's made all the difference in my lifestyle. Kiss ootsie-wootsie Rutherford for me," she said. Marie made wet, slurpy kissing noises and hung up.

Zalman smiled happily to himself, thinking of Marie gnawing away on gelatinous bacon slices, and although he refused to kiss ootsie-wootsie Rutherford, he did rumple the dog's ears a few more times on the long, long trek back to the Hollywood Hills.

Two hours later, Zalman and Rutherford were happily ensconced in Zalman's living room watching TV. Zalman had stopped at Trader Vic's on the way home and picked up some sweet-and-sour ribs for himself and a big plate of steak tartare for Rutherford, and now they were watching *Dead on Arrival*. The original, not the remake.

Zalman looked around and felt a warm, pleasant glow spreading over his entire being at the sight of his gleaming new living room. Thanks to the adorable Miss Thrasher, he'd recently made a large amount of money quite by accident after Marie and his cuckoo ex-wife Tracee sold a Toulouse-Lautrec lithograph of his and invested the proceeds in World O' Yip, a New Age health food emporium in Santa Barbara. World O' Yip was owned by Tracee's husband, a meditate-and-levitate entrepreneur whom Zalman fondly thought of as Yip the Dip.

Since he'd suddenly happened on a big chunk of disposable change, Zalman had decided it was time to update his image. Gone were the oriental rugs and the dark furniture; now it was all pastel, postmodern, and tubular steel, gray carpet, and gleaming silver walls. Plenty of crystal, lots of silver. Zalman liked it. It was cheerful, it was energetic, it was the sort of house that proved a guy was ready to take the plunge into the nineties. It was just the joint a Bev Hills lawyer on the up-o-later ought to have, he mused dreamily as he looked around.

Maybe he wouldn't go in to the office tomorrow. "Maybe we'll just sleep late, whaddaya say, Ruth?" he asked the Doberman. Rutherford rolled over on his side at the sound of his name, burped, and closed his eyes. One thing about Rutherford, Zalman thought, he was a fool for steak tartare. Zalman wiggled his toes and sank into a pleasant Sunday-evening reverie. Maybe he'd zip over to Knobby, his tailor, and get a suit or two. Maybe some shirts. Relax. "Master of all I survey, huh, ootsie-wootsie? Christ." He shook his head. "I gotta watch that."

He settled back on the couch, wondering just how long it was gonna be before Edmond O'Brien tumbled to the news that his goose was cooked, when he thought he heard a soft, scraping noise on the patio outside. He listened, didn't hear anything; then he heard it again.

A sandy, rhythmic patter on the bricks. Then the low but unmistakable sound of a man's voice, humming. "DUM-dum, dum-dum. Diddle dee diddle dee DUM . . ." Zalman felt his heart shrivel up like a California raisin; all of a sudden he knew just how Edmond O'Brien felt, cold tentacles of fear wrapped around his chest like a thirty-foot octopus, heart rocketing like a heavy metal back-beat. There it was again, and there was no mistaking it. "DUM-dum, diddle diddle all around, dum-dum. Dum-dum, diddle dee something, something else is blah blah blah . . ." the voice chirped.

Slowly, Zalman got up, clucking futilely at Rutherford. Rutherford belched. Zalman went to the sliding glass door and pulled open the drapes, somehow hoping against hope that it wasn't so, that he was hearing things, imagining things, that maybe it was only Norman Bates humming "East Side, West Side" on his patio. Zalman flipped on the outside lights and peered through the glass.

A sixty-year-old man was doing a soft-shoe on the bricks, accompanied by the bossa nova rhythm of crickets scritch-scratching their legs together. His face was tinted pale aquamarine by the flickering pool lights and he was exactly Zalman's height, five foot four and a half, and he still had a full head of black, curly hair, just like Zalman. He was wearing a well-cut dark gray suit, a snappy gray Come-Fly-with-Me hat with a white band on it, a red and white polka-dot bow tie, and rimless bifocals, and behind those glasses gleamed the bright eyes of a man who knew the score. "DUM dum dum diddle dumpling . . ." he sang as he came to a finish on one knee, then segued into a nasal, Jolsonesque version of "California, Here I Come." He grinned when he saw Zalman peering at him through the glass and gave him a snappy salute. "Jerry! It's me!" he called, spreading his arms wide in welcome.

"Hi, Dad," Zalman said, kissing the thought of a long, slow Monday in bed good-bye. "Great to see you." He smiled as he opened the sliding glass door and let his father into the house. "How'd you get in the back gate? I thought I had it locked."

Earnest K. Zalman grinned happily at his one and only son. "A snap. I gotta lockpick on my keychain . . . it was nothing. Easy as one of them chain locks, if you know how to—What the hell's this?" he said, pointing at Rutherford, who was still lying on the floor, filled with steak tartare. "You got this thing for protection? Don't look too scary to me." He laughed as he crouched down on the floor next to Rutherford and stroked his sleek flank. "Hey, pooch! How 'bout a kiss for Ernie?"

"His name's Rutherford and he's a professional coward. Belongs to my girlfriend—"

"Ba-bing!" Earnest said, cocking a forefinger at Zalman. "The new girlfriend. Lucille told me all about her. Your sister thinks she's a great girl, and you know what a toughie Lucille can be. . . . Where is the girlfriend? Marie, that's her name, huh?" Earnest embraced his son, then sat down on the couch and spun his hat across the room like a Frisbee.

"She's not here—" Zalman began, but his father interrupted him.

"Don't tell me you broke up already and you got custody of the mutt," Earnest said, staring at Rutherford like the dog was a sack of wet meat. "Doesn't seem like a fair deal to me, tell you the truth. . . ."

"We didn't break up. She's in Eugene, Oregon."

"They got a track there? I never heard of it."

"She had to go to a wedding—"

"Ba-bing!" Earnest said, flipping his forefinger. "A wedding! That's why I'm here. Now look, Jer, level with me. You're thinking of getting married again? I thought maybe you were, that's why I came in from the East Coast early. Horses were still running at Aqueduct, but family comes first to Earnest K. Zalman. I thought maybe I'd like to get a look at the girlfriend, especially after what Lucille said. . . . My bags are outside, by the way. I got a rented car. . . ."

"You're staying with me?" Zalman asked weakly. He loved his father, it wasn't that he didn't love his father. It was just that somehow, whenever his father was around, Zalman found himself getting a little nervous. Nothing two weeks in Baden-Baden wouldn't cure, but still, a teensy bit edgy. "Won't Lucille be upset you're not staying with her?" he said, hedging.

Earnest regarded his son with paternal warmth. "Jerry. I love your sister. I love her kids. But at my age kids are too noisy—and besides, that schmuck Phil Hanning she married, him I can live without. Besides, you have better cigars. . . ." Earnest said, fumbling in his breast pocket for his cigar case.

"Well, God knows that's true," Zalman said with a laugh. "In that case, welcome to L.A."

A FEW MINUTES LATER, ZALMAN, EARNEST, AND RUTHER-ford strolled outside to collect Earnest's luggage. The warmth of the afternoon had given way to a cool evening, a faint reminder that the City of Angels was merely a momentary oasis hacked out of the center of a harsh desert by legions of greedy developers. As Zalman hauled Earnest's eight-piece set of matched Mark Cross luggage out of the trunk of the rented Mercedes, he began to remember why Earnest always made him a little nervous.

Earnest K. Zalman was a nutty kind of guy, but he was a great guy, a guy who always paid up on his markers, a guy who'd never stiff you on the lunch tab, a guy who'd always pop for a bottle of champagne when there was a lady present. Along about the time he hit puberty, Jerry Zalman had realized that he and his father were very much alike, and the similarity was too close for Zalman's comfort. Besides the strong family resemblance, both men were gamblers. But while Jerry Zalman had channeled his love of adventure and risk-taking into his wacky law practice, Earnest was strictly a professional. Vegas, Monte Carlo, London, cards, dice, the track, he'd played 'em all and managed to make a darned good living in the process. For although Earnest was a confirmed grasshopper who staunchly believed that life oughta be nothing but fun, he was old enough and wise enough to comprehend the ice-cold beauty of a stack of U.S. Treasury bonds bringing in ten percent per annum. "At my age, I like an ace in the hole," he always said.

They brought the bags inside and stashed them in Zalman's guest room, then went out into the living room for a drink.

"Hey! I just realized, you redecorated, right?" Earnest said as he looked around. "I like it. Looks more, I dunno, more relaxed, or maybe it's less stodgy. You look good too, relaxed, yeah? I think the girlfriend is good for your health, Jer. You don't want to work too hard. Kills the enjoyment, know what I mean? Jesus H.," he said, his mouth dropping open as he stared across the living room at the far wall. "What the hell is that junk?" he asked, pointing at a cobalt blue mirrored art deco shelf crammed with salt and pepper shakers. "What the hell's that—Mr. Peanut, for Chrissake? Whaddayou, crazy? You got Mr. Peanut in here?"

Zalman sighed. Marie had given him the salt and pepper collection when he redecorated, and Marie's taste in interior decor ran to "Star Trek," Elvis, demented collectibles, and Dagwood Bumstead furniture. It was a sore point between them. "Yeah, I got Mr. Peanut," he told his dad. "I also got Nipper, and Willie and Millie, the Kool Penguins, and I also got the Poppin' Fresh Doughboy. Marie gave 'em to me. She keeps saying I ought to stay in touch with my roots. . . ."

"The girlfriend thinks you got roots in the Poppin' Fresh Doughboy? Ay-yi-yi," Earnest said, shaking his head. "You sure you wanna marry this dame? I'd think twice, I was you, Jer. Can you live with Mr. Peanut on a long-term basis?"

"Don't start with me, Dad," Zalman warned. "I asked her to marry me. She doesn't want to get married."

Earnest sat down on the couch, took out a handkerchief, and began to polish his glasses, squinting at his son. "She doesn't, huh? Smart move. I think I like this girl. I can tell she's got brains. You been married twice, Jer, you paid enough alimony already. You might as well skip the aggravation, is my advice. Say, you gotta drink for the old man?" he asked, settling his glasses back on his nose.

Zalman went over to the bar. "Bullshot?" he asked his father.

"You still drinking those?" Earnest said. "You oughta switch to a lighter drink, Jer, more modern, more up to date. But yeah, okay. Gimme one cold. But I tell you, the place looks great." He nodded. "Silver walls, though, jeez, I'd think you'd get a headache. . . ."

"Business okay?" Zalman asked, ignoring the criticism. You wanted to retain your sanity around Earnest Zalman, you had to have a tough skin. He took a pitcher of cold bouillon out of the bar fridge, poured it into a pair of Waterford glasses, and splashed vodka on top of it.

"I'll tell you, Jer, the track's changed," Earnest said sadly as he took his glass. "Not as much fun as it was in the old days. . . . Used to have a great crowd out there, every day of the year. Now, guys are too young, all too busy on Wall Street flogging junk bonds, for Chrissake, they think you can't make a decent living at the track. So serious, all these young guys! No time for fun. Girls are worse, now that they gotta have careers, too. Yeah, I was up to Saratoga a few weeks in August. You remember the horse gambler's calendar I taught you when you were a kid?" he prompted.

"Sure," Zalman said. "April, May, June, July, Saratoga . . ."

"Hey, you do remember." Earnest laughed. "That's nice, Jer. Don't want to lose touch with family tradition. Yeah, I won a few, lost a few. Did okay. Nice track, Saratoga. Used to be straight class, still is pretty swell, your rich crowd likes Saratoga. Belmont, had a few nice wins at Belmont. Played a little gin. Makes a nice indoor game, classy crowd plays gin. I'm thinking maybe next year I'll start working the cruise circuit. Take it easy, check out the Bahamas. I heard Omar Sharif does okay with bridge, so how bad can it be? Plus you get the sea air as a bonus. It's not too late to learn bridge, even at my age. But, hey! I don't think much about age, you wanta know the truth. All in the mind," he said, tapping his skull. "Yeah, I'd like a cruise in the wintertime, get outta New York. Float around the ocean on some damn boat just like you're in a bathtub! Take a little sun, play a little cards. . . . You know what, Jer," he said, sipping his Bullshot. "I got a great idea. It's early yet. I think I'll call Lydia. . . ." Earnest jumped up and went over to the phone. "Great girl," he said enthusiastically as he punched the buttons. "You're gonna love her. Yeah, backstage, please," he said into the phone. "Yeah, Lydia Devanti, please. Earnest K. Zalman. I'll hold. Jer," he said, "I tell you, this girl . . . gorgeous. Fabulous condition for her age, too, I'm telling you. One in a—Yeah, I'm holding. . . ."

Zalman looked at his Bullshot and rotated the ice in his glass. Was there a faint discord sounding in those crystalline tones? Wind chimes of warning drifting through the air? He gave his father a speculative glance. "Okay, Dad, I'll play. How old is she?"

"Forty. But I'm telling you, gorgeous!"

"That's pretty old, Dad, for you. . . ." Zalman teased.

"Still holding—Christ, I hate phones. Jer, you misunderstand me. If your mother, God rest her—"

"She's not dead, Dad."

"In my heart, she's dead. It's over, finished. But if that wonderful woman were still at my side, if she hadn't left me—"

"Don't start, Dad!" Zalman warned. "You can't blame Mom for walking out after she found out about that redhead! I mean, man to man, Dad, you shoulda been a little more careful. Little more discreet. . . ."

Earnest waved at his son, frowning. "Details. A guy makes a mistake . . . But if your mother was still with me, I'd never look at another woman again, so help me— Yeah, baby, it's me! Just got in! Yeah, you too. . . . Everything go okay at rehearsal? How's Simone? Yeah? Sergeant Pepper? Yeah? What time you go on? Yeah, I'm with him now," Earnest said, his eyes gliding speculatively across the room to Zalman. "Yeah, don't worry about it. Yeah, yeah. It's done. Yeah, I said yeah, didn't I? Okay, babe. See you soon."

Earnest put the phone down and smiled at his son, smiled the warm, open smile of a man with something on his mind, a man with a plan, a man who wants something and intends to get it. . . .

Zalman could see it coming. He could feel trouble barreling down on him like a runaway train on a steep mountain grade. "So, Dad," he said warily. "Now it's Lydia? Tell me about Lydia."

"Great girl," Earnest repeated, rubbing his hands together briskly and looking around the room like he'd forgotten something. "You see my cigar case?" he asked. "She's going on in a few minutes. Saaay, listen," he said, as if Zeus had suddenly impaled him with a bright thunderbolt of unexpected inspiration. "Whaddaya say we run on down to the club? Huh? Is that a great idea? Catch her act. You'll love it, Jer. Laughs a million, and she knows some pretty good tricks, too."

"What does Lydia do, Dad?" Zalman asked. He knew he didn't want to know. He just knew it. "She's a comedian?"

Earnest put his hand over his heart, sighing like he was Archie mooning around after Veronica. "Nah, I'd-a thought an around guy like you would recognize her name right off! She's Lydia Devanti, the Princess of Prestidigitation, the Mistress of Magic! She's a magician, a big star! Sings, dances, the whole nine yards. A headliner! She's a great magician, 'cept she calls it 'magicienne.' Get it? Magicienne," he repeated. "Cute, huh? Come on," Earnest said as he picked up his snappy chapeau. "It's early yet. She's playing the Magic Cavern, you know the big place right above the Strip? We'll run down there, check out the act. Have a coupla drinks, it'll be fun. Whaddaya say, Jer?"

Zalman got up and went back to the bar. "You can have a drink here, Dad. Besides, it's late and I've got a killer week staring me in the kisser. Meetings up the wazoo. The law grinds on, you know," he said sententiously.

Earnest shook his head sadly. "Jer, Jer, Jer, life is short! You gotta enjoy every minute. These are the golden years, kiddo! You gotta seize every opportunity! C'mon, take some time out with your old man, have a little fun! It won't kill you, take my word on it. We'll run over there, have a nightcap. . . ."

Zalman looked at his father, who was fiddling with his

polka-dot tie. "Why do I get the feeling there's something you're not telling me, hmmmm? You left Aqueduct early just because Lucille tells you Marie is a nice lady and maybe I'm getting married again? Why don't I believe that, Dad? You wouldn't leave a hot horse unless you had the winning ticket on Lotto America, this much I know for a solid gold fact. Besides, you want to know about my love life, you could have called me, asked me over the phone, saved yourself a couple grand." Zalman stared quizzically at his father, who was now making a great show of fumbling for his cigar case.

"You got a cigar, Jer? I guess I left mine in the car. . . ."

"I'm right! I knew it!" Zalman said as he flipped his father a cigar from the big humidor on the bar. "There is something else! Now look, Dad, I'm glad to see you, happy to have you stay as long as you want. The guest room is yours in perpetuity, maybe longer. The maid's name is Isobel and she comes in twice a week, if she feels like it. Just don't go into business with her, that's my advice, she's too smart for you. But you might as well tell me what's going on, save us some time. You need some dough, is that it? It's no problem, Dad. You're faded."

Earnest waved Zalman down. "Nah. Christ, I'm loaded. Remember that tip sheet I went in on with Tommy the Tyke? Guy who does the midget act, dressed up like a little kid? Thing's coining money. I could retire, for Chrissake, except it would be too damn boring. Nah, Jer, it ain't money. It's Lydia."

Zalman wished Marie was waiting for him over at her house, in her bedroom with all the antique dolls with their freaky glass eyes. In her living room with the circus posters and the carousel horse. In her kitchen with the "Star Trek" collection and the magnetized robots on the fridge. He sighed as he looked at his father, then shrugged, went over to the couch with a fresh drink in either hand, and sat down. He'd seen it coming and now it was here, and it felt just like the twister that had taken Dorothy to Oz. "Why don't you tell me all about it, Dad?"

EARNEST LIT HIS CIGAR AND LOOKED AROUND THE ROOM, nodding with the paternal solidity of Ward Cleaver after a tough day on the links. "Good you're settling down, Jer," he said warmly. "Got a nice house even if you do hafta live with Mr. Peanut," he added, shaking his head. "Kids, who understands 'em? Got a nice girlfriend, even got a dog. Things going okay at the office?"

Zalman smiled. "Yeah. Doing great, Dad. Everybody needs a lawyer sometime."

"Glad to hear it. Y'know," Earnest said with a confidential air, "me and Lydia are thinking about getting married. Maybe!" he added quickly, holding up a warning hand. "Just maybe. A guy like me, a gambler, hanging around the track all the time, and she's got a big career ahead of her, she has to travel every week of the year . . . Doesn't seem like we'd have a shot at true love and happiness, but she's a great girl, Lydia, and I'm thinking maybe it's time I tried to settle down again. She's very successful, y'know. Big act. Got this other girl named Simone who works for her, got this little monkey in the act, Sergeant Pepper is his name. See, people really like monkeys. Monkey's very well trained. Does tricks you wouldn't believe. They call 'em 'illusions,' though, in the magic dodge. Don't like you to call 'em tricks, sounds kinda like snake oil, know what I mean?"

Zalman put a pillow behind his head and his feet up on the coffee table, and settled back on the couch. He figured his dad would get around to the story of Life with Lydia sooner or later. Oh, it would take fifteen or twenty minutes, a little hemming, a lot of hawing, but because Zalman was a lawyer and because his practice consisted of people who had oddball problems they couldn't solve without the benefit of his particular brand of legal brilliance, the detached part of his mind knew that he was in for a tangled tale.

Every human being on this crazy old planet has a story to tell, eight out of ten have a confession to make, and ten out of ten don't want to cop to it. This was a fact Jerry Zalman accepted just as if Moses had handed it down to him as a birthday present, hand-carved on two tablets of stone.

Even his dad—who was right up there next to Clarence Darrow and Fred Astaire in Zalman's personal pantheon of heroes—even his dad had a confession to make, and like every other troubled soul who'd burned a sorry trail of footsteps across Zalman's office carpet, he'd take his own sweet time getting around to it.

Zalman had practiced law in Beverly Hills for quite a while now, and in the course of his checkered career he'd listened to lots of confessions, plenty of sad stories, and more than one tale of woe. Guys and gals who cheated on their partners; guys and gals who'd walked out of Cartier with this darling little bracelet they'd neglected to pay for; guys and gals who'd forgotten that Las Vegas was a no-kidding-around force of goddamn nature, for Chrissake, and unless they wanted to see a large and unpleasant-looking gentleman tooling off down Wilshire Boulevard in their brand new Mercedes they were going to have to pay up; guys and gals who had the kinds of problems you only found in Beverly Hills, CA, 90212.

"So . . . ?" Zalman said easily. Even though Earnest was his father, he knew he had to help him over the hard part of the confession. And the worst was always the beginning. "Tell me about it, Dad," he prodded gently.

"Yeah," Earnest said as he puffed happily on Zalman's Dunhill cigar and blew a thin stream of smoke into the air. "Beautiful cigar, this," he said with delight. "So, like I said, we're thinking about marriage. Now, I want you to know, Jer, ever since your mother, God rest her, left me in the lurch—"

"Dad! I'm telling you, don't start about Mom, okay? I'm your son, I love you, but don't start about Mom."

Earnest ignored Zalman's protests. "Ever since that sad day, I've known a few girls. That's life, right? But it was never serious. I never connected with that certain something a guy like me looks for in a lady. Now Lydia, she's something else again. She's a lot of fun and she likes me just like I am. Doesn't want me to change, settle down. At my age, some fat chance of that, right? Like, whaddamy gonna do, be a plumber? Nah, Lydia's realistic. She sees me just the way I am and she likes it! Knock wood, when we decide to get married, you'll be there to see it, son. . . ."

"Dad . . ." Zalman nudged. It was getting late and he knew he had miles to go before he hit the happy trail to dreamland. "Tell me about it, okay? You got a problem? I'm your son, you can trust me. . . ."

"If not you, who else?" Earnest said. "Okay. So, anyhoo, you'd expect a guy like me's been around the block a few times, and so has Lydia. Hey, I don't blame her for nothing, we've all made our mistakes, right? Right, Jer?" he challenged.

"Right, Dad."

"Besides, everything that happened, it all happened before she met me. Ancient history. Past tense."

"Ummmmm. . . . How'd you meet Lydia, you don't mind my asking?"

"Met her last year in Miami. I was at Hialeah, she was playing one of them big hotels. Tommy the Tyke, he introduced us. Great guy, Tommy! He was opening for her act. See, he comes out in this Little Lord Fauntleroy outfit with this big pink ruff around his neck and then he goes into a clog dance and then he—"

"Dad, please, can we make the jump to hyperspace here?" Zalman pressed. If he didn't get things rolling, he'd never sleep.

"I'm getting to it! I'm getting to it! So I meet her, we start going out, pretty soon, you know how it is, Jer, we're going out pretty steady. Pretty soon, we're going out every night. Pretty soon, we start staying home some nights, having meat loaf, a nice brisket. Good cook, Lydia. Makes a difference, Jer, a girl who can cook. Remember that when you think about setting up housekeeping with the new girlfriend. Anyhoo, then we start getting serious. We get to the part where we start telling each other everything about our past, know what I mean, Jer? Getting up-close and personal?"

Zalman sighed. "You mean like when the girl tells you all about the sad, sad time she came home early from her day job down at the five-and-dime and found her first husband Eddie in the sack with her best girlfriend Doreen, and they weren't watching 'General Hospital' like they swore up and down they did every afternoon? Is that what we're talking about here?"

Earnest grinned and twiddled his cigar in his manicured fingers. "I can see you're a man of wide social experience, Jer. That's exactly the part I'm talking about. So I told her all about you kids and your mother, and she told me about her old boyfriends. . . ."

"Ahhhhhh . . ." Zalman said. "This *does* sound like a serious relationship."

"I'm not making a commitment," Earnest said, a tinge of terror creeping into his voice. "Not yet! So anyhoo, it didn't mean too much at the time, y'know, a girl's entitled to a past, even though Lydia—well, she's got quite a past, Jer, if I say so myself."

"You know, Dad," Zalman said with what he hoped was a man-of-the-world flair, "it can make a woman more interesting. A past."

"You ain't kidding, sonny!" Earnest grinned. "And don't think I hold it against her, either. Y'know, nowadays, most dames don't know how to have any fun. They read too many magazines, worry about having a relationship. In the old days, you hit the Daily Double at the track, you'd take a girl over to El Morocco, have a swell dinner, some laughs, take in a show. You met a great dame, ba-bing! You fell for her! Love was a lot more fun when you didn't hafta have a relationship to go with it, in my opinion. Today, you meet a girl, she's too busy with her career to fall in love with a guy like me! Work is no life for a girl. They're always tired, they gotta get up in the morning! They got no time for dancing! So when you meet a lady like Lydia, you appreciate her all the more. First off, she's a night person like me, especially being as she's in show business and all. But I gotta admit, she's been around. She's had lots of boyfriends in the past and, well, people learn things about each other. There you are, you're eating your meat loaf, you get close. You tell each other all your secrets. And since Lydia's known more than one guy . . ."

". . . Lydia knows quite a few secrets, is that what you're trying to tell me, Dad?" Zalman asked carefully.

"Right on the money, Jer. Lydia knows quite a few secrets about quite a few people. Guys, we're talking about," Earnest stressed, just in case Zalman hadn't figured it out for himself. "Big guys. Important guys. One of them's this guy Bland, by the way."

"Bland? Lucille's client Bland?" Zalman asked. Suddenly he was getting that bad Rolaids feeling in the pit of his stomach. Lucille Zalman Hanning, Zalman's feisty sister, was an important manager in the world of rock and roll, and Bland was her primo, all-star, top-of-the-line act. "Oh, boy. I think I'm beginning to hate this. . . ." he said, rubbing his stomach.

EARNEST STARED AT HIS SON WITH THE STRAINED EYES OF an old pug who's taken too many heavy hits to the head. "Don't get crazy on me, Jer! I'm just getting started here! So anyhoo, one of 'em is Bland, one of 'em is this guy Tom somethingabunkus, guy who has all these nitwit family shows on TV?"

Zalman shook his head, uncomprehending. How had he lost control so quickly? His father had only been in the house for twenty minutes, and already he felt the ground buckling and swaying under his feet, like he was up to his ankles in aspic. His father generally had that effect on him, but how did it happen so fast? Why had he thought this time things would be different?

"You know! You know!" Earnest urged. "Stuff with a bunch of kids and they all live together in a big Victorian house with Mumsy and Grampy, making smart cracks and eating cupcakes after school! What the hell do you call that show?"

Zalman realized what Earnest was raving about. "Personally, I call it a fantasy," he said, "but I think you're talking about 'Thicker 'n Water,' is that the show?"

"Yeah, yeah." Earnest nodded up and down like he was bobbing for apples. "Tom Kellar, that's the guy's name. How people can watch that mush is beyond me. Anyhoo," Earnest went on, "back to Lydia. And then there's this other guy—"

"Jeez, Dad . . ."

"—Lenny Dunn. You hearda him? Big guy, like a body-builder? Used to be an actor in TV Westerns, but it turns out the schmo had the talent of a chair. But then, for the first time in his life, Dunn actually got smart. Started making chairs. Tables. Furniture, know what I mean?"

"Yeah, Dad. I know what furniture is. Okay, okay, so Lydia . . ."

"Don't rush me! I'm getting to it! I'm getting to it! So Lydia meets me, all this stuff is behind her, right? All in the past. But a couple months ago, she's out here by herself, she's lonely, you know how it is with girls, she starts going to this psychic she meets on the beach out in Malibu."

Zalman raised an eyebrow. "She meets a psychic on the beach? Is this for real?"

"Hey! This is your town!" Earnest said defensively. "Don't blame it on me, okay? Besides, first thing she tells me is that she ain't fooling around with the guy, and I believe her! You meet her, you'll see. Lydia's a great dame. She's just like a guy, but she's a girl, know what I mean, Jer? Anyway, you know how it is with girls, they like to get their palms read, that sort of thing. In the old days there was this dame, Madame Lulu, some such name. She had a little joint over a Chinese laundry on Second Avenue in New York, used to read palms. All the girls went there. Now they call 'em psychics, they do this channeling stuff where they talk in funny voices? Same deal as getting your palm read, you ask me. So Lydia starts going to this guy, name's Roy Caldwell. Got a big joint out near the Malibu Colony, so you figure he's raking in the bucks, right?"

"Right, Dad," Zalman sighed.

"Sooooo . . . Lydia goes to him, he claims he's a channel, right? Claims he's got a two-thousand-year-old Scotsman named MacTavish living inside his head. Can you beat it? Mr. MacTavish, he calls him. Like he thinks the guy in his head is really there and he has to be polite to him and call him mister! So this guy Roy Caldwell, he goes into a trance and then he talks in a funny voice like a damn Scot and all the girls go crazy. Tell him all their secrets. . . ."

"Secrets, huh? Somehow I think I'm beginning to get the picture. Go on, tell me the rest."

"You can see it coming, right, Jer?" Earnest said sadly. "Too bad Lydia didn't. Woulda saved us both a lotta aggravation. So the girls tell him all their secrets about their boyfriends and what the guy said and what deal he's making over at CBS and what stock he's buying or what he likes to do in the—".

"I get the picture."

"And Roy Caldwell gets it all on tape and then he blackmails 'em."

"And that's how he gets the big joint out in Malibu," Zalman said.

"He didn't get it making chopped liver and talking like a damn Scot, I can tell you that! So Caldwell calls up this guy Tom Kellar and puts the bite on him, says he's got these tapes of Lydia talking all about their love life, and Tom Kellar freaks out because he doesn't want *TV Guide* to know he likes to—"

"Don't tell me something about this guy I don't want to hear, Dad, okay? I don't care what he's doing in bed. I don't care if it's chickens—"

"Chickens! Yeeeccccchhhh! Now, that's disgusting! Nah, it ain't chickens, he likes to play games with the velvet ropes, is all—"

"I told you not to tell me! Now I'm gonna run into this guy at a party or something and I won't be able to keep a straight face! I'm gonna keep thinking of him strapped to a lawn chair yelling, 'Ooooh, Mommy, please don't spank me!'" Zalman got up and began to pace. He liked to pace, it used up his nervous energy, a commodity that was currently in abundant supply.

"And he's gonna put the bite on the other two guys, Dunn and Bland. So you see, you were right, Jer, I didn't come out just to see you—hey, I love you, you're my son, right? But when I found out this jerk Caldwell's gonna blackmail Bland . . . hey, I dropped everything. Bland's a big client for Lucille, so we gotta do something for your sister's sake, right? Right, Jer?"

"I'm thinking," Zalman hedged. "I need a minute to think here."

"And this is the bad part . . ."

"There's more?" Zalman groaned. "Say it ain't so! How much more can there be?"

"Caldwell's also got pictures of Tom Kellar and Lydia. See, Kellar—"

"Do I have to hear this?" Zalman moaned. "I know I don't want to hear this. . . ."

"Kellar wanted some snaps, y'know, Polaroids of him and Lydia so's he could look at 'em when she wasn't around. . . ."

"That one's Paleolithic! She fell for that old gag?"

"Yeah. She did," Earnest said sadly. "What can I tell you? Lydia's very trusting. Too damn trusting, you ask me. But here's the funny thing about the pictures. After they broke up a couple years ago, she asked Kellar for the pictures back and he gave 'em to her. No problem. And she kept 'em, which was damn silly of her in my personal opinion. Then all of a sudden this situation with Caldwell starts up and the pictures disappear! Somebody pinches 'em out of Lydia's trunk, and then, ba-bing! They turn up with Roy Caldwell. Well, that's the story. Whaddaya think?" Earnest asked.

"I think it stinks," Zalman said.

"Jer, you think I like this? This is the girl I'm thinking about marrying. Maybe," Earnest said, holding up his hand, cigar smoke trailing through the air. "Just maybe."

"Dad. I'm a lawyer—"

"You think I don't know that? Who the hell put you through law school!" Earnest demanded.

"Hey, I paid you back! With interest! Now, listen to me like a client, Dad. I gotta ask you the obvious question. Why doesn't Lydia go to the police? Why doesn't Tom Kellar go to the police? I mean, so they like to get together and play the slave girl and the Roman emperor, and so Caldwell's got some compromising pics. That's not exactly a stop-press situation these days. I don't even think it would make 'Oprah,' you wanta know the truth."

31

"That's what I think, Jer. I mean, hey, we're all living in the material world, right? But this guy Tom Kellar is a real lunatic, you know how these Hollywood guys are with the big egos, you say hello to 'em, they give you their credits. Kellar thinks that if the pictures get out, it'll ruin his family image. Like no one will believe he's a true heart-warmer if 'Entertainment Tonight' finds out he's a human guy with one or two human foibles. And Lydia, well, pictures like that, girls see things differently. It's a problem for her. Roy Caldwell says he's gonna flog 'em to the *Snoop* or the *National Peeper* or the *Big Eyeball Weekly.* Whatever. And Lydia's convinced it'll break her mother's heart. See, her mom's a very conservative old lady. Lives in one of them homes for old missionaries."

"Her mother's a missionary?"

"Yeah, can you beat it? Retired, of course. But Lydia thinks that if the pictures get into the papers, it'll kill the old lady, the other oldies'll kick her out of the home, she'll have to move in with Lydia, it'll wreck our romance." Earnest sighed. "Get the picture? It's a tough situation all the way around, you gotta understand that. Look, these kind of pics, actually, it'd be a great career move, but Lydia's old-fashioned and we got the problem with her mother. I told you, she's trusting, she's sincere. Hey, why else would I be thinking about marriage, right? She just doesn't wanta see those nasty photos staring her in the face when she's at the checkout counter buying her burger, know what I mean?" Earnest stared hopefully at his son. "So, whaddaya say we run on down there? Catch Lydia's act. She really wants to talk to you about it, Jer. Give you all the details. Besides which, I want you to meet her." Earnest shot his cuff and looked at his watch, a gold Rolex.

"You see! I paid you back!" Zalman said, pointing at the watch. "That's the watch I got you!"

"And I wear it every day, son. I don't even give this watch as a marker, that's how much it means to me. So whaddaya say, huh?" Earnest jumped up and rubbed his hands together. "You wanna drive?"

Zalman shook his head. "Did I say I'd go?" he asked. "Did I say I wanted to get involved in this mess? Huh? Did I?"

"Darling," Earnest said, smiling, "you didn't have to."

ZALMAN AND EARNEST WENT OUTSIDE AND CLIMBED INTO Zalman's Mercedes. The night air was cool and the Hollywood Hills felt unusually soft and quiet. Only the distant but ever-present hum of the freeways ringing L.A. like a concrete wedding band reminded Zalman of the gleeful threat of the city all around him.

Zalman was used to the wildcat spirit of L.A.; he'd grown up in the city and never felt quite comfortable unless he was fighting his way through the impossible traffic, inhaling an orange lungful of smog, or battling the greed and ambition that orbit the movie studios, TV empires, and record companies that've made L.A. their drug of choice. Some people say L.A. is only a state of mind; for Jerry Zalman the city was a state of war, his own personal battlefield. He loved the fight, and even more than that, Jerry Zalman loved the spoils of war. In the darkened car, he smiled as he sensed the teasing, tangy smell of money that drapes L.A. like the finest, softest cashmere shawl.

Zalman zipped down the hill, twisting and turning his way through the canyon, and swung the car onto Sunset Boulevard, bright with lights and cars, though a little quieter than normal since it was a Sunday and a lot of the street trash had clocked out for the night.

Earnest sat quietly, staring out at the Strip as it rolled past the window, drumming his fingers on the dashboard to the soft jazz on the radio, humming along to Mel Tormé's version of "New York, New York." In contrast to his son, Earnest K. Zalman never felt at ease unless his soles were pattering down the concrete highways and byways of the Big Apple, and he was happiest when he was cursing the mayor. Earnest didn't care for combat, but he did need the daily give and take of the aggravation inherent in New York life in order to feel fully alive.

Zalman cruised slowly down the Strip past Tower Records and thought about all the time he'd spent growing up on the sidewalks of Hollywood. When he was just a kid in elementary school out in Mar Vista, he used to hop the bus into town once or twice a week and hang around outside the Unicorn, one of the first L.A. coffeehouses, hoping to see a black-clad beatnik. Later on, when he was a wiseass teenager, he spent his summer vacations goofing around with his pals at the Club Renaissance listening to jazz, having a bad burger at Googie's, or checking out the scene at Schwab's.

After that phase ended, during his fleeting romance with Peace and Love, he and his then-wife Tracee used to frug the night away at the Whiskey a Go Go, their eyes bleary in the sea of colored lights, their ears permanently damaged by the blast of the band. Afterward, when both his marriage and the waters of psychedelia began to run cold, he'd cruise the clubs with his sister Lucille as she ferociously scouted for talent in the highly competitive, shark-eat-shark world of rock and roll.

Zalman shook his head, trying to knock the memories out of his mind. Once again, the past was creeping up on him. . . . For Zalman, the Strip was like the old college buddy who shows up drunk on your doorstep in the middle of the night, wanting to relive the Big Game. Zalman had successfully managed to stash this part of his past in the yearbook up on the top shelf, and he damn well didn't want to haul it down and reminisce. He sighed. Once again, Jerry Zalman realized that he just never felt happy when he was slap up against the Good Old Days.

Zalman turned off the Strip and wound his way back up into the Hills toward the Magic Cavern. Like many old-line L.A. nightspots, the Cavern was a huge, lumbering joint with a long and convoluted Hollywood history. Perched high on a hill overlooking the glittering lights of the Sunset Strip, it had been built in 1929 by Cyrus T. Cornelius, Jr., a lonely little lunatic with a vision of architectural grandeur conceived as the moody boy mused away his childhood in darkened nickelodeons while silent movies spooled their endless tracks across the white screen in front of him. So, by the time he was ten, Cyrus Junior knew every frame of *Intolerance* and *Flesh and the Devil* as well as he knew the face of Katie, his Irish nursemaid.

Cyrus Junior was the scion of a well-known Chicago meat-packing family, and as soon as he grew up he moved to California and became a toga-wearing vegetarian, perhaps because of some ugly childhood experiences when his father, Cyrus Senior, forced him to pass his otherwise halcyon summer days hard at work in the family slaughterhouse. Cyrus Junior always said that he had a tough time looking a rib in the eye.

When he turned twenty-one, Cyrus Junior came into a

big pile of dough and he decided to live his childhood dreams to the fullest. He sank every inherited nickel into the Magic Cavern, determined that he would create a glittering nightspot that would outshine every other gin joint in Hollywood. And for a few brief, shining days, his dream came true.

Cyrus Junior conceived the Magic Cavern as a showplace, an homage to the vision of lush and lonely splendor he'd imagined as he sat drinking in the beauty of the stars of the silent screen. He passionately hoped to create a watering hole for those very same faces of magical mystery, a palace of pleasure where not only was every man a king, but every extra was a star.

Cyrus Junior, who never really grew up, wanted the Magic Cavern to be a true-to-life version of his favorite film of all time, *The Thief of Baghdad,* which was made in 1924 by director Raoul Walsh and starred Doug Fairbanks and Snitz Edwards. And since he had money to burn, he spared no expense to bring his boyhood fantasy to life.

When it was completed, the Magic Cavern was a vision, an *Arabian Nights* reverie complete with silk hangings on the walls, alabaster urns in every corner, and pink marble floors inlaid with delicate gold art nouveau tracery that made the guests feel they were walking on clouds right out of a Maxfield Parrish pipe dream. But although every corner of the Magic Cavern was an art director's idea of a little bit of heaven, it was the main dining room that knocked your socks off.

It was a gigantic room complete with a big stage that boasted a pair of motorized turntables for the many nightingales Cyrus Junior believed would twitter ceaselessly in his golden cage. The stage also featured a trapdoor, in case a pretty little thrush wanted to make her entrance from the lower depths, chirping all the way, or disappear amidst a sea of fire. Cyrus Junior installed gas jets to insure spouting plumes of flame.

The dining room had a pale frescoed ceiling painted in exquisite pastels by a pair of Italian artistes who had been laid off over at Metro; the ceiling was illuminated by a clever lighting man Cyrus Junior had wooed away from Cecil B. DeMille himself. The lighting designer had created a system that allowed the stars in the sky to drift slowly from day to night, so that at midnight in the Magic Cavern a starlet could gaze over her lover's dinner jacketed shoulder and see exactly the same scene she'd be looking at if she were flat on her back in the middle of the Sahara Desert.

The dining room walls were faced in pink granite left in its natural, rough-hewn state and many a showgirl scraped her backside when she moved a titch too close to the wall as an over-eager suitor breathed heavily down her cleavage. Little gilt chairs, pink silk tablecloths draped over round tables, and golden dinnerware put the finishing touches on the big room, and for the first time in his solitary young life, Cyrus Junior felt completely at home.

But the deadly combination of the stock market crash and the waning of silent movies put the kibosh on both Cyrus Junior and his dreams of heavenly glory for the Magic Cavern. The club opened ten days before Black Tuesday and closed promptly ten days afterward, just another victim of the stock market collapse. The dream of Cyrus T. Cornelius, Jr., his dream of romance, class, and culture all shaken into one single Hollywood martini, went down the tubes just as his father's meat-packing empire passed into the hands of some flat-nosed types who weren't fit to be seen in the country club. Cyrus Junior died, a broken entrepreneur, and so the Magic Cavern passed into receivership and gathered dust until the beginning of World War II, when it became a whorehouse.

Not your cheap, two-bit, hello-sailor-dating-tonight establishment, but a sort of officers' club run by an enterprising lady from Duluth, who saw the entry of the United States into the burgeoning world conflict as an event guaranteed to turn her life as an unsung member of the Screen Extras Guild into a paying career.

Lily DuBarry, as she called herself, had carved out a tiny niche for herself as a dress extra playing faded blondes in the gangster films that Warner Brothers cranked out all through the thirties. But when her wealthy boyfriend, a real estate broker who'd done darned well for himself buying up orange groves in the San Fernando Valley, croaked in her arms one sweaty night, she found herself the sole proprietress of the wreck of the Magic Cavern. Lily was smart enough to realize that this was her last, perhaps golden opportunity to grab hold of a decent living for once in her life, and she ignored the advice of her newest close, personal friend, her dead boyfriend's partner, and reopened the Magic Cavern.

With the help of a few of her other close, personal friends, Lily redecorated the Magic Cavern, started serving sandwiches, beer, and company to Our Fighting Men, and made herself a comfortable fortune by V-J Day, when she married a chief petty officer who thought she was a living doll and retired to San Diego where she, her CPO, and a cocker spaniel named Friskee lived happily ever after.

Dormant in the fifties, the Magic Cavern became the Psychedelic Cavern in the sixties, then a disco, then a punk hangout for the local head-bangers, a sad, moth-eaten relic without a flicker of its former glory. Finally, in the mid-1980s, the Magic Cavern was purchased by Mitzi Melbourne, a five-foot-two, two-hundred-pound redhead known affectionately as Little Miss Four-by-Four. The Cavern's luck had changed at last.

Mitzi Melbourne was married to Marty Melbourne, a second-rate magician whose mitts were getting a trifle shaky for sleight of hand due to his all-consuming interest in the bottle, and Mitzi, who was a lot smarter than her husband, decided they better settle down before they ended up yanking gerbils out of hats at kiddie birthday parties in the hinterlands of Encino. Like Lily DuBarry before her, Mitzi saw the Magic Cavern as her own personal last shot at show-biz success and, like Lily, she made the most of it.

Mitzi glommed on to the dusty old plans for the Magic Cavern and redid the joint according to the original specs. She hired a troupe of traveling wood-carvers, stonemasons, and craftspeople who lived in an Arkansas commune during the summer and worked their restorative miracles in the winter. The Karvers, as they called themselves, specialized in bringing the past to life, and they did a bang-up job on the Magic Cavern, which reopened in 1988, looking like a zillion bucks.

Mitzi's timing was perfect. After decades of somnolence, there was renewed interest in big-time glitzy magic shows. Siegfried and Roy were packing 'em in in Vegas, David Copperfield was hot on Broadway, and the Magic Cavern was socko on the Strip. Cyrus T. Cornelius, Jr., smiled happily in his grave and Mitzi Melbourne got the show rolling.

Besides the big floor show featuring the best of magic's many faces, Mitzi had wandering magicians, sleight-of-handsters doing card tricks at the bar, and pretty magic misses with short skirts grabbing coins from behind guys' ears, not to mention a grandma named Irma who did a disappearing turtle routine that everyone adored. Even Marty Melbourne had a place; he opened for every big act that played the Cavern, while Mitzi sat contentedly at her table in the back simultaneously applauding her twitchy husband and keeping a sharp eye on the bar receipts.

And Mitzi ran a terrific joint. She had a friendly bartender and a serious Southwestern chef whose chili put Chasen's to shame, and for the first time in its long and colorful history, the Magic Cavern was a star.

Zalman pulled the Mercedes up at the door and got out. The big parking lot was filled with expensive cars and there were ten or twelve bored chauffeurs hanging around in the far corner, reading *Variety*, clipping their nails, and shooting craps.

"If I see one scratch on it when I come back," Zalman told the skinhead attendant, a pimply kid wearing a star-and-crescent cape right out of "The Sorcerer's Apprentice," "you die."

"No big," the kid said disdainfully as he ran a loving hand over the Mercedes' silver-gray finish. "I win the lottery, I'm gettin' one just like it."

Zalman rolled his eyes at the simple ambitions of the young lad as he trotted up the stairs after Earnest, who had already hustled out of the car and was standing on the steps, waiting impatiently for his son.

"I haven't been here since the place changed hands," Zalman said as they went inside and stood in the hallway admiring the decor and waiting for the maître d' to show up. "I gotta say, the joint looks fantastic so far."

"I heard great things about it," Earnest said. "Lydia says this dame Mitzi Melbourne is a smart cookie, done real well fixing it up and all."

The entrance hall was covered with sparkly silver rock, with little flecks of mica glittering on every surface. Huge pierced brass lamps smoldering with incense filled the corners and there was a thick red satin curtain over the doorway that led to the main dining room. Deep red and blue oriental rugs covered the floor, piled haphazardly one on top of another, so that the room seemed like a wealthy Bedouin's tent, a children's storybook version of what life would look like if only life had the good taste to imitate art.

The maître d' sauntered up and looked them over appraisingly, like he wanted to pat them down but knew it wasn't classy. He was a tall, thin man with a hooked nose and black eyes that were too close together, and he looked like he had a permanent squint. Like the parking-lot kid, he was wearing a star-and-crescent wizard's cap, a matching cape caught around his neck with a large rhinestone brooch in the shape of a star, and black satin trousers stuffed into black kidskin boots. "Something I can do for you, gents?" he said, fanning a deck of cards with one hand and riffling a stack of pink and gold menus with the other.

"Cute," Zalman said. "Dad, you want to sit down or—"

"I want a table down front for Miss Devanti's act," Earnest told the maître d', peeling a ten off his bankroll. "But first I want to go backstage and see her. I'm Earnest K. Zalman. She's expecting me," he said as the maître d' started to raise his eyebrows.

"Oh, yeah, she told me," the maître d' said. "I got the table all ready for you, sport. She goes on in about half an hour. You want to see her, you go backstage to her dressing room, it's through the kitchen, follow your nose," the maître d' said, pointing at a side door that opened off the entrance hall. He reached behind Zalman's ear, winked, pulled out an ace of hearts, and handed it to Earnest. "Tell Miss Devanti Sammy gives her the big hello. . . ."

Earnest took the ace and grinned at Sammy with camaraderie. "I'll do that little thing. Let's go, Jer."

Zalman and Earnest went through the kitchen—Earnest

41

thought that the sole looked pretty good—and followed their noses to Lydia's dressing room down the hallway. Earnest scratched on the door with the ace of hearts.

"Oh, poooookie!" a woman's voice called happily from inside. "You're here!"

Earnest smiled sheepishly at Zalman and shrugged. "She calls me pookie," he explained. "You know how women are, they got these silly nick—"

The door opened and a six-foot-tall blue-eyed blonde wearing a short red sequined costume, red net stockings, and four-inch red sequined heels threw her arms around Earnest, nearly knocking him over. A jaunty little red satin top hat rimmed with sequins and a matching red satin bow tie completed her fire-engine ensemble. "Oh, poooookie, I've just missed you sooooo much," she whispered as she bent down and nuzzled his neck.

Earnest, who at five foot four and a half came up to her armpits, stuck his head out from under her arm and grinned at Zalman. "Dame's crazy about me," he said. "But who can blame her? Okay, okay," he told the blonde. "Cut the mush. Don't you want to meet my brilliant son? This is Jerry, and this, of course, is Lydia Devanti, the Princess of Prestidigitation, the Mistress of Magic! By the way, Sammy asked me to give you this," he said as he handed her the ace of hearts. "Guy's nuts for you, and who can blame him, either?"

Lydia took the card, arced it gracefully in her hand, and as the card burst into flame she produced a slim red cigarette from out of the air. "I'm always asking him for a light," she said, winking as she exhaled a dainty plume of red smoke. "Please come in and sit down, Jerry," she said. "I just can't tell you how much this means, that you'd take time out from your busy law practice just to come down here and help poor me." Lydia frowned, sighing heavily.

"It just means everything to me, that you're going to help me with this awful mess. Honestly," she said, puffing red smoke like an angry dragonette, "I don't know how Roy could do this to me! After all the meaningful sessions we had! After all the deep soul work we did together! Why, I thought he and I were in complete spiritual harmony!" The cigarette suddenly disappeared as she leaned forward and took Zalman's hand in hers, squeezing it sincerely. "And now he has the gall! The nerve! He wants money! From me! I can't believe it," she said as she turned and went into her dressing room.

Zalman and Earnest followed her inside. A long row of glittering, sequined costumes hung on a rack against one wall and a large black steamer trunk filled a corner. There was a little mirrored dressing table with jars and bottles and an open makeup case on it and a red velvet couch and a matching poufy red velvet ottoman.

"Look, Miss Devanti," Zalman said, hoping that he could guide this encounter back onto a professional level. "I'm not sure I'll be able to do anything for you. Blackmail is a dangerous business. Shouldn't you go to the police?" he asked, though he knew in his gut it was hopeless. Earnest had already promised Lydia his help; this much was horribly obvious, and Zalman could feel that old sinking feeling slipping up on him from behind.

Lydia's blue eyes misted over with big fat tears. "Oh, Jerry, I know you can help me, I just know it! Erniekins told me you were a legal genius, and I believe him! I do!"

Zalman looked over at Earnest, who raised his hands and rolled his eyes in an attempt at Gallic nonchalance.

Lydia dabbed at her eyes with a lacy red handkerchief. "You see, Jerry, I made a big mistake when I met Roy Caldwell. I trusted him. I know I shouldn't have, I know it was silly, but I did. I was lonely," she said as she turned to

Earnest and patted his hand. "I was out here by myself, Erniekins was on the East coast. . . . And then Roy said he could help me work through some of my . . . oh, dear, I don't know how to say this. You see, I wasn't very smart when I was younger—not that I'm so smart now. But when I was younger, men made promises to me and I believed them and, well, I guess the problem is that I've known too many men. And I told Roy Caldwell too much about my, oh, what do you call them?"

"Indiscretions," Earnest said gently. "Honey, I don't blame you for anything, you know that! We've both put all our mistakes behind us."

"I know you don't," Lydia said, smiling at him. "And I love you for it. I shouldn't have told Roy so much, but I felt so guilty about my past! He told me that Mr. MacTavish could eliminate all the stress and guilt that was hanging over me, discoloring my aura! You see, after I met Erniekins, I felt so guilty about all the silly things I did when I was younger. But I hadn't known true love! I was just waiting for Erniekins to come into my life!" she said. "And now I blame myself for this whole awful thing! If something terrible happens and those awful pictures get out, or people I've known in the past are hurt because I talked to Roy, I just don't know what I'll do. And then there's my mother." Lydia sighed, her face like that of a crushed Barbie doll. "Did Ernie tell you about my mother?"

"He gave me a rundown," Zalman said. "Just the basics, though."

"My mother is, well, she's sort of very conservative? She never even approved of my going into show business in the first place. She thinks it's right next door to being a you-know-what. On the streets," Lydia said primly. "And those pictures! If she sees those terrible pictures of me in

those costumes! She'll have a stroke or die or have to move
in with me! It would be worse than death! Now, after all
these years, when I've finally found Erniekins. . . . You
just have to help me, Jerry, you just have to!"

Despite himself, Zalman felt sorry for Lydia, and as
soon as that happened, he knew he was trapped. The noose
was tightening around his neck. . . .

"Now, baby, don't worry about one little thing," Earnest
jumped in. "Jerry can handle it. He's my son, isn't he? A
Zalman, and there's nothing a Zalman can't handle. Take
my word for it."

"It means so much to me, Jerry," Lydia said. She sat
down in front of her dressing table and began to stare criti-
cally at herself in the mirror. "Do you think the red eyeliner is too much, Ernie?" she asked. "I don't want to look
rabid, you know."

Earnest studied her reflection. "Looks great, doll," he
said. "More glitter, it couldn't hurt."

Zalman sat down on he poufy red ottoman and laughed
hollowly. "Look, Miss Devanti—"

"Lydia," she insisted, a dove peeking out of her cleavage. "Get back in there," she muttered at the bird. "Look, I
just have to finish loading up. These damn doves . . .
Tonight's our opening here and I want to make sure nothing
goes wrong. Did you see Mitzi?" she asked Earnest. "Has
she done wonders with this place? Wonders? I could play
here twice, three times a year, then Vegas, then Reno, then
back to Florida. . . . Don't you think it would be a good
life, Ernie darling?" she said wistfully. The dove squirmed
out of her cleavage again. "Quiet down!" she told it. "No
more birds after this," she said as she added a soupçon of
red glitter under her pale eyebrows and blended it in with
her finger. "They tickle too much. Simone!" she called.
"We're on after Marty! Now, are you two darlings going to

watch from out front or do you want to stand in the wings or—Simone!" The dove popped out again and she pushed it down absentmindedly. "Damn birds . . ."

"Did you call me? Oh, hi, Ernie! Great to see you!" A heavily freckled redhead dressed in a pink sequined outfit that complemented Lydia's poked her head out of the dressing room next door. A small monkey togged out in a pale blue satin Lonely Hearts Club Band suit was sitting on her shoulder. As soon as the monkey saw Lydia, he leapt from Simone's shoulder, and Lydia caught him expertly in midair, one-handed. The monkey draped himself around Lydia's neck like an old lady's fur piece, bared his teeth, and snarled viciously at everyone.

"That's Sergeant Pepper," Earnest said, sticking out his finger to the monkey, who lunged at it playfully.

"No biting, now," Lydia said with a laugh. "He always tries to nip people, he's such a bad boy!"

Zalman nodded hopelessly.

Earnest stuck out his finger and tried again. "Hello, boy! Good monkey!" This time, Sergeant Pepper took Earnest's outstretched finger and shook it gravely with a delicate paw. Earnest turned to the redhead and gave her a friendly peck on the cheek. "And this is Simone, Lydia's assistant. This is my son, Jerry," he told the girl. "My famous son."

Zalman shook hands with Simone and, just to be polite, offered a cautious finger to Sergeant Pepper. The monkey regarded it hungrily but didn't bite. Zalman wondered if he could possibly be having a nightmare, but somehow, everything seemed so real, so lifelike! Dreams aren't this concrete, he thought, once again feeling that awful sensation of quicksand sucking at his Guccis.

Earnest plopped down on the little red couch and looked around the room approvingly. "Hey! This is pretty nice, y'know! Bigger than the one in Miami, huh, babe?" He settled a pillow behind his head and put his feet up on a small trunk that was stacked with magical paraphernalia. Five fake bouquets, four trick hats, three crystal balls, and a box filled with chirping chicks were scattered on the trunk, along with a top hat, a fold-up cane, and a long red feather boa that was shedding all over the floor.

"I've got to go check the equipment," Simone said as Sergeant Pepper settled himself back on her shoulder. "Anything else you want me to do, Lydia?"

Lydia shook her head, distracted. "I think we're all ready, dear, don't you? We're on right after Marty. . . ."

"See you all after the show then," Simone said with a smile. She waved good-bye to Zalman and Earnest and went out into the corridor with Sergeant Pepper.

Earnest crossed his fingers and waved them in the air. "Knock 'em dead, doll," he called out as Simone left. "Nice girl," he said to Lydia. "Now, look, we've given Jer the lowdown on the situation, but he's gonna want details from you, right, Jer? So, as soon as you're through tonight, I think we oughta go back to Jerry's place. I know, I know, you'll be tired after the show, but maybe you can have something to eat on the way. Hey, maybe we can pick up some Chinese around here, take it back to Jerry's. Then you two can thrash this thing out together, whaddaya say, doll?"

Zalman started to protest, tell Earnest that it was late, he had a big day tomorrow, but no luck. Before he could open his mouth, Lydia threw herself into his arms, tipping his poufy perch.

"I'd love that, Jerry," she sighed, staring deeply into his eyes. "I can tell you're a man I can communicate with. Already, even though I've only known you a few minutes, I have this need to unburden myself completely to you, can you understand that? Tell you everything. Bare my soul."

Some brief thought breezed over her pretty face and she sighed again, went back to her dressing table, and peered at her reflection. "The red isn't too much?" she asked anxiously, watching their reactions in the mirror. "I could soften it a little bit, would that help?" She lost her train of thought again. "You know, it's a real treat for me, performing with Marty, poor old thing. He got me started in the business," she said a little wistfully. "I was working as a waitress in a tiny little club, which I didn't mind but it's just hell on your feet because you have to wear four-inch heels all night long and boy, do your feet hurt at the end of your shift! Anyway, I was working at this saloon in Chicago, it's gone now, I think they put up condos or something, and Marty was the star. He was playing the club for a two-week run. I was going out with this guy, well, I didn't know it at the time, but he was, well, a sort of a criminal?"

"A sort of a criminal?" Zalman asked cautiously. "What sort of a criminal?"

"Oh, not a bad one! He didn't kill people or anything, I don't think! I think he was in protection, which at the time I thought was a branch of law enforcement. He was older than I was and we had a good time together for a while, but then he wanted me to move in with him, and I was so silly then, I just told him no thank you. I mean, I thought we were going to get married! I thought nice girls didn't do that sort of thing! I was so naive," she said. "And was he mad! He told me I was gonna do it. That's just what he said: 'You gonna do it!'" Lydia growled out an imitation of her criminal cutie's gravel delivery. "And I didn't know what to do! But Marty straightened everything out for me. He and my boyfriend just sat down and had a nice game of poker together, and Marty told me later there was no way he was going to lose when there was so much at stake!

Wasn't that sweet?" she said. "And then everything was all right! I quit the club and got a job selling perfume, which was much easier on my feet because you could wear flats since you were behind the counter all day long. Then a month or so later, Marty called me up and said his assistant quit on him to get married and would I like the job? Well, I certainly did want the job! Poor Marty, he was a real star back then. It's so sad that things haven't worked out too well for him, except he's married to Mitzi and she kind of"—Lydia lowered her voice—"takes care of him when he needs it, if you know what I mean. But working for a big star like Marty was a big break for me. He changed my life. I'd probably still be a waitress or maybe living with a criminal! Marty taught me a lot. He's a wonderful man, really. But lately . . ." She frowned and shook her blond head. "He thinks his age is catching up with him. Silly, isn't it? He's younger than pookie. . . ." She got up, kissed Earnest on top of the head, and pulled the ace of hearts out of his ear. "Now," she said, "we're doing the Metamorphosis routine and I've improved it just loads since we rehearsed it in Miami, so you watch out for the changes, okay? I want to know what you think. What you *honestly* think. I've got to go, I promised I'd watch Marty's act." And with that the Princess of Prestidigitation rushed out of the room in a cloud of glitter.

"What's the Metamorphosis routine?" Zalman asked, just for drill.

"Famous illusion in the magic world," Earnest told him as he lit one of Zalman's cigars. "Houdini did it, lots of magicians do it. It's kinda like passing the bar exam was for you, know what I mean? It's a first for Lydia, and she's a little worried about it."

"So what happens?" Zalman asked.

"It's like you have the magician in one place and the

assistant in the other and you tie them both up and put each of 'em in a big strong trunk with plenty of chains and padlocks to prove they can't get out and then, when you open the trunks, presto chango, they've switched places! See? It's magic."

"It's a transposition," Zalman said.

"Is that what it is? I thought they just changed places. Ahhh, the hell with it. Let's go siddown in front," Earnest said. "I know you're going to enjoy this, Jer. . . ."

Zalman opened his mouth, but thought better of what he'd been about to say. "You bet, Dad," he said. "I love it already."

ZALMAN AND EARNEST WOUND THEIR WAY BACK THROUGH the Cavern's steamy, bustling kitchen—Earnest definitely decided on the sole—and out into the entrance hall, where Sammy was leaning up against the wall, fanning a stack of menus one-handed just for practice.

"So?" the maître d' said. "You saw the beautiful Miss D?" He doffed his wizard's cap and held it reverently over his heart. "One of the great dames of all time, and I mean great! You're a lucky man, sport," he told Earnest, tapping him on the shoulder. "And don't you forget it. I got your table all ready for you."

"Down front?" Earnest asked.

"Sure, down front, whaddaya think? For a friend of Miss D, only the best," Sammy said, pulling aside the red satin curtain that led to the dining room. "Follow me, gents." He grinned as he settled his peaked cap back on his head.

The big dining room was overflowing with people laughing and talking and having their dinner. The pink granite walls were glowing with light and the ever-changing stars in the ceiling glistened like the spray a kid shoots up from a garden hose to kill the heat of summer. The Magic Cavern was a popular place, both with the wealthy tourists who flocked to see the big, Vegas-style shows and with hard-core Hollywood foodies. Mitzi's culinary shrewdness insured that a chic coterie of glitzy locals would frequent the Cavern as well as the awed out-of-towners. But tonight, no tourists were in evidence. The Magic Cavern's big dining room was thick with a gaggle of well-dressed Hollywoodniks trying to scarf down their dinners before the show began, and the room was alive with the low mumble of deal-making, accented by the Muzak of busy forks. Agents were table-hopping, producers were refusing, studio execs were saying yes, maybe next week, probably it's definite. Their wives were bored and their best friends were trying to look interested and wondering what was in it for them. Every seat in the house was full and there were plenty of dinner jackets and lots of low-cut gowns accentuating creamy cleavage and sparkling Paloma Picasso jewelry. The elite were meeting to eat, and it wasn't the Morton Downey, Jr., crowd by a long chalk. At least half the house was there on an expense account, and by the way they were chowing down it was obvious they were determined to get the company's money's worth.

"So?" Earnest said as they sat down. "You like her, Jer? You can level with me. Speak your mind, know what I mean?"

Zalman had been around the track enough times to know that whenever someone wanted you to level with them or asked you for your sincere personal opinion, they really wanted you to agree with them. Failing agreement, a big fat lie would do just as well, but in this case, he had no trouble telling the truth. Even though she had big, big problems, Lydia Devanti seemed like a lovely lady—a little ditzy, but hey, these days every being on the planet had a shaky brain; ditzyness was no disqualification.

"Great dame," Zalman told his dad, giving him a light sock on the arm. "Nice-looking, and a very sweet nature."

"Hey!" Earnest said defensively. "A poodle can have a sweet nature—this dame's got a mind! Now, we can help her out here, right, Jer?" he asked. "It's not gonna be a big problem, this thing with the psychic? I'm asking for your professional opinion, like as a lawyer, got it? And I want you to level with me."

"Hmmm," Zalman hedged. This time the truth didn't come so easily. "Let me think it over and we can talk about it tomorrow. I'm gonna need more information before I can get it figured—"

"Great!" Earnest said. "That's really great! Hey, there's Mitzi Melbourne, over there, see? At that table next to the bar," he said, pointing across the room. "Great gal. I gotta go say hello." Earnest jumped up, and Zalman watched as he snaked his way through the overflow crowd toward Mitzi's table, meeting and greeting as he went. A couple guys said hello to Earnest and introduced him to their ladies, and Earnest shook hands and kissed hands and slapped guys on the back like he'd been in town ten years instead of ten minutes.

When he was a kid, Zalman had figured his dad knew everybody in the world, and now that he was a grown-up, he was sure of it. Zalman smiled ruefully and shook his head.

His dreams of a peaceful week cleaning up details at the office, having a couple of new suits made, getting a shirt or two—shot. Lydia had a problem and that meant Zalman had a problem, because it was obviously true love between Earnest K. Zalman and the Princess of Prestidigitation. There was no way Earnest would stand still for the possibility of letting his lady love in for a public blackmailing or having a missionary mother-in-law moving in on him when there was a hope in hell his son could figure an angle.

And there was an added, highly unpleasant complication, and that was Lucille and her dopey client Bland. Zalman knew he ought to call Lucille and find out if she'd had any nasty communications from the blackmailing psychic, but he didn't have the heart to ruin his sister's Sunday evening at home with Phil and the kids. Besides, it was late and Zalman didn't want to deal with his sister's hysteria at this point in the evening. He already had too many problems on his plate without Lucille.

Anyway, he'd call Lucille first thing in the morning, and she'd probably invite them over for roast beef or maybe Chinese. Lucille couldn't cook worth squat because she was always on the phone and didn't pay attention to anything except business, but her schmuck husband, Phil Hanning, was a regular gourmet, and Zalman usually had dinner with them once a week. Yes, tomorrow was definitely better. If Bland was being blackmailed, Lucille's screams would resound all over the Greater Los Angeles Basin. Right now, Zalman had other things on his mind.

He glanced over at Mitzi Melbourne, winced, and looked away. Mitzi Melbourne, Little Miss Four-by-Four, was one of the ugliest human beings he'd ever seen. She looked like a two-hundred-pound frog with a red Brillo pad on top of its head, and the green satin bat-wing outfit she was wearing didn't do anything to improve her overall image of loveliness. Mitzi, who was lifting a dripping fork piled high with a mountain of cheese blintzes into her maw, put the fork down and shook hands with Earnest as he came up to her table. He sat down, pointed at Zalman, and Mitzi peered over at him through her green-framed Coke bottle glasses and began to wave furiously, one green satin bat-wing trailing into her blintzes. She looked like a refugee from a Saint Paddy's Day celebration in the heart of Boston.

Zalman got up and went over to her table. Even though she looked frogish, Mitzi Melbourne had a solid rep all over town. People said she was a tough negotiator and she'd take your shoes, socks, and shorts away with her if you didn't pay attention, but she was fair and not a bad person, especially if you could do business over the phone and didn't have to look at her much.

"Mitzi, you know my son, Jerry Zalman?" Earnest asked. "My famous son? The lawyer?"

Mitzi Melbourne peered up at him through her green glasses, her eyes shrewd as an old hen's behind the thick lenses. "I've heard about you, Jerry," she said, extending a pudgy hand. "I met your brother-in-law the other night. He came in with some people, we got to talking about this Wild West Museum he's promoting. Is it a good investment? What do you think?" Mitzi Melbourne asked.

Hanning the albatross, Zalman thought. Hanning the dead weight on my back. "Phil's a great guy," he said, hoping he sounded neutral.

Mitzi laughed, a short bray like a choking donkey. "Yeah, and he's got nice suits, too. Looks good in clothes. Didn't he used to be an actor?"

"Among other things," Zalman said easily.

"Okay, so he's a great guy, but what about the museum?" Mitzi pressed.

"He hasn't spoken to me about it," Zalman lied. He hated it when Phil put him on the spot and he had to lie. Not that he minded lying, he just didn't like to waste energy lying for Phil. Phil and his crackpot schemes. Why the hell didn't Lucille increase his allowance? Maybe if the guy had a little more spending cash, he'd lay off the so-called business deals, the desert land in Newhall, the hair transplant factory on the Yucatan Peninsula, the miracle mood pendant that read your aura. "Nice to meet you, Mitzi," he said as he left the table and threaded his way back toward his seat.

A lady agent named Annie Pepper waved at him enthusiastically from the far side of the room and Zalman waved back. Lots of waving, he thought as he realized that she was sitting with Tom Kellar. "Verrrrrry interesting," Zalman said under his breath. He wondered if the lady agent represented Kellar, or if they were just getting together for some gymnastics that involved lawn chairs. . . .

Kellar didn't look up. He was a big guy with a thatch of white hair and he was wearing a yellow satin sweatsuit and mirrored sunglasses. From across the room, that's all Zalman could see. He'd never met Kellar, but he knew the guy by reputation. Kellar was a well-known traveler on the Hollywood Hiway. He produced sitcoms, and most of his shows were simpleminded half-hour playlets that were enough to send any person with the intelligence of the average newt into sugar shock. Like Earnest had said, they usually involved a white-bread family who lived in a cute little country house and had vexing problems when the Immigration Service came around and wanted to repo their hardworking Guatemalan maid, or when dear old Grampy didn't want to go into the home. They always ended the same way, the happy family laughing heartily as Consuelo spilled soup all over the floor, and if you'd seen one, you'd seen enough. But Kellar's formula was fantastically successful; his shows played endlessly, night and day, all over the world via satellite. So, it you were stuck on safari in the wilds of darkest Mazingaland, chances were the natives would be gathered around the campfire, yukking it up to "Thicker 'n Water," "Cast the First Stone," or maybe "The Kunning's Kids."

A few minutes later, Earnest came back to the table. "Showtime!" he said, rubbing his hands together happily as he slipped into his chair. The lights dimmed, the curtain opened on a five-man combo, and they began to slaughter Cole Porter as the room quieted down to a feral roar.

After the combo had worked their way through a cha-cha medley of "Night and Day," "You're The Top," and "Brush Up Your Shakespeare," a skinny guy with a receding hairline, a pencil moustache, and buck teeth came onstage to a polite round of applause and began to do card tricks. "That's Marty Melbourne," Earnest said. "Poor guy. Must be tough, when you used to be a pretty big act and now you're a yutz. Kinda sad to see him go downhill like this. Like Lydia says, he taught her a lot, but now . . ." Earnest shrugged. "I don't like to say it about a guy, but Marty drinks a little too much and his hands shake. Mitzi's the brains of the outfit, but I guess you can tell that right off, huh?"

"Yeah," Zalman said. "Mitzi looks like nothing too much gets by her."

"She oughta cut down on the chow, though," Earnest said absently, tapping his heart. "Not good for the pump." He waved for Sammy and ordered sole for both of them, but told him to hold the food until after Lydia's act. "Just bring us a couple Bullshots and some salad for now, okay, Sammy? Fish okay with you, Jer?" he asked as Sammy disappeared across the room. "You oughta be watching your cholesterol. Stay away from your red meats, stick with your lighter foods. Y'know, couple months ago Lydia made me get my cholesterol checked and it was way over two-forty! Now, I got it down to one-ninety. God, I hate fish! And it was tough to give up ice cream, but I can live with ice milk, when I get the craving."

Onstage, Marty Melbourne went through his card routine, did a little close-up coin work at the edge of the stage, then a few bits with the cup and balls, but Zalman could tell his heart wasn't in it. Earnest was right—his hands shook and he had that shell-shocked look of an old warhorse who'd faced the Gatling guns across the footlights one too many times. Finally, Marty finished up onstage to a polite smattering of applause and the jazz combo took over again, this time murdering Gershwin.

Earnest waved for another round of drinks and began to chew thoughtfully on his salad. "So, Jer, whaddaya think? Way I see it, we gotta go talk to this guy Roy Caldwell tomorrow and get Lydia's tapes and photos off him." He shook his head and frowned, his eyes sharp behind his glasses. "We gotta threaten him," Earnest said darkly. "That's the way to do it. Lean on him a little, know what I mean? Throw the fear-a-God into him."

Zalman looked at his father in disbelief. He had the feeling that his mouth was hanging open wide enough to catch a swarm of killer bees, but he checked and it wasn't. Threaten him! He couldn't believe what he was hearing! Was this his father speaking? The man who'd taught him that you never draw to an inside straight? "Dad, are you crazy?" Zalman sputtered. "I'm a lawyer, I only threaten people when I can back it up in court! Don't let anybody hear you talk like that, okay? Threaten him! That's nutsy talk, Dad!"

Earnest smiled with the innocent guile of a cherub on a church window. "Don't lose control, Jer! I didn't mean we should punch him out or anything! I only meant that, within the confines of strict legality, completely within the bounds of the Constitution of these great United States, we should threaten him. That's all."

"Well, that's better," Zalman said sulkily. "I don't want you doing anything crazy, okay, Dad? Listen to me on this, we'll figure something out. Okay, Dad? You listening?"

Earnest smiled peacefully and continued to chew on his salad. "Good dressing," he remarked.

"Dad! . . ."

"No problem, Jer."

"Listen," Zalman said as he picked up his fork and began to shove his greens anxiously from one side of his plate to the other, "tell me this. You said Lydia had these photos locked up in her trunk, right? So how—"

"I know what you're gonna say," Earnest said, waving his hand deprecatingly. "Look around you, for Pete's sake. Lydia's always playing joints like this. Why, there's guys in here—ladies, too, y'know—who could pop open any bank in this town in ten minutes flat. Opening a little old trunk is like eating cheesecake to these guys. See that guy I just said hello to?" Earnest pointed to a conservatively dressed, gray-haired man sitting with an equally conservative wife. "Magic is a hobby with him, and he's a good mechanic, too. . . ."

"Mechanic?"

"Cards. Got fast hands. Guy can deal seconds, deal from the bottom, the side, stack a deck, you'd never know it unless you're a mechanic yourself. He's strictly legit, though, the grandkids love it for parties. Think he's a guy in the rag trade. . . . So when you talk about opening a trunk, that's nothing. Hell, I popped open that gate of yours and I bet you paid plenty for that lock, am I right? Locksmith told you it couldn't be opened by man nor thief."

Zalman nodded.

"See? And I'm not even half as good as him." Earnest waved at the gray-haired man with the fast hands.

"I get it," Zalman said thoughtfully. "So anybody in any of the magic clubs could have . . . "

"Yeah, sure, anybody Lydia knows, for Pete's sake. And they got these kinda clubs all over the country, y'know. Magic is very popular, even with kids. You ever seen Penn and Teller? Funny act. Ahhh, here come the girls. . . ."

Everyone began to applaud as the lights dimmed, then blazed up brightly as Simone came running onstage, illuminated in a pink baby spot. She was pushing a small gilt cart dripping with multicolored ribbons, and Sergeant Pepper, wearing an apricot uniform, was sitting on top of it on a little gold throne like he was the Monkey King. Simone began to wave her pink feather fan slowly back and forth, a network of pink rhinestones glittering in her hair, and the Sergeant handed her a stick which she instantly changed into a huge bouquet of silk flowers and tossed into the audience.

Dressed in her pink spangled costume, her red hair backlit, Simone looked very glamorous, very theatrical, very self-assured. Zalman had hardly noticed her backstage in Lydia's dressing room, but now, as she swung into her warm-up routine and did several tricks with large colored silk scarves, Simone looked right next door to beautiful. Zalman had often noticed that only a few performers had the same magnetism offstage that they were able to conjure up at will once their feet hit the boards. Bland, Lucille's rock-and-roll client, was a case in point. The kid was a huge international star, but he was almost invisible unless he had a guitar in his mitts. Like Bland, Simone was self-effacing offstage, but once safe on her own turf she was able to switch on the single most important tool of her trade—charisma.

Simone continued to warm up the audience for Lydia, and after a fairly standard routine with the scarves and a cute bit juggling fruit with Sergeant Pepper, she invited a volunteer from the audience to come up onstage and try to lift her off her feet. It looked easy—Simone couldn't have weighed in at more than one-ten—but although two or three guys snuggled up to her and did their best to pick her up, not one of them could budge her.

"Old routine," Earnest whispered, "but an audience pleaser. Works every time."

"You gonna tell me how she does it?" Zalman whispered back.

"I could," Earnest said, grinning, "but I won't. Wouldn't be fair to the trade, y'know. Gotta know how to keep a secret if you wanta hang out with magicians. That's the first thing I learned. Ahhh, here comes Lydia."

Zalman switched his attention back to the stage. Lydia made her entrance, and right from the start, it was obvious that she had the makings of a big star. While Simone had picked up a warm professional glow, Lydia shone like a galaxy. The combo kicked into her music and Lydia began to sing—

> Lovey Dovey,
> Who's my sweetie?
> Don't fly away,
> Darling tweetie . . .

—as she danced around the stage, pulling a multitude of doves from out of nowhere and releasing them into the dining room, where they flapped back and forth over the tables, then settled in the flies above the stage. Zalman was amazed—even though he'd seen her stashing the birds in her ample bosom, he couldn't for the life of him figure out how she got them out.

Slowly, as he watched the lovely Lydia and as her doves fluttered overhead like ticker tape, he began to have the wonderful, dreamy sensation that he was lost in a nightclub scene in a Fox musical. Usually, Zalman's taste ran to classic gangster flicks and film noir with bang-bang-bang dialogue and harsh, contrasty lighting, but he realized he had the mad desire to go home and put some old Betty Grable flicks on the VCR, kick back, and dissolve his troubles in a Technicolor world. . . . Everything was so beautiful, so soft-focus! Lydia, onstage in her fire-engine costume, the white doves over her head like snowflower petals adrift in a light winter mist, the cavernous pink walls of the Magic Cavern, the black-tie patrons seated in the audience . . .

Zalman sighed happily, and it suddenly occurred to him that if you were going to keep your head on straight in this crazy modern world, a strong sense of fantasy was better protection than a suit of armor.

SIMONE RAN BACK ONSTAGE CARRYING A FLAMING TAPER and lit a long row of torches that were lined up along the back of the stage, the spotlights catching on her pink sequined costume and throwing off tiny chips of sparkling light. Then she began to fling the torches to Lydia one after another and the two women juggled the blazing torches, pitching them high into the air, catching and hurling them back and forth across the stage to the accompaniment of some wild tiki-god music from the combo and tremendous applause from the audience. The whole shtick was hokey as hell, but the combination of the two beautiful women catching and tossing the fiery torches quickly captured the attention of the jaded Hollywood audience and they willingly forgave the schmaltz. Lydia and Simone ended the juggling portion of the act by flinging each torch high into the air above the stage, where it simply disappeared in a harsh whoosh of flame.

The audience cheered happily as they applauded Lydia and Simone and there were quite a few wolf whistles as Lydia stepped to the front of the stage, bowing modestly. "Well, folks," she said as she fluffed up her blond hair and smiled prettily over the footlights at the audience. "We hope you like what you've seen so far, but we're not finished yet! Tonight Simone and I want to try something special for you. It's a new illusion for us, and we've been working on it for quite a while. We hope you'll like seeing it as much as we like doing it. Tonight," she went on, "Simone and I are going to give you our special, all-new version of the great Harry Houdini's own most wonderful illusion, Metamorphosis!!!"

The audience cheered and whistled again as Lydia and Simone stepped to opposite sides of the stage, and a curtain opened behind them to reveal a huge silver iron maiden gliding forward under its own steam. It was an ugly thing, horrible and frightening, with a fat body and a knobby, vestigial head with a toothy metal smile pasted on its featureless face. Zalman didn't like it and neither did the rest of the audience; all of a sudden the applause died down, and a small shudder made its way across the room as the metal monster rolled forward and stopped in the center of the stage between Lydia and Simone. Zalman realized that the maiden's smooth, impassive grin reminded him of the *Mona Lisa,* never one of his Top Ten pictures. The maiden was easily eight feet tall and its studded silver skin looked cold to the touch. The audience sucked in its breath and gave a collective shiver, as a frisson of terror raised every neck hair in the room.

Simone flourished the huge pink feather fan that matched her pink spangled costume while the drummer gave out with a low drumroll. Then Lydia gestured again and another curtain opened, revealing a second, golden iron maiden, which slowly rolled forward to greet its sister.

Lydia and Simone walked forward and stood next to the great beasts, each woman caressing her terrible twin. Simultaneously, they touched concealed buttons and both of the metal monsters yawned open to reveal a thick forest of deadly teeth, rows of sharp steel spikes protruding from the doors that meshed with a second set of spikes in each maiden's belly. It was clear that when the door was closed, anyone inside would be punched full of holes.

The audience sucked in its breath again, and Zalman felt an uncomfortable tingle flip down his spine like a tiny green snake. Lydia smiled playfully, then reached out to touch one of the ugly spikes with her red-nailed finger. "Ohhhhhhh," she said in a little girl's voice, "that's sooooooo sharp!" The audience rippled with nervous laughter, but they didn't like it. Perhaps it was too real, Zalman thought. Perhaps the sight of the ugly ladies of metallica made them wary.

"Simone, the dolls, if you please!" Lydia said. Simone ran over to the little gilt cart and brought out a pair of large, smiley-faced dolls dressed in spangled pink and red costumes. One of the dolls was a blonde and the other was a redhead, and they were obviously meant to look exactly like Lydia and Simone.

Simone trotted over to Lydia, who took the dolls with a flourish and set them inside the two iron maidens as the audience laughed nervously. "Now," Lydia told them, "just to prove to you that these spikes are real . . ." Quickly, she slammed both doors shut, then opened them again just as quickly. The two dolls swung forward, impaled on the doors, glittery pink and red sawdust stuffing pouring out of their poor, mutilated toy bodies.

The audience laughed again, and this time the laughter was all nerves. Zalman looked over at Earnest, just to check things out. His father's face was composed and he was watching Lydia intently, but Zalman wondered if his old man had the jitters. If you were in love with the Mistress of Magic, did you worry every time she got sawed in half or climbed inside an iron maiden? Could you? Even though Earnest knew it was a trick, an "illusion"—hell, the whole audience knew it was a trick—there was always the awful possibility that it could go wrong, and there was something very, very nasty about the iron maidens. . . .

The two pretty ladies were going to climb inside those horrible maidens, a bad-tempered pair of vestal virgins doing an imitation of the shark from *Jaws* and, okay, it was a trick. Just a stage show. It wasn't for real. But yet . . .

Marty Melbourne came back onstage, bowing crablike as he ran, and the drummer went into a loud, ominous drumroll. "Watch closely, everyone!" he said, holding open the door of the silver iron maiden for Simone. She smiled out over the footlights and stepped inside, waving her fan. Marty slammed the door shut, giving it a theatrical push with his shoulder and a grunt as he did so.

Then Lydia stepped into her own, golden iron maiden.

"Now," she told the audience knowingly, as she settled herself in the monster's embrace. "we'll see if the lady is quicker than the maiden. . . ." And as Marty pushed the door closed on her, a few red feathers from her fan caught in the crack and one floated gently to the floor.

MARTY MELBOURNE GRABBED HOLD OF THE EDGE OF THE curtain and trotted across the stage like a one-trick pony, pulling the curtain closed as he ran. Then, without missing a beat, he trotted back again, reopening the same curtain. Both the silver and the golden iron maidens were still standing grimly in the center of the stage and the red feathers from Lydia's fan were still caught in the door. Apparently, the maidens hadn't budged.

"Now," Marty said, "which one should I open first?" He grinned slyly at the audience, teasing them, inviting them to choose between Lydia and Simone. "The silver? Or the gold? Tonight," he said with a laugh, rattling a huge jailer's key-ring on the end of his forefinger, "I think we'll open up . . . the silver maiden first! Now let me see," he said, drawing it out, "I forgot. Who was in the silver iron maiden? Miss Lydia or Miss Simone? Miss Simone, wasn't it?" he asked the audience. "Didn't we all see Miss Simone get into the silver iron maiden?"

"Yeah," a man in the audience yelled. "We did!"

Marty laughed, tipping an imaginary top hat, then quickly inserted the key in the big padlock and snapped open the silver iron maiden to reveal Lydia, now dressed

entirely in pink. She struck a campy pose with one hand
flung high, and the audience applauded wildly.

"But now!" Marty cried. "Look who we have here! Miss
Lydia!"

"There's the new touch Lydia was talking about," Earnest whispered to Zalman. "They've never done the costume switch before, just changed places."

Lydia stepped out of the iron maiden with a flourish and
the audience went nuts, clapping and giving out shrill wolf
whistles. She bowed left, right, and center, flipping her
pink fan with theatrical abandon. "Thank you, Marty," she
said, kissing him on the cheek. "Marty Melbourne, ladies
and gentlemen!" she called out as Marty bowed and was
accorded a respectable hand. Marty handed Lydia his big
key-ring and went over to the side of the stage, his rabbity
teeth gnawing his lower lip. Swiftly, Lydia ran to the
golden iron maiden, keys jingling as she took the padlock
in her hand. "Now, who can we have in here, I wonder?"
Lydia asked as she slipped the key into the padlock.
Slowly, she pulled open the door of the golden iron
maiden.

The audience saw it first, and a harsh gasp ran through
the crowd. Several women screamed in shock and there
was a crash of breaking glass as a waiter dropped a tray of
martinis in the back of the room. Zalman and Earnest
jumped to their feet at the same time and Earnest grabbed
his son's arm. "Jesus, Jerry," he said in a thick whisper,
and looked away.

Simone, now dressed in Lydia's sparkling red costume,
swung forward as the heavy door of the iron maiden
opened, spindled on the sharp steel spikes like an overdue
bill on a deadbeat's desk. Her body dangled helplessly,
rivulets of bright blood pouring from each wound like
thick, gooey syrup. In the brief second before the full hor-

ror hit him, Zalman thought she looked very much like Saint Sebastian, showered with a rain of arrows.

Her face was twisted toward the audience, and as she hung mutely on the spikes Zalman thought he saw a look of anger and disbelief in her eyes, a reflection of her surprise when, at the exact instant of her death, poor little Simone realized that this was one trick that was no illusion.

Rosy blood the color of raspberry soda streamed down her body and over her spangled red costume, and the colors had meshed so completely that it was difficult to tell where the blood left off and the costume began. Hanging there, she had the limp, formless droop of a crushed cat on the side of the freeway, and though she had died only a moment ago, she looked shriveled, like a wrinkled old bag of skin. Zalman shivered when he realized that her auburn hair reminded him of Marie.

Lydia shrieked in horror and clawed the air with frantic hands. She made a convulsive move toward Simone's bleeding body, but Marty Melbourne rushed over to her from his post at the side of the stage, grabbed her, and took her in his arms, shielding her face with his hand. He stared helplessly out into the audience, his eyes searching across the footlights, and Zalman realized he was looking for his wife, hoping that Little Miss Four-by-Four would handle this situation just the way she handled everything else.

Mitzi Melbourne didn't fail her husband. "Bring down the goddamn curtain," she boomed in a voice that could melt bricks. Zalman turned and saw Mitzi standing at her table in the rear of the Magic Cavern, one fat arm extended in command, green bat-wing waving. "Bring the sonafabitch down!" she brayed. Slowly, a hidden stagehand obeyed, and the curtan was unceremoniously yanked closed on the frozen tableau of Marty Melbourne, Lydia

Devanti, and the helpless body of poor little Simone, dripping with blood.

All around, people in the audience were grabbing their belongings and chattering in harsh, excited voices as they streamed out of the Magic Cavern before anyone could stop them. Zalman figured at least five hundred people had seen every detail of Simone's murder, and not a one of them knew how it had happened, not even himself. So much for eyewitnesses, he thought grimly. A thought hit him and he looked back toward the table where he'd seen Annie Pepper sitting with Tom Kellar, but they were gone.

"Damn," Zalman muttered under his breath. "The trouble with murder is it always happens before you know it."

"What'd you say?" Earnest asked, grabbing at his arm. "C'mon, I gotta go backstage and see Lydia. She's gonna need me. This is terrible. . . . What an awful thing to happen, and on her opening night! She'll never get over it—never! I told you she was sensitive! Terrible!"

"Simone probably thought so, too." Zalman mused as he and Earnest fought their way through the crowd, heading toward the kitchen and the dressing rooms beyond. Sammy, the maître d', grabbed Earnest's arm. "Hey, sport!" he said sharply. "Don't you two guys try to cut and run! The cops're gonna wanta talk to you!"

"No problem," Zalman said. "I'm an attorney."

"Yeah?" Sammy said. "You do personal injury? A dentist in a brand-new Caddy rear-ended me and I gotta whiplash you wouldn't—"

"Talk to me later," Zalman said, handing him his card. "Right now we gotta see Miss Devanti."

Backstage, Lydia was in hysterics. The Mistress of Magic was seated at her littered dressing table, her makeup a sloppy mess from her vague attempts to rub it off, her blond hair tousled. Marty Melbourne was at her side, patting her arm in a pathetic attempt to comfort her.

"Don't worry, Lydia," he was saying as Zalman and Earnest came through the door. "It wasn't your fault. I know you're scared, I know you blame yourself, but these accidents happen, even to the best of us. Magic can be a dangerous profession. . . ."

Lydia jumped up and threw herself at Earnest. "Oh, Erniekins! Darling!" she cried as Earnest took her in his arms. "Oh, God, how could this have happened? Did I do something wrong? I didn't, I know I didn't. We did everything the same as always! We'd been over it a hundred—"

Earnest sat her back down at her dressing table, bent over, and kissed the top of her head. "Now, babe," he said sternly, staring into her eyes, "You gotta stop this right now, before you get crazy. This wasn't your fault. Are you hearing me? This was terrible, a horrible accident, but it wasn't your fault. Simone checked the apparatus herself, didn't she? Just like she always did? I heard her say she was going to do it. . . ."

Marty Melbourne looked sadly at Zalman, his buck teeth cutting into his lower lip. "Poor kid," he said under his breath, indicating Lydia. "I told her magic could be dangerous. This isn't the first time something's gone wrong onstage. Beginning of the century, Chung Ling Soo got himself shot onstage doing the Gun Trick! Even Houdini didn't do the Gun Trick after that! I told her magic could be dangerous! I've known Lydia for years, she tell you? Me and Mitzi, we been like the folks she never had. This is gonna be terrible for her, just terrible! She always blames herself when something goes wrong, y'know? Takes stuff on herself. It's a crime."

"Yeah, I think so too," Zalman said.

Marty looked at him blankly. "Huh?" he said.

"Ohhhhhh . . ." Lydia began to cry softly. "We did everything just like always, just like always," she snuffled into Earnest's sleeve. "But did I do something wrong? What could have happened? Oh, God, I never should have tried Metamorphosis, this is all my fault! Ambition! Ambition is murder! Why did you let me do it, Marty?" she asked him. "I wasn't ready! I knew I wasn't ready! And now Simone is dead!"

"You *were* ready," Marty told her. "You got what it takes, Lydia. You could be at the top of the world of magic! But you gotta keep reaching! Try new things! Otherwise, you end up like me!" Melbourne's rabbity teeth chewed at his lower lip again, like he was Bugs Bunny after a juicy carrot. "I didn't try hard enough!"

"No offense, Marty, but you're right," Earnest said. "You wanta hit the top, babe, you gotta keep aiming high, just like Marty's telling you! You didn't do anything wrong, something *went* wrong. But you didn't do it, okay? Trust Erniekins?" he soothed, stroking her hair.

"Ummmm, yessss . . ." Lydia whimpered, nestling in his arms.

Earnest looked over at Zalman. "Now what, Jer?" he asked.

Zalman sat down and fished his cigar case out of his breast pocket. "Well," he said as he offered cigars to Earnest and Marty, selected one for himself, and carefully manicured the tip. "We might as well get comfortable, boys and girls, 'cause we're in for a rocky night."

"WHY ME!!" CAPTAIN ARNOLD THRASHER BELLOWED AT the top of his lungs. Marie's dad had put on a few pounds since Zalman had seen him last, and his tummy was hanging out over the black vinyl belt of his baby blue polyester pants and peeking out between the buttons of his matching baby blue wash-'n'-wear short-sleeved shirt. He was wearing a jolly yellow tie with a design of crabs on it. The big cop had a weakness for crustacean neckwear, and in odd moments, Zalman often wondered where in the world he managed to find 'em. Was there a special barnacle boutique for cops who dug crayfish? Lobsters R Us? Arthropods Only? He'd never had the guts to ask.

Thrasher, who was six three and weighed in around twotwenty, had arrived only moments ago, and now he stood staring angrily around the Magic Cavern, horrified to find his son-in-common-law at the scene of yet another crime. Clearly, Captain Arnold Thrasher was not a happy copper.

He'd first met Zalman and Zalman's scruffy pal Doyle Dean McCoy years ago when Zalman was goofing around the picket line at UCLA, trying to pick up tall blondes, and Thrasher knew right off the bat that he hated both Zalman and McCoy. Zalman managed to elude his claws, but Thrasher successfully sent McCoy to San Quentin for a brief vacation after McCoy allegedly kidnapped the dean of men and stashed him in a broom closet for a nap. McCoy, who still brooded about his trip to the slammer, thought of himself as a redneck version of Jean Valjean and claimed it was a bum rap.

Many years later, when Jerry Zalman met Marie Thrasher and they fell in love, Thrasher couldn't believe his bad luck. It was like Freddy from *Nightmare on Elm Street* had moved in next door, in 3-D. The fact that Marie was crazy about Zalman meant nothing. The fact that Zalman was crazy about Marie meant nothing. The fact that Zalman was a real, grown-up lawyer with an office in Beverly Hills, a classic Mercedes, and an upscale lifestyle meant nothing. Thrasher adored his daughter, and it figured that no man in the entire universe was good enough for her, especially not a short, smart-mouthed onetime troublemaker whose best pal had done time at the cross-bar hotel.

"I'm glad Marie isn't here to see this," Thrasher snarled. "On the other hand, maybe if I shot you now and put you out of my misery, she'd learn to forget, get involved with a guy who does honest work. Like running a hardware store or a barbershop or something."

"Cut the comedy, will you, Arnie?" Zalman said. It was always a mistake to take Thrasher too seriously. "This is murder here!"

"Don't call me Arnie or I *will* shoot you," Thrasher said, breathing as heavily as a rodeo bull coming out of the chute. The big room was empty; other than the cops, who were photographing Simone's crumpled body and poking around backstage hoping to see a naked girl, everyone had beat it. Mitzi and Marty Melbourne were hiding out in Mitzi's office down the hall from the dressing rooms, Sammy was lounging around the back of the dining room walking a coin back and forth across his knuckles, and the cooks and waiters were cowering in the kitchen.

Thrasher rubbed his prickly Marine haircut and looked

balefully at Zalman. "Damn," he said. "Even though I hate talking to you, Zalman, you were a witness. So I guess you better tell me what happened here."

"Why don't we sit down and have a drink, Arnie?" Zalman said, gesturing to Sammy. "I bet you're gonna want one. Look, before we go any further, you'd better meet my father," he said as he maneuvered Thrasher down front toward his table. "Arnie, this is Earnest Zalman. Dad, this is Marie's father, Captain Thrasher."

Thrasher stared down at Earnest in anguish. "I don't believe it!" he said in a pained voice. "I don't believe you have a father! I thought you was hatched!"

Earnest looked from Zalman to Thrasher and back again. "Ay-yi-yi! This guy is the girlfriend's father? A cop? Why didn't you tell me before?" he moaned. "Jer, I think we're in top trouble." Nevertheless, he flashed Thrasher a wide grin and stuck out his hand for a shake. "Earnest K. Zalman. Pleased ta meetcha."

Thrasher took the proffered hand and shook it limply. He stared long and hard at Earnest, then at Zalman, then back at Earnest "Oh, God," he groaned. "There's two of them! I can see the resemblance! I don't believe this is for real! Two of them!" He sank down at the table, his bulk nearly snapping the tiny gilt chair, and put his head in his hands. "It's bad enough my little girl says she's crazy about you, you shrimp sonofabitch," Thrasher said in a muffled voice, "but now you have to go and have a father? Oh, God, this is awful." He sighed heavily and lifted his head from his hands. "How did this happen to me? Where did I go wrong?"

"Don't tell him, Jer," Earnest advised. "Believe me, he don't wanna know."

Thrasher looked at the two men, blinking like a big white rat. "Well," he said with a philosophical air as he loosened his crab tie, "the policeman's lot ain't a goddamn happy one, lemme tell you. Okay, Zalman, let's have it. What happened this time?"

Zalman sat down at the table as Sammy came over with a tray of Bullshots. "I brought one for you, Captain," the maître d' said. "I allus figured that no-drinking-on-duty stuff was a crock."

"It is tonight," Thrasher snapped, and drained his glass. "I'll have another. I'm waiting, Mr. Zalman," he said combatively. "Let's hear it."

"Arnie! I'm an innocent bystander, I swear it! My father just flew in from New York and he suggested we drop by to see his friend Miss Devanti, who's performing here for a three-week run. Miss Devanti and her assistant, the young lady who died, came onstage to do their act, and something went wrong. The young lady falls out of the iron maiden, and she's dead. That's all I know," Zalman said in his most sincere voice. Of course, that wasn't all he knew, but he wasn't about to volunteer any information unless Thrasher oiled up the rack and trotted out the thumbscrews. After all, why should he tell Thrasher about the blackmailing? Or that it was true love between Earnest K. and the Princess of Prestidigitation? Why should he bring up the psychic who thought he was a Scotsman, or mention the stolen porno pics of Lydia and the big-time Hollywood TV producer who liked to play stocks 'n' bondage? Why should *he* be the one to tell Thrasher about the possibility that Lucille Zalman Hanning's biggest client, Bland, had also been involved with Lydia? Why should *he* be the one to bring up these things? After all, the information overload would only drive Thrasher certifiably nuts, so why say anything until he had to? Zalman smiled honestly, a warm, caring-and-sharing smile, and hoped desperately that Thrasher would fall for it and let him the hell out of this lunatic asylum so he could drag Earnest K. Zalman home and proceed to beat him to a pulp. Zalman smiled again, a real Liberace, "Sincerely Yours" smile.

Thrasher lifted an eyebrow and looked slowly around the room. Very carefully, he folded up his crab tie and put it tenderly in his pocket. "Didn't this joint usta be a disco or something?" he asked conversationally, completely ignoring Zalman's little litany. "I usta work Vice here in Hollywood, y'know," he confided, "before they transferred me out to the Valley. They said I wasn't in tune with the times, they said I was out of touch with today's kids, so they transferred me. Jeez, though, you usta see all kindsa weird stuff on the Strip in the old days. You know, one day I was comin' outta Schwab's after lunch—they made a pretty good BLT there—and I hear this clippity-clop, clippity-clop," Thrasher said, looking at Zalman and Earnest with expectation. "Yeah, clippity-clop. So whaddaya think it was?"

"A horse," Earnest said.

"Yeah! A horse. How'd you know?" Thrasher said.

"Well, when you said clippity-clop you sorta gave it away," Earnest told him. "See, that's a real horse kind of noise, clippity-clop. One thing I know about is horses."

"Hmmm, yeah, I can see where clippity-clop would sorta be a dead giveaway," Thrasher said. "But yeah, it was a guy driving a big covered wagon with a sign on it that said 'Alaska or Bust,' and he had on a cowboy suit and a lady with him with one of them big sunhats? I wonder if the guy ever made it. . . ." Thrasher said thoughtfully. "So you see, I'm usta seeing weird stuff. Then they send me out to the Valley. Like you don't see weird stuff in the Valley these days, what with all the gangs and crap," he snorted. "Now they've decided the little buggers need guidelines—that's what they call it, guidelines!—they think I'm in touch again, so they transferred me the hell back. But I don't mind," he said with a knowing air, "I like working in Hollywood. You see all kinds here," he said, looking straight at Zalman. "All goddamn kinds."

Zalman wished he'd had time for the sole. It looked like Thrasher wasn't going to let them go until the dawn's early light, and he always hated to face a police grilling on an empty stomach. It also meant he'd have to wait until later to commit patricide, but there was plenty of time for that. Besides, when Lucille found out that Earnest had been in town for an hour or two and was already involved in a murder, maybe he'd get lucky and she'd do it for him.

ZALMAN, EARNEST, LYDIA, SAMMY, AND THE MEL-bournes hung around the Magic Cavern for the next four hours chatting with Captain Arnold Thrasher. Everyone swore up and down they didn't know nothing from nothing, hadn't any idea how Simone got herself punched full of holes inside the iron maiden, nor did they have any idea who did it or why, but Thrasher kept on asking them anyway, over and over and over again.

Zalman hung around acting like Mr. Casual and listening to Thrasher nibbling away at the alibis of his victims, but the big cop wasn't getting anywhere. Marty Melbourne had been up on stage, right next to Lydia, in plain sight during the whole sequence. He claimed he'd seen nothing unusual, even though he swore he was being super-duper vigilant because he wanted Lydia's first shot at Metamorphosis to be perfect. "Look, Captain," Marty explained, "me and Mitzi, we been like parents to this girl! This was a big night for her, so I was on the lookout, understand? Everything was going great right up until Simone falls out of the maiden! Whoever did it, they did it good, that's all I can say," Marty said, shaking his head with professional awe. "I may be a little past the old prime, but up until now nothing in the magic line ever slipped by me! This killer? He's good."

Mitzi said she was at her table during the entire evening, and the kitchen staff backed her up. "Listen, Captain," she snorted, her chins wagging one after another, "I'm no sylph, get it? Once I get myself parked for the evening, I don't budge unless I gotta answer an urgent call of nature, see? Sure, I saw Lydia and Simone go onstage, but I don't pay much attention to the acts, tell you the truth. That's Marty's department. I was too busy counting the house. That's *my* department."

Sammy said he was in the kitchen berating a hapless waiter. "Can you believe this guy?" the maître d' asked. "One of the customers says he wants the chops rare, a side-a sliced toms, no fries? This waiter I got? He brings the customer steak medium with onion rings! Then he starts up giving the customer a hard time about it! Only thing worse than cooks? Waiters, I tell you. . . ."

Nothing from nothing. The endless evening was duller than humanly possible, and Zalman, who thought boredom was the worst kind of police brutality, hung around just in case a deranged lunatic burst into the room shrieking, "I'm the killer, Captain! Book me and let's all go home!" but no such luck. He decided to keep his mouth shut. Even though Captain Arnold Thrasher suffered from brain drain, he'd only take so much punishment before he'd leap on you and rip your head off with his bare teeth. Zalman thought it wise not to push the old stoat too far.

Luckily, even without any coaching, both Earnest and Lydia were smart enough not to mention the blackmail scheme. Lydia's lovely blue eyes filled with tears every time Thrasher got near her, and finally the captain quit asking her questions in disgust. "I don't know, Captain," she wailed. "I blame myself! We did everything just the same as we did it in rehearsal! What went wrong?"

Earnest played it cool. He hovered over Lydia when Thrasher questioned her, offering her little sips of water and urging her to try to stop crying and tell the captain what he wanted to know. After all, Captain Thrasher was only trying to help, right?

As for Zalman, he simply let his eyes glaze over and kept repeating his story every time it was his turn to be drawn and quartered, and finally, around three-thirty in the morning, Thrasher morosely decided that he didn't have a hope in hell of stringing up the Zalmans, père et fils, and told everybody to go home.

"But don't leave town!" the big cop bellowed.

"Is this guy kidding?" Earnest whispered to Zalman. "Don't leave town? Did he really say that? I hope the girl-friend is better-looking than her father, Jer, 'cause if she takes after that hippopotamus I'm gonna have you committed."

"Shut up, Dad," Zalman whispered back. "I'll talk to you later. You're in deep enough already. Go get Lydia and the little ape and let's get out of here before Thrasher changes his so-called mind." He turned to Thrasher and smiled winningly. "I'll be glad to take Miss Devanti back to her hotel," he told the cop.

"Yeah, yeah," Thrasher said unhappily. "Just get out of my sight, all of you. Buncha damn nuts," he mumbled.

Silently, Zalman ushered Earnest and Lydia into the Mercedes, which was waiting unscathed in the empty parking lot. Earnest hopped into the back seat and Lydia, who had Sergeant Pepper draped around her neck, got in front and instantly began rummaging in her purse for her lipstick. "I look awful!" she moaned. "I'm all wizened!"

"No, you're not, babe, you look tired, is all," Earnest said, trying to comfort her.

Zalman got behind the wheel, started the car, and drove away from the Magic Cavern. *"All right!"* he exploded. "What's going on here! Dad, I'm giving you about ten seconds . . ."

"I don't know a damn thing!" Earnest responded hotly. "The girl got herself killed! I had nothing to do with it! I'm an innocent bystander!"

Lydia broke into tears again and Sergeant Pepper made a hissing noise like an unhappy reptile, then bared his fangs at Zalman.

"I'm warning you," Zalman told the monkey, "I hate you. Stay away from me. . . ."

"Now look what you've done!" Earnest said with indignation. "You made Lydia cry! It's all right, babe," he said, leaning forward to stroke her shoulder. "Jerry didn't mean it." Lydia continued to wail with the decibel level of an air-raid siren.

"Is it too late to kill myself?" Zalman wondered aloud as he swung down onto the Strip. "I think the gardener left some snail-bait lying around the pool. Maybe there's enough left to do the job. Probably be all over in a matter of . . ."

Lydia continued to howl, and Sergeant Pepper adjusted his little cap and spasmodically plucked at Zalman's sleeve in a simian attempt to protect his mistress.

"Get away from me!" Zalman warned the monkey. "I told you before! I hate you! I hate all monkeys! What hotel are you staying at? Where am I going? Please, some directions before we turn into the *Flying Dutchman*."

"I'm staying at the Chateau Marmont," Lydia said, snuffling wetly. "Please, Jerry, you mustn't hold this against me . . . I didn't know Simone was going to be killed. Honest! I had nothing to do with it!"

"I believe you! I believe you!" Zalman said. "Thousands wouldn't, but I believe you!"

"There, there, pookie, don't cry," Earnest said. "I told you Jerry would take care of everything, didn't I?"

"Ummmm, yes," Lydia whimpered.

"And does Erniekins ever lie to Lydia?"

"Ummmmm, no," Lydia said.

"So Erniekins promises Jerry will fix everything up, okay? Now, feel better?"

"Terrific," Zalman groaned. "Just terrific."

They dropped Lydia and Sergeant Pepper off at the Chateau Marmont—she had a very nice bungalow, she said—and Zalman took Earnest back to his house to kill him.

As he walked in the door Zalman saw that his answering machine was blinking, and he remembered that Marie had said she'd call when she got to Eugene. It seemed like centuries ago that he'd dropped her off at the airport, and he missed her terribly. Marie was so smart, she had such a level head on her shoulders! He punched the button on the machine and there was some giggling, then someone—who could it be?—began to sing "Hats Off to Larry" in the voice of Alvin the Chipmunk. The singing ended and Marie said, "I'm going to sleep, call me tomorrow. Good night, ootsie-wootsie! Umms Mommy misses umms good wittle boy . . ."

Rutherford, who'd been napping on the couch, jumped up and began to howl pathetically at the sound of Marie's voice, whimpering and whining and rubbing his snout on the armchair.

"Hah!" Earnest cried from the kitchen. "And you're giving *me* a hard time! At least Lydia talks English!" Triumphantly, he settled down on the couch, a cheese sandwich in one hand, a cold bottle of Tuborg in the other "The hell with my cholesterol," he muttered. "I'm starved!" Rutherford, his eyes pinned on the sandwich, sat down at his feet and began to drool on the carpet. "You wanna cheese sandwich, Jer?" Earnest said with his mouth full. "I may have another when I'm through with this one. You got some nice-looking salami in the fridge."

Zalman stared at his father, peacefully munching his cheddar. "How well did you know Simone, Dad?" he asked, trying to sound like he was in control.

Earnest shrugged and continued to chomp. "Not well. She's been with Lydia for maybe eight, nine months. Lydia was happy to get her. It's tough to find a good assistant, Lydia says. They always wanta be stars, upstage the headliner. But Lydia, she's the star of her act, so she just needed Simone for a second banana. But Simone seemed happy—besides, Simone told me once you can learn a lot from Lydia. Nice girl. Quiet, friendly. Can't imagine why someone would want to kill her. . . ."

"Dad!" Zalman said with exasperation. "You gotta face facts! This has something to do with the blackmailing, right? Now, the way I see it, we have three possibilities. Numero uno, somebody wanted to kill Simone for some reason we don't know about. If so, the deed is done, right? Numero dos, the killer was after Lydia and he missed and got Simone!"

Earnest looked up from his sandwich. "Whaddaya mean?" he asked sharply.

"The girls were doing this switcheroo act, right? They

even switched costumes, and you said yourself it was a new touch. So maybe the guy blew it and got the wrong dame! In which case it's possible he tries again, and that means we're in big trouble, got it?"

"That creep Roy Caldwell, I'll kill him!" Earnest yelled, dropping his cheese sandwich to the floor. Rutherford lunged for it and skulked off by the bar with his prize. "It's gotta be him! And if it is, I'm gonna rip that bastard's lungs out!"

"Dad, listen up! I told you before, we ain't ripping out anybody's lungs and that's a fact! Besides which, we don't know it was Caldwell. It could be one of the other guys. Could be Bland. A horrible possibility for Lucille, since Bland pays a lot of bills around the Casa del Hanning, but it could be him. Could be Lenny Dunn. Also, it could be Tom Kellar. He was there tonight, you notice?"

Earnest shook his head. "Kellar? Good thing I didn't see him, I woulda ripped *his* lungs out. . . ."

Zalman thought about throttling his father, but remained calm. "Yeah. Kellar was with a lady agent I know. Cute, huh? I'll give her a buzz tomorrow, see what she's got to say for herself. And don't forget numero tres, which is that the answer is none of the above."

"I guess it wasn't an accident, huh?" Earnest said slowly. "Any chance it was an accident?"

Zalman shrugged. "It could happen. I knew a guy once, he was driving under an overpass on the Ventura Freeway and an RV fell off the top and killed him deader 'n disco. Things happen. . . ."

"Things happen. Right. And disco's coming back, by the way. But the point is, you don't believe it was an accident."

Zalman shook his head. "It was no accident. Took too much planning, too much thought."

"Damn," Earnest said slowly. "I was enjoying that sandwich and now I've lost my appetite."

"You've lost the sandwich, too," Zalman said, pointing at Rutherford, who was contentedly gnawing away at the remains of the sandwich. Zalman got up and went into the kitchen to make himself a sandwich before he turned in. Luckily, since he started hanging out with Marie, she'd taught him the wisdom of a well-stocked fridge, and there was a wide assortment of goodies waiting for him, mostly deli. "I guess you're right. Some salami would go good with the cheddar," he said as he stood in front of the open fridge and thought about murder.

ZALMAN MADE HIMSELF A SALAMI AND CHEDDAR SANDwich lathered with Chinese sweet 'n' hot mustard and managed to eat about half of it; Rutherford had the other half and a nice big bowl of water. Rutherford had a mutant fondness for Chinese sweet 'n' hot. Then they got Earnest bedded down in the guest room and finally managed to climb into the sack around five. Rutherford, who had territorial ambitions, took up most of the bed, and Zalman woke up at ten, shoved over to one side with Rutherford's head next to his on the pillow. Rutherford gazed at him adoringly, panting. "You're so beautiful in the morning, sweetheart," Zalman said caustically as the Doberman stared longingly into his eyes. "But you smell like fish." Zalman jumped out of bed and headed for the shower, hoping he could wash the sludge out of his brain before the day attacked him.

When he was dressed, Zalman phoned Esther Wong, his beautiful Eurasian secretary. She wasn't in the office yet, so he tried her at home.

"Esther?" he said when she picked up. "Is that you? You sound like you're underwater."

"Oh, hi, Mr. Z.," Esther said sleepily. "Ohhh, what time is it? I guess I should be in the office, huh?"

"Why do you think that, Esther?" Zalman said. "It's only eleven, why bother to go in when it's almost lunchtime?"

"I had a late night," she explained. "I went to a concert at the Music Center? And then I met a great guy at this party backstage? So we went down to the Pantry after and had steak and eggs and I don't think I got home till three. Have you ever been to the Pantry? It's neat."

"Esther," Zalman explained patiently, "this is not the time. I don't suppose you happen to remember what my schedule is today? Any chance of that, Esther?"

Esther was silent for a minute. "Somebody or other is supposed to come in this afternoon . . . I forget who . . . just give me a minute and it'll come back to me."

"I'll tell you what, dear," Zalman said, sighing. "I want you to throw on your clothes real fast and race into the office and cancel everything, okay? This is an emergency, so I need your help, pronto."

"A real emergency? You're not just saying it's an emergency so I'll go in to the office without my makeup and then you'll laugh at me, are you?" Esther asked. Suddenly she sounded more alert; that was the great thing about Esther and that was why Zalman put up with her general ineptitude. Esther hated the daily grind, she didn't like to write down messages, filing bored her, and she couldn't stand typing because it ruined her nails. Dictation? Hopeless. However, just ask her to race to the office on a moment's notice, then drive out to the airport and hop a plane to Hong Kong and back overnight, give her something difficult or exciting to do, and Esther Wong wouldn't let you down. Thus, to Jerry Zalman, she was invaluable.

"Yes, a real emergency. My dad's in town and—"

"That's an emergency?" Esther sounded disappointed.

"—and we were witnesses to a murder."

"That's an emergency. Okay, I'll be right in. Don't worry, Mr. Z.," she said. "I'll take care of everything."

"I'm depending on you, dear." Zalman hung up, then phoned his sister Lucille. Her schmuck husband answered the phone.

Lucille and Phil Hanning were an exceedingly modern couple. Lucille, who was ferociously ambitious, was very successful as a personal manager in the record business and had quite a few big acts, although Bland was her meat and potatoes. So she went to work every day, made all the money, fought with the accountant, and wondered if she should play it safe with the thirty-year Treasury notes or take a flyer and invest in a retirement home in Santa Fe. And, because she and Phil loved each other very much, she had a home and a family and a happy life waiting for her and didn't feel she had to be Superwoman once she kicked off her shoes at the end of the day.

But although he adored his wife and kids, househusbandry chafed at Phil Hanning like an itchy red rash cortisone couldn't cure. Phil had wanted to be an actor and had actually managed to plant his handsome mug on the screen once or twice, before Lucille got the bit in her teeth about building an empire of personal management that would someday circle the globe. So, because he'd never been a very good actor or made more than ten, fifteen bucks at it, Phil Hanning stayed home, took care of the kids, and cooked fabulous gourmet dinners that Lucille said made it a pleasure to give a dinner party. Still, his role chafed, and Phil was always involved in some dumb business scheme that he claimed would make everyone involved a huge pile of money with absolutely no effort whatsoever. Invariably, the scheme went bust and Phil lost his shirt, so Lucille was very, very careful about cash and kept the poor guy on a short financial leash.

"Zally!" Phil Hanning said joyfully. "How's every little thing! Say, you know, I tried to call you the other day but you weren't home and I got ahold of Isobel, your cleaning consultant?"

"You mean Isobel, my maid?"

"Hey, she's very sharp! Got a lotta big plans! So she told me about this Jack the Zipper franchise she's investing in —the high-class soft-porn thing? She tell you about it?" Hanning asked anxiously. Hanning was always anxious. "So I'm wondering if maybe you'd like to kick in a little dough, you know, like get involved in a monetary sense?"

Zalman shook his head. If it weren't for the fact that, in a moment of uncharacteristic bravery, Phil Hanning had once stopped a bullet that would have permanently ended Zalman's career, Zalman would have had him put to sleep a long time ago.

"Not a cent, Phil," Zalman said cheerfully. "And watch out for Isobel, she'll take you to the cleaners. Lucille around? I got news."

"Uh-oh," Phil said "Yeah, she's here. *Lucille!*" he shrieked. *"It's Jerry!"*

Zalman yanked the phone away from his ear. "Jesus, Phil. . . ."

Lucille picked up the extension. "I got enough problems, Jer," she said. "You give Phil any money, that's your lookout."

"Are you kidding?" Zalman laughed. "I love Phil, but

like I told him, not a cent. Look, Dad's in town. Came in last night."

"He's staying with you?" Lucille shrilled. "What's the matter, he hates his grandchildren?"

"Lucille," Zalman warned, "we've got a problem. . . ."

"How can we have a problem?" she said, her voice rising higher. "He just got here! Look, come for dinner, I'll tell Phil to make Chinese. I gotta get in to the studio. Bland's cutting the new album out at his place in Malibu and all of a sudden he tells me he wants to do a gong track. Can you bee-leeeve it! Gongs, he's giving me, gongs! Like he's some New Age woo-woo jazz artist!"

"Shut up, dear, and listen to me. Bland is part of the problem."

"Oh, no. . . . Don't do this to me, Jerry, I can't take it. Not now. . . ."

"Pay attention, Lucille! This is serious. Dad's got a new girlfriend—"

"Is that all!" Lucille said with relief. "He's always got a new girlfriend, that's no big deal! What else is new. . . ."

"Lucille!" Zalman shrieked. "Listen to me! The new girlfriend is Lydia Devanti, the Princess of Prestidigitation, currently appearing at Mitzi's Magic Cavern."

"Yeah, yeah, I know the Cavern."

"Lydia Devanti used to date Bland. Answer me this, Lucille. Has Bland said anything to you about needing extra money? Big chunks of money?"

"No . . ." Lucille said slowly. "I pay all his bills through the office, he just charges whatever he wants. Besides, he thinks money ain't spiritual. What's this about, Jerry? I think I'm getting nervous here."

"I'll explain it to you if you'll keep quiet a minute! Lydia Devanti went to a psychic and got herself hypnotized, and while she was in the middle of some damn past-life regression she tells the psychic all about Bland and all her other ex-boyfriends, and she's had plenty! So now the psychic's threatening blackmail and it looks like Bland could be in for some trouble. I met Lydia and she's a great dame and Dad thinks she's the greatest and blah blah blah, but I think we got big problems. You haven't heard anything about blackmail?"

"Blackmail! Jerrrrrrry!" Lucille whined. "This is awful! No, Bland hasn't said anything."

"Listen further, my pet, 'cause it's gonna get a whole lot worse. Last night, Dad hauls me down to the Magic Cavern to see the show and Lydia Devanti's assistant gets croaked—"

Lucille sucked in her breath. "Dead? You mean she's dead?"

Zalman ignored her. "Now, me, I've seen 'Mannix' and 'The New Mike Hammer' and 'Simon and Simon' so I'm up on the ins and outs of detective work, and I figure the murder and the blackmail are connected. Maybe the killer was after Lydia and missed, maybe he was after Simone and made it, maybe it was something else entirely. I don't know yet. But I do know this: either way, it's trouble. To add to all this fun and frolic, Captain Arnold Thrasher—"

"That slob!"

"True, but I'm stuck with him. Anyway, Porky Pie Thrasher is on the case and you know how he hates my guts."

"Poor Marie! She's so darling! How did she get such a dork for a dad?" Lucille wondered. "Maybe Darwin was wrong . . ."

"Lucille, I don't have time for this! So whaddaya think? Are we having fun yet?"

Lucille was silent. Zalman figured she was mulling, because that was the only time Lucille was ever silent. "You think if I just went to bed for a week and cranked the electric blanket up to ten, any of this would go away?" she asked hopefully.

"Not a chance. Not even if you went to Switzerland and got sheep gland injections and the sleep cure."

"Oh, God, why do these things happen to me!!" Lucille howled. "I've spent years building up Bland's image! His fans think he drinks puppy blood for breakfast! Slaughters virgins on a black marble altar looped with chicken entrails! Nobody in the world knows what a pussycat he really is, and if MTV finds out he's really Clark Kent and not a heavy metal monster, he'll be a joke! And I'm in the middle of some big contract negotiations," she added, lowering her voice as if record company lawyers were scurrying around the kitchen. "And I mean big negotiations! I can't afford to have his image blown at this point in time! Murder is not Top Forty!"

"Well, he's not involved so far, Lucille," Zalman said reasonably.

Lucille was not interested in reason. "Used to be, this sort of thing was good publicity. Post-Reagan, it doesn't play in Peoria. This is no longer the Age of Aquarius, Jerry, you should know that better than anyone! We're facing the dawn of the Age of Affectation! Form is all! Content sucks the big weenie! Image is everything! You gotta help me out here, Zally. I'm your sister."

"Yeah, and he's our father, Luce, don't forget that. Look, what's your afternoon like? Let's get together with Bland and torture the truth out of him."

"Yeah," Lucille agreed dreamily. "I like it. If this deal goes in the dumper, I'm in big trouble. My expenses at the office are killing me and I just took back a second on the house you wouldn't believe. It's like having a balloon payment the first of every month. . . . So meet me out at Bland's place—at two, okay? Bring Dad. I got a few things to say to him. . . ."

"You're on." Zalman hung up, then dialed Marie's number in Eugene. She and her cousin Sally were out shopping, so he left word with Sally's mother, Mrs. Wishniak, who said that Marie had told her all about him and he sounded like a very sincere person and just right for Marie and wasn't Marie so clever to have made all that money investing in World O' Yip? Zalman listened patiently and agreed.

Afterward, he went out into the living room, where Earnest and Rutherford were lounging about, drinking coffee, and watching "Thoroughbred Digest" on ESPN.

"Well, Jer," Earnest said as Zalman came in and poured himself a cup of coffee from the pot on the table. "I got it all figured out."

Zalman regarded his father ominously as he sipped his coffee. Earnest was wearing a red silk dressing gown with tumbling dice on it, a red ascot, and red velvet slippers with a royal flush embroidered on the toes. Zalman sighed. "Dad, do me a favor and don't figure anything out, okay? Get dressed, have a bite to eat, and then you and me's gonna take a little drive. You wanna call Lydia? See how she feels?"

"Nah. She'll be asleep until two or so. Don't want to disturb her after all the action last night. I'll talk to her this evening before the show. Where we going?"

"See Lucille. See Bland. I'll do the talking, you keep quiet and observe. Got it? Don't have any bright ideas, don't figure anything out. Just watch. Okay? Do it my way, Dad, I'm begging you." Zalman wagged a warning finger at his father, went back into the bedroom, and called Doyle Dean McCoy. If there was anyone who would understand the problems that Jerry Zalman was having with Earnest K. Zalman, it was McCoy.

McCoy was a six-foot-tall, hard-drinking Irishman who lived way the hell out in Newhall in a broken-down mobile home with a kennel full of mutts, including Rutherford's many brothers, which McCoy claimed were highly trained guard dogs and which he sometimes managed to rent out for a few paltry bucks. In order to make ends meet, McCoy often did legwork and odd jobs of a dubious nature for Zalman—following unfaithful wives, digging up dirt on people, or asking dumb questions down at the DMV or the Hall of Records. He was a great guy with a professionally bad attitude, and though Zalman and McCoy were two very different guys and they often disagreed on matters of style and taste, they'd been friends for a lot of years, and that cast-iron loyalty came before anything else.

Zalman punched in the number and McCoy answered at once, the muted sound of barking resonating behind him. "McCoy!" Zalman said, trying to sound like a no-problem guy. "How's it going?"

"Man, I am in love. L-U-V, love," McCoy exclaimed. "Me and Eddie Ramirez went bar-hopping last night and I met this girl, she's an exotic dancer? Jerry, let me tell you, you don't know how exotic it can get. . . . She's gorgeous, she's the woman of my dreams, she's everything a man lives for—"

"Dean, this is your lucky day!" Zalman interrupted. "I got a job for you. Things go right, you'll be able to take your new true love away for the weekend, see something really exotic. Like the inside of a motel room in scenic Oxnard."

"Oh, yeah? For how much?" McCoy's deep voice rumbled. "I gotta kill anybody for it?"

"Please don't talk like that, Dean, you don't know who could be listening! I've asked you before!"

"You're too paranoid, Jer—"

"I'm not paranoid! I'm careful! Now look, this is a serious situation here. My dad's in town—"

"That's serious," McCoy said. "Tell him hello for me."

"—and last night, he and I were witnesses to a murder."

"What, again? Murder is getting to be a bad habit with you, Jer. Hey, anybody I know?"

"No, Dean, nobody you know. Now look, I want you to ferret out some information on some guys . . ." Zalman gave McCoy a brief rundown of the situation and rattled off his list of names. "Get the real deal on these guys, all of 'em. But especially Caldwell, okay? The old lowdown —like every sleazy thing they ever did since they cheated on the phys ed final in high school, know what I'm talking about?"

McCoy laughed. "Sure I do, Jer. Think I'm stupid?"

"We'll let that pass, Dean."

"Usual rates, chief?"

"Of course, of course! Just get out there and dig up some dirt before Arnie Thrasher's dreams come true and you get to sit on my lap when he throws the switch on the electric chair. Besides which, Dad is driving me nuts. . . ."

"Thank God I'm an orphan," McCoy said. "But listen, Jer, do me a favor. Ask Ernie who he likes for the daily double at Santa Anita on Saturday, will you? These canines could use some extra kibble—"

"Shut up, Dean," Zalman replied as he hung up. "Talk to me later."

THAT AFTERNOON, ZALMAN DROPPED RUTHERFORD OFF AT Doggie Do-in's—formerly Woof World—to have his coat groomed, and then he and Earnest drove all the way down Sunset Boulevard to the beach, then out Highway 101 to Bland's huge house just past the Malibu Colony.

Horace Edward Albert Bland lived a protected life in the center of a double-platinum island of bliss, surrounded by an ever-changing entourage of kats and kitties who couldn't believe that a tall, skinny, jug-eared kid like Bland was one of the biggest rock stars in the universe. Bland, who hailed from the wilds of East London, looked like an underfed sixteen-year-old who'd passed out in a tattoo parlor, and even though his fans thought he was a vicious, Satan-worshiping devil who really dug sacrificing virgins on a bloody altar while wearing a horned goat mask, his hideous criminal image was strictly publicity conjured up by Lucille. Actually, Bland was a very mellow fellow with a taste for needlepoint and cake decorating, skills he'd learned as a tot at his mum's knee.

Lucille Zalman Hanning, who was a very tough piece of action in the big-money world of pop music, had engineered Bland's entire career from its inception. Lucille had turned the kid from a backup singer in the Songfrogs, a meek, post-Beatles elevator band, into a heavy metal hero, a studded, black leather villain who wore a necklace of rat skulls and drove every member of Mothers Against Rock right up a tree. Now, after umpty-seven platinum albums, ten years on the road, and a boffo box-office performance flick, Bland was the brightest star in Lucille's empire of personal management.

A Neanderthal at the steel gate surrounding Bland's compound took Zalman's name and eventually buzzed him in, and Zalman tooled up the long, palm-lined driveway to the house.

Zalman and Earnest got out of the car just as Lucille came charging through the front door. "Dad!" she cried. "The kids want to know when you're coming over! Jason wants to learn how to do a time step!" Lucille and Earnest embraced, and he rumpled her dark hair and gave her a big squeeze.

"Lucille, darling," he said fondly as he held her at arm's length and took a long look at her. "You look great, darling! Honestly great. You're not working too hard? Take some time out, enjoy life a little. I've missed you."

"I've missed you, too," she said with a smile, kissing him on the cheek. "Hey, Jer," she said, turning to her brother with a warning frown. "We gotta talk. . . ."

Zalman looked at his father and his sister, who were staring at each other eye to eye. One thing about los tres Zalmans, there was a definite family resemblance. "Yeah, we do. Where's Bland?" he asked.

Lucille shrugged. "Meditating."

"Oh, yeah?" Zalman snapped. "Let him meditate on the fact that I'd like to talk to him about his relationship with Miss Lydia Devanti. Or maybe he'd like to meditate on the fact that unless he gets out here in twelve seconds, I might punch him in the mouth and he'll never bleat again. How about he meditates—"

"Jerry, puh-leeese!" Lucille groaned. "Let's discuss this inside, okay?" She led them up the low steps and into the house.

Bland's house was gigantic. It lay sprawled on a cliff overlooking the Pacific Ocean, and Bland claimed that on a clear day you could see straight across to Mount Fuji, no lie. The place featured an open-air living room with a pool and several tiny hot tubs scattered around like marbles, endlessly open to the California sky. One wall displayed a mural of Bland wearing one of his death's—head and rat necklace costumes and looking ever so frightening, and the other was stacked with enough state-of-the-art sound equipment to blast the reverberation of a drop of dew hitting a blade of grass clear to Miami.

"Dad, sit down, will you?" Lucille said, gesturing to a circular arrangement of sofas and chairs where five or six kids with glassy eyes were watching *Village of the Damned* on TV. "Jerry, let's you and me go see Bland, huh? Dad, we'll be right back."

"No problem," Earnest said jovially. "I'll sit here, enjoy the TV. Maybe take a little sun, a swim. It's no problem, you two kids go ahead with your business, don't worry about me, I'll be fine right here."

"Great," Lucille said as she led Zalman away. "We'll be right back."

"JERRY! THIS IS SERIOUS!" LUCILLE SNARLED AS SHE LED Zalman down the hall toward Bland's meditation chamber. "Look, Bland's a doll, we both know that, but he's got the brain of a stoned limpet! How did this happen! And when did he have the time? I watch him like a mother! Oh, God," she groaned, her eyes wide with a sudden, hideous blast of realization. "I was in Europe last summer and I left him with Phil! Phil, how could you do this to me! I'm doomed! I told Phil not to leave him alone and look what's happened! Now he's being blackmailed by a bimbo!"

"Strictly speaking, she isn't a bimbo," Zalman said mildly. "And she isn't doing the blackmailing, either."

"Is this my brother the chauvinist speaking?" Lucille said, laughing. "Okay, so she's not a bimbo. So she's a girl gone wrong. That's not important right now! What's important here is that I've worked my tail off, building up Bland's image, getting talk-show hosts to play his records backwards, paying kids to do these dumb demonology demonstrations outside his concerts! You think this is easy? Bland's fans think he's the devil with socks on, and if they find out he's strictly from 'Ozzie and Harriet,' he goes down the tubes. I've worked too hard to let that happen!" she snapped. "You seem to forget, Jerry, I've got a husband and children to support!"

"Lucille, will you calm down and just let me talk to him?" Zalman said. "I've already got Dad on my case, I don't need you giving me aggravation too! I'll do what I can, but I gotta tell you, Bland's lousy career isn't exactly my main concern."

"We're not talking about Bland, we're talking about me! You think an act like Bland grows on trees? I got my life invested here!" Lucille cried, her dark eyes flashing. "Bland's career *is* my career! I saw him when he was just a mewling backup singer in the Songfrogs and I knew he could happen! I molded him! He's my little Frankenstein, and if anything happens to him, who's gonna pay for my kids' orthodonture, huh? You don't seem to understand; there is no Bland, there's only my little monster!"

"Lucille, you're the one who doesn't understand!" Zalman told his sister. "Dad and I were witnesses to a murder.

Can you fast-forward your brain, please? Murder. You savvy murder? This isn't a sidebar in *Billboard*, Lucille, this is death!"

Lucille ignored him. "Jerry, you gotta help me out here. . . ." she begged as she stopped in front of a door covered with silver stars and stared intently at her brother. "Bland is my life!"

Zalman took her hand. "I'm here, right?" he said.

Lucille smiled at him. "Right."

"So don't worry about it, okay?"

"If you say so, Jer."

"I say so," he said with a certainty he didn't feel.

"What's Lydia like?" Lucille asked.

"What are they always like! Big, blond, great figure, makes a terrific meat loaf! Dad says they're thinking about getting married."

"Big deal, he always says that. How old is she, twenty-two?"

"Forty," Zalman said as Lucille knocked gently on the door.

"Whoa! That's pretty old, for Dad. . . . Maybe it's serious this time. Bland? Blandie, it's me. . . . Can we come in, sweetie?"

Slowly, Horace Edward Albert Bland opened the door and peeked out. "Oh, hullo, Mr. Zalman," he said with the innocent smile of a kindergartener fresh from naptime. He was wearing only a baggy pair of white shorts, and his skinny chest and arms were covered with lurid tattoos of witches and death's-heads and snarling monsters with fangs dripping bloody drool. "Thanks for 'elpin' me sister wif 'er green card," he said sweetly as he stepped back and ushered Zalman and Lucille into the big white room. One end of the room was a huge wall of windows lined with glass shelves that held a colorful array of mineral specimens glinting in the afternoon sun. In the center of the room was a ten-foot uncut amethyst on a teak stand, and a blue Zen meditation pillow lay facing it on the floor. Nothing else. "Like she's startin' 'er own band, y'know? More laid-back than me, more middle-of-the-road. Somefing for the older folks, and she knew she could make it big 'ere in the States."

"Sure, Bland, that's great," Zalman said "But look, we got some serious business, okay? We gotta talk and you gotta be straight with me. Did Lucille tell you what happened last night? At the Magic Cavern?"

Bland's skinny arms shivered, and he slowly took a ripped undershirt off the blue pillow and pulled it on over his head. The undershirt said "Chuck E. Weiss and the Goddam Liars" on it, and it hung on Bland like a wet dishtowel on the back of a kitchen chair. "Yeah, she did." He nodded. "Me and Lydia's old mates from way back, and I 'ates to see 'er in any trouble, Mr. Zalman. She was 'elpin' me wif me meditations, is all," he said. "I'm tryin' to program me thoughts, step into an 'igher state of consciousness. . . . Lydia, she and I were into some cosmic vibrations together. . . ."

"You know this guy Roy Caldwell?" Zalman asked casually.

"Roy? Sure. Lives up the beach 'ere. Big white house 'bout an 'alf mile up? Big golden torch in front? You couldn't miss it. Me and Lydia ran into him on the beach at dawn, like he was clearin' some crystals in some seawater? Very good for crystals, seawater," Bland said pensively. "Like, is Lydia in real trouble? I'd 'elp 'er if I could. Tell 'er that for me, will you, Mr. Zalman?"

"Have you heard from Caldwell recently?" Zalman asked. "Seen him?"

"Oh, yeah," Bland said happily. "'E called the other

day, talked to one of me chums. 'E said 'e 'ad some tapes I ought to 'ear—but, like, everybody's got a tape they want me to 'ear, y'know, Mr. Zalman? I didn't want to 'urt 'is feelings so I was gonna ask our Lucille 'ere what to do about it. . . ."

Zalman and Lucille looked at each other. Lucille looked sick. "Tapes, huh?" Lucille said slowly. "But you didn't hear these tapes?"

Bland shook his head.

"So you don't know what was on them, right?" Zalman asked.

Bland shook his head again. "I dunno. Like what wif Roy being a psychic and all, I figure it's some kind of New Age music, kinda like what I'd like to get into," he said, rubbing his tattooed arms thoughtfully. "Someday . . ."

Lucille rolled her eyes and elbowed Zalman in the ribs.

"How'd you meet Lydia?" Zalman asked.

Bland scratched his head "Meet 'er? You mean like, 'ow we got together and all? I dunno. . . . It was a couple years back—I kinda forget. . . . Somebody musta brought 'er round 'ere, I guess. Then she called last summer and like we did some meditating. Lucille? You remember when she was 'ere?"

Lucille shook her head and sighed. "I didn't even meet her, Bland," she said. "This was last summer, right? I was in Europe all of July and August setting up your tour and you were with Phil. Can't you remember? This is important!" she said, tearing at her cuticles. Lucille was getting nervous. It didn't take one whole helluva lot to get Lucille going, and murder, blackmail, and an impending catastrophe with Horace Edward Albert were quite enough to send her shrieking over the edge and into the abyss of looney-toons terror.

Bland stared blankly. "Well, like a few years ago, we

used to be close. Then we weren't close anymore, but we were still . . . well, close. Just not close-close. What wif Lydia bein' like a spiritual person and all, we were still close even after we weren't close-close. Last summer, we were just close. But not close-close. See?" he said hopefully.

"Yeah, I see. But the point is, you were with Lydia when you met Roy Caldwell," Zalman said gently. It was clear Bland couldn't handle any high-level stress and Zalman's usual tough-guy act wouldn't work with the poor dumb simp.

"Sure," Bland said happily, a smile flicking over his thin face. "On the beach, like I said. 'E's all right, Caldwell is. Got a big place, lotsa girls live there wif 'im and all. Calls 'em 'is sisters. You know, like it's a spiritual-type relationship?"

"Oh, yeah. Right," Zalman said. "Go on. . . ."

"Well, so Roy, 'e's a channel. 'E gives you messages from the beyond and all. You talk to 'im privately, tell 'im your problems, and then 'e pops into this trance? Like 'is eyes rolls back in 'is head? It's somefing, innit? And then 'e turns into Mr. MacTavish like right there! Like you're watchin' 'im and 'e turns into somebody else!" Bland shook his head, amazed. "Too cosmic. And then Mr. Mac-Tavish gives you advice and tells you what sort of crystal you ought to be meditatin' on and like 'ow you ought to be livin' to attain an 'igher state of being and 'armony." Bland shrugged. "You oughta try it, Mr. Zalman, it's somefing! Mr. MacTavish, 'e knows a lot!"

"Did Lydia know Caldwell? Did she walk up to him and say, 'Oh, hi, Roy, great to see you, buddy'?" Zalman asked carefully.

Bland looked blank. "I don't unnerstand," he said.

Zalman tried it again. "When you ran into Caldwell on

the beach, did you have the feeling that Lydia knew him already?"

"Nah." Bland shook his head emphatically. "Like I said, 'e was standin' in the surf, gettin' his crystals cleared, and we was meditatin' on the purity of the dawn. She didn't know 'im. Lydia's straight-ahead, she is. I know it for sure."

"YOU DON'T TRUST ANYBODY, DO YOU, JER?" LUCILLE REmarked with a laugh as they walked slowly down the hall and back to the living room.

"Huh? Whaddaya mean?" Zalman asked defensively. "I trust Marie! I trust you!"

"I'm family! You damn well better trust me! And you're in love with Marie, so that doesn't count either," she said. "But didn't you tell me you thought Lydia was okay? That she was telling the truth?"

"Yeah. So?"

"So you were asking Blandie a lot of junk about who met who and when. . . ."

"Lucille," Zalman said, spreading his hands wide in a plea for sisterly understanding, "even though I'm a lawyer, I have feelings. Somebody tells me something and I respond instinctively, just like any other human person. I think Lydia's okay, but we're dealing with crime and punishment here! I still gotta check up on her, right? I could be wrong. . . ."

"You? Never."

"It's happened! Look, I think she's telling the truth, but

the truth isn't all black and white like a damn zebra, y'know! This is the end of the twentieth century, and believe me, the truth is a nice flat gray, like a mule. And it's sterile, too." He grinned. "Just like a mule. Trouble with the truth is, it reminds me of one of those math problems they used to keep me after school with. It's so boring! Who cares if you ever figure it out? You take my meaning?"

"I love you, Jerry." Lucille laughed. "Trust me?"

Zalman smiled at his sister. "Hey, you're family, right? I trust you. . . . Enough metaphysics, Luce. Just explain to me how Bland makes twenty zil a year, will you?"

Lucille grinned. "I keep trying to tell you, Jer, *I* make the dough. Blandie just stands there and sings. . . . He's a nut case, but he's a monster act and he's on my caseload and I gotta take care of him. Besides, the kids adore him. You shoulda seen the cake he made for Jason's birthday, a chocolate three-decker with big red robots all over it—"

"Lucille!" Zalman yelled. "Don't start! I don't care about Bland's skill with a pastry bag! Everyone around me is insane! I'm convinced of it! I can't be the only non-psycho in Southern California, I just can't be!"

"What makes you think that, Jer?" Lucille said, and laughed.

Back in the living room Earnest was watching the race results from Pimlico on ESPN. "Okay," he said to the group of awed teenagers sitting on the floor at his feet, "now watch the two horse as he comes out of the turn. Okay, okay, see that? There he goes . . . yeah, yeah, yeah, into the stretch . . . ba-bing! He's home free! Beautiful race!" He leaned down, picked up the phone, and punched in a number. "Tommy! See the race? Gorgeous, huh? Yeah, Kitchen Police to win in the fifth for tomorrow. Hey, we're goin' all the way on this one, pal!" He chuckled as he hung up. "Oh, hi, kids!" He beamed as he saw

Zalman and Lucille standing in the doorway watching him. "Just hadda check with my turf accountant for tomorrow's race. Me and Tommy the Tyke, we got some serious money down on this horse Kitchen Police. Nice filly."

"But why did you think that horse was going to win, Ernie?" a kid with a blue rooster cut asked in obvious wonderment.

Earnest grinned happily. "Years of study, my child," he said. "You want to be a success in this dodge, study the past performance sheet every day like it was the Bible, that's my advice to you as a professional. Say, you ready to go?" he asked Zalman. "I could use a sandwich. Maybe we could cruise over to the Kibitz Room at Canter's, huh? Sound good? A little smoked whitefish would go good right now. . . . Anyhoo, you kids remember what I told you. Bet to win, got it? Your place bet, your show bet, that's for dodos. Take it from Earnest K. Zalman, always bet to win." Earnest picked up his gray fedora and twirled it on one finger, then set it jauntily on the back of his head. "Jer, let's hit the road," he said as he kissed Lucille good-bye.

Zalman and Earnest walked outside and got back in the Mercedes. "How 'bout that sandwich?" Earnest said as they pulled away from Bland's house.

Zalman shook his head. "We got a lotta work to do today, Dad. First I buzz McCoy. See what kinda poop he's scooped." Zalman punched McCoy's number.

"Dean, any news?" he said when McCoy answered.

"Got the dope on Lenny Dunn you wanted. Lives in the Malibu Colony," McCoy rumbled. "I gotta girlfriend, a waitress works down the highway at the Come Inn? She says Dunn's not too bright, but makes this very trendy furniture. Every rich dame in Brentwood, Bev Hills, and Bel-Air thinks his wares are the greatest, but it ain't his table legs they wanta turn. Lenny makes house calls, like during the day when Dad's away? Delivers the coffee table and the rest of the goods, too. Get it, Zally?"

"Yes, Dean, I get it. You're not known for your fine Italian hand," Zalman said patiently. "What else?"

"My waitress friend claims he's dreamy, looks just like Joel McCrea, 'cept he never bought any real estate so he ain't quite as handsome. He had this one Western series where he was the second banana—'Gunshy,' remember that?"

"The only Western I ever liked was 'Have Gun, Will Travel,'" Zalman said. "What else? What else? C'mon, Dean, I'm swimming in gumbo here!"

"But the problem was, the guy was too phony."

"Too phony for TV? C'mon, Dean, no such animal."

"Hard to believe, but that's what happened. The guy came across like a frightened politician. So the series folded," McCoy went on, "he went into the furniture biz, and you wanta go see him, here's his address." McCoy gave Zalman a number in the Malibu Colony.

"Nice everybody lives in the same neighborhood," Zalman said. "Makes it convenient for Caldwell. So Dunn services the ladies, and if their husbands should find out . . . I get the picture. All right, Dean, but please, dig up some dirt on the other guys, will you? I know I'm gonna find Arnie Thrasher hiding under my Barcalounger when I get home, know what I mean? Talk to me later," he said as he hung up.

"No whitefish, huh?" Earnest said.

"Nope. Now we go blitzkrieg the Malibu Colony," he said as he pulled to a stop at the Colony gate and leaned out the window to hassle the bored guard.

Lenny Dunn's house looked like it had been decorated by John Wayne on a bad acid trip. Maybe once it had been a regular California adobe bungalow, but Dunn had painted the place in thirty shades of pastel so now it looked like a faded Navajo rug. There was an ugly cactus garden in a small sandy plot of ground outside the front door and every gnarled plant was draped with tiny Christmas lights in the shape of chili peppers, red and green. Smack in the center, there was a toothy totem pole that looked like it had been put there to give the birds heart attacks.

Inside, everything howled Old Wild West. Eye-dazzler rugs in Day-Glo colors plastered one wall; a large collection of carefully framed barbed wire filled another, surrounded by a gay selection of purple velvet sombreros with all the gold trimmings. Lenny Dunn's handmade furniture was everywhere, all of it in an elaborately carved eccentric neo-Western style.

Perched on the edge of a huge green chair with wraparound arms, Lenny Dunn looked like the ultimate fifties Western star in his silver concho belt, tight faded jeans, and pink embroidered cowboy shirt. His tanned bodybuilder muscles bulged like knockwurst as he leaned forward in his chair and stared at Zalman with pain on his chiseled face.

"Yeah," he bellowed, flashing a set of pearly white choppers that were a dental hygienist's dream. "I usta go out with Lydia Devanti, and no offense, Mr. Zalman, but now all of a sudden, I've got big problems because of that broad. This guy Caldwell, he calls me up and says he's got something I might like to hear, and then he sends me a tape of Lydia spilling her guts, pardon the expression, all about my private life! I gotta great setup here, Mr. Zalman, I don't want anything to happen to it. Okay, I didn't do so good in TV, but now I got a whole new career, a whole new image! I got a lifestyle! See, I'm a craftsman! A hardworking craftsman," he said as he waved proudly around the room, pointing at his wares. "I make furniture for a living, but hey, women go for me, is it my fault? Huh? I can't help it . . . I know it's wrong, but I'm weak! And if their husbands get wise, I could lose my shirt! I'm just about to pop! I had a spread in *Architectural Digest,* my stuff is rockin' hot! See, the ladies do the shopping but the husbands pay the bills, and if they find out their old ladies like a little taste on the side, I'll be finished! It's a tough world," Lenny Dunn said moodily, his handsome face contorting bitterly as he realized the manifest inequity of life in his little corner of the galaxy.

Zalman leaned back gingerly on the couch, which was a ten-foot version of a Conestoga wagon, complete with a carefully torn ragged canvas awning done in multicolored serape stripes. "Have the police talked to you yet?" he asked, cautiously laying a loafer on the papier-mâché coffee table sculpted to look like a boulder. "It wouldn't surprise me if they showed up at some point—"

"The police! I didn't kill Simone! I swear! Anyway, why would I want to kill her when it was Caldwell who was giving me gas!" Dunn pointed out triumphantly. "And he's still giving me gas! What am I gonna do, Mr. Zalman?"

"This guy's not playing with a full deck," Earnest said under his breath. Zalman had tried to persuade Earnest to wait in the car on the grounds that maybe he was going to pick up some news about Lydia that he wasn't going to like, but Earnest had insisted on coming in.

"You gotta help me," Mr. Zalman," Dunn moaned. "I'm in too deep! They're closing in on me! There's no escape!"

"Calm down, Lenny," Zalman snapped. "We don't have to circle the wagons yet."

"You gotta be my lawyer," Dunn said, a crafty gleam of hope in his eyes. "You gotta help me!" He sprang to his feet and ran over to a large desk that looked like a free-form version of a saguaro cactus, its arms waving in the wind. He grabbed for his checkbook and scribbled out a check. "Here," he said, thrusting the check at Zalman, "this be enough?"

Zalman glanced at the figure Dunn had scribbled on the face of the check. "For a while." Zalman smiled as he pocketed the check. "For a while."

"NOW CAN WE GO FOR A SANDWICH?" EARNEST ASKED AS they got back into the car and pulled out onto Highway 101. "I'm starved!"

"We got another stop to make," Zalman told him. "Besides, you just ate. How can you be hungry again so soon?"

"Dog ate my whole breakfast," Earnest said moodily.

"Well, Dad, why did you let the dog eat your breakfast? You're a human being, you're supposed to be in control of the dog, not the other way around."

"He was too fast for me," Earnest complained. "I turn around, ba-bing! He's licked my plate clean! Just a quick stop, Jer. I'm starving to death here! What about the place used to have the sea lions swimming in a big tank out front? You and Lucille used to love that place when you were kids." Earnest laughed. "Bet it's gone, though."

"Yeah," Zalman said. "L.A.'s changing fast. Every time I turn around, there's a new building going up. They tore down Schwab's Drug Store, y'know. They were selling the bricks for ten bucks a pop. I shoulda bought one for a paperweight, but the idea of paying ten bucks for a brick grated on me, know what I mean?"

Earnest laughed. "Ten bucks for a brick! Some crazy world! Ten bucks!"

Zalman pulled into a little café he knew called Fruits de Mer and they went inside and sat down at a table overlooking the ocean. The place was half empty, and as he sipped his Bullshot, Zalman thought that this would be an opportune moment to raise a ticklish subject with Earnest.

After the waitperson brought their lunches—Earnest thought crab salad sounded tasty—Zalman leaned forward across the table. "Dad," he said in his best lawyer's voice, "I'm only gonna ask you this one time, okay? One time only. And you know I gotta ask, right? It isn't something we can let slide since all of a sudden you and I are involved in some serious soup, and with Captain Arnie Thrasher on our tails, I need to make sure we're in the clear. Okay? One time only, then we don't have to mention it again. So I want you to think before you answer me, okay?"

Earnest nodded. "Ask. I know what you're gonna say, but ask me anyway."

"You're sure about Lydia? Right down to the wire, you're sure about her?"

Earnest nodded again. "Right down to the wire, Jer. I'd bet the limo on it."

"Then we don't have to worry about it anymore, right? You're sure, right?"

"Right."

"You're sure?"

"I'm sure."

"How's the crab?"

"I love crab."

"You're sure?"

"I'm sure."

"Then eat up and let's hit the road. We got another stop to make."

"Where we going now?" Earnest asked.

"Now we go see Roy Caldwell, see what that blackmailing scuz has to say for himself."

"Great!" Earnest said enthusiastically, a romantic fever burning behind his bifocals. "I'm looking forward to this."

"I'M WARNING YOU, DAD," ZALMAN SAID AS HE CRUISED down the highway looking for the turnoff to Roy Caldwell's place, "you keep your yap shut! You're just along for the ride, get it? Don't have any bright ideas. Are you listening to me, Dad?" he asked. "Why do I get the feeling I'm talking to a wall?"

"I hear you, Jer," Earnest insisted. "Every word you say, I hear."

"I hope so, Dad. Ahh, yes, this must be the place!" Zalman said as he pulled up in front of a big white colonial house with a twenty-foot golden torch on the lawn in front of it. "Just look for the torch. . . ." he sighed.

Zalman jumped out of the car and went up to the door, Earnest right behind him, but before he could knock, the door opened.

A lady wearing a yellow caftan stood there, a pocket calculator in one hand and a legal pad in the other. She was about sixty, with salt-and-pepper hair cut short and heavy black glasses pushed down on her nose.

"Yes?" she asked, staring over her glasses at them with hostile brown eyes.

"I'm Jerry Zalman, I'm Lydia Devanti's attorney," Zalman told her. "I'd like to see Mr. Caldwell."

The lady was not happy about this unplanned interruption. "He can't see you now!" she said. "We're doing the estimated taxes and we're late already! We're very busy! Some other time."

She started to shut the door, but Zalman stuck his foot in the way and smiled. "Tell him I'm here, please?" he said, trying to sound like a nice friendly fellow. He didn't take his foot out of the doorway.

"Will you stop that!" she said, whacking his foot with the door. "Honestly, you're being very annoying!"

Zalman pushed the door forward a little and tried to step inside, but she had a firm grip on the handle and pushed back. Behind him, Earnest snorted at their brief contest.

"What's going on, Martha?" a man's voice called from inside the house.

"Somebody named Zalman to see you, Roy," she answered over her shoulder. "Says he's Lydia's attorney."

Zalman heard the man groan softly and say, "Great. Just what I need." Then the door opened fully and a six-foot-tall, powerfully built man with a head as smooth and white as a cue ball was standing in front of him, staring down at Zalman and Earnest with a thin smile playing across his face. He was wearing a flowing white caftan and a long necklace of faceted crystals, and he had long Fu Manchu gold fingernails and gold glitter peppering his eyelids like a dusting of pollen. More than anything else, he looked like a young Daddy Warbucks in drag. The man arched a gold-flecked eyebrow and continued to stare down at Zalman. "Yeesssss?" he said finally, drawing it out.

"Roy Caldwell, I take it?" Zalman asked, unfazed.

The man smiled slightly, revealing a gold front tooth

with a diamond set in it. "You're Lydia's attorney? Who's this, your bodyguard?" he asked, indicating Earnest.

"I'm Jerry Zalman; this is my father, Earnest K. Zalman. I'd like to talk to you about my client, Lydia Devanti."

"Ahhhh, Lydia," Caldwell said. "A lovely person, an old soul. . . . I heard about last night. You two better come in."

"Roy, we don't have time for this!" Martha snapped. "We're facing big penalties if we can't clear this up with the IRS!"

"Don't get testy, Martha! It's a very unattractive quality you have! I'll be through in a few minutes," Caldwell said. "Just keep going without me, okay? Mr. Zalman and I won't be long, will we, Mr. Zalman?"

Zalman didn't answer. "Cops been here yet?" he asked as he and Earnest followed Caldwell through the marble entry and into the living room. The room was big, fronted with glass all along the far wall; the blue sea glittered in the distance and lots of colored pillows were scattered around the room where a normal person would have chairs and sofas and tables. Caldwell had nothing but pillows and plants.

"Cops?" Caldwell intoned. "Why cops? What do I have to do with cops? I'm respectable, I'm a pillar of the spiritual community, I'm—"

"Oh, lay off, will you?" Zalman groaned. "Can't we just talk this over like regular guys? Number one, Lydia Devanti's assistant Simone got herself killed last night. Number two, you're threatening to publish some photos you stole from Lydia, and number three, you're threatening to blackmail some ex-sweeties of Lydia's with those tapes you've got. This is illegal, immoral, and further, I kinda doubt any of these guys want to be blackmailed. So maybe you oughta rethink the situation, Caldwell."

Roy Caldwell sank down on a scarlet pillow and plucked at the fringe with a gold nail. "Do sit down, won't you?" he said. "Some sparkling water, perhaps?"

"Yeah. Sure," Zalman said as he sat down cross-legged on a pillow across from Caldwell. He hoped he wasn't making the knees of his trousers all baggy. He hated baggy knees. He glanced over at Earnest, who was being unusually quiet. His dad was hovering across the room at the window, just staring out at the ocean.

Caldwell put two fingers in his mouth and gave a New York taxi whistle. Instantly, a girl in a pink caftan flowed into the room, the stunned look of a clubbed baby harp seal in her eyes. "Something for you, Brother?" she asked in a cloying voice.

"Three Perriers," Caldwell said shortly. "With a twist." He turned his attention back to Zalman, rubbing his smooth head thoughtfully. "You're representing Lydia on this?" he asked. "I've heard about you, Mr. Zalman. People say you're a heavy piece of machinery. Can Lydia afford you?"

"How'd you hear about me?" Zalman asked curiously, sidestepping Caldwell's question.

"The spirits tell me many things, Mr. Zalman. Besides, I read the trades, and your reputation precedes you."

"Well, at least you do your homework," Zalman said.

"Mind if I use the gents'?" Earnest asked.

"Not at all," Caldwell said. "Around the corner, down the hall, to your right."

Earnest nodded and left the room, whistling "Take the A Train" under his breath.

The girl in pink rolled back in, set a silver tray laden with three glasses of fizzing water and a pink hibiscus on the floor next to Caldwell, and silently rolled out again.

Zalman stared thoughtfully at Caldwell, who sipped his

designer water and stared back, his eyes smooth and blank as a flat river stone. "So?" Zalman pressed. "What about it, Caldwell? The photos? The blackmail?"

Caldwell shook his head and smiled like he'd just cured cancer. "Mr. Zalman," he said with an attitude that just begged for understanding, "I'm a completely legitimate channel. Believe me . . ."

"Yeah. Sure. You close your eyes and turn into a Scotsman named Mr. MacTavish? Save that noise for your sisters," Zalman said cynically, jerking a thumb toward the door, "and don't expect me to buy it. It's an insult."

"Mr. Zalman, please! Why are you picking on me? Being a channel is the same as any other business! You think I don't have overhead? Crystals don't come cheap, y'know! You heard Martha, I pay taxes and I got money problems just like every other small businessman in America! I got an accountant bleeding me dry, the lease is up on my car, this house is a killer! Look, I come out here about fifteen years ago, try to get into the movies, right?"

"You and the rest of the planet. . . ." Zalman snorted.

"Now I know that!" Caldwell said, sounding wounded. *"Now* I'm sadder but wiser. Back then, I was just a kid with a crazy dream! After a while, I realized it wasn't going to happen for me. I went bald young, and Telly Savalas was already big with 'Kojak'—he had the bald slot covered. My agent says to me, 'Hey, there's only room for one chrome-dome at a time.' So I got into meditation, kinda took the edge off my failure as an actor. . . . I played Othello once," he mused, his eyes misty with memory. "In summer stock in Ohio—I still think I was pretty good. . . . So then I started leading these meditation groups, one thing led to another, and here I am. I fit right in! After all, Southern California's got a tradition to main-

tain—it's the nut group capital of the world! Do you know," Caldwell said, leaning forward confidentially to deliver his spiel, "there've been nut groups in L.A. ever since 1880 when a band of fun-loving sun worshipers fled the persecution of a self-righteous gang of East Coast intellectual snobs! We're talking tradition! I've got spiritual ancestors here!" Caldwell huffed, and swigged his water defiantly.

"Lydia Devanti—" Zalman began, hoping he could maneuver Caldwell back on track.

"Lydia and I were best friends. I admit that," Caldwell interrupted, holding up a hand with a ruby on it the size and color of a maraschino cherry. "My . . . sisters know I have close relations. I don't pretend to be a saint—"

"Gee. That's swell."

"—and Lydia and I are still good friends. We share . . . secrets in common." He smiled. *"Blackmail* is such an ugly word, Mr. Zalman. I don't see myself as a blackmailer. Nothing of the sort. People tell me things while they're under stress, and sometimes, with the aid of Mr. MacTavish, I can relieve that stress. I'm like a doctor. People often don't want to come to see me, sometimes they wait until it's too late. But after they've had a session or two with Mr. MacTavish, it makes all the difference in their poor, pathetic lives. Often, they're so thrilled with their new knowledge that they want to make a contribution to me. I don't charge," he squawked. "I'm a nonprofit foundation! I take donations! But people can be very generous, especially after a session with Mr. MacTavish! Lydia's been a dear friend; why would I, or Mr. MacTavish, want to hurt her? Matter of fact," Caldwell said, narrowing his golden eyes, "I just spoke to Lydia a few minutes ago and she's promised to do me a great favor.

She's going to perform at a party I'm having tomorrow night. I do hope you and your father will be able to join us?" he said magnanimously. "It'll be a lovely gathering. I'm going to invite all Lydia's friends," Caldwell said slyly. "I've already called Tom Kellar about it, and I'm going to ask Bland, and what's that other fellow's name? Lenny Dunn? Don't you think that'll make an interesting mix of people, hmmm? That's the key to a good party, an interesting mix. And perhaps, if we're lucky, I can persuade Mr. MacTavish to put in an appearance. Then you'll see that I'm a professional, an honest man!" Caldwell said with pride.

"Lydia's going to perform, hmmmm? Somehow I think I know how you persuaded her to show up, but it's a cute trick all the same." Zalman shook his head. "Caldwell, I gotta hand it to you. You got a great act here."

Caldwell arched his golden eyebrows. "In L.A., all business is monkey business," he said with a secret smile. "You'll join us?"

"It's an invitation I can't refuse," Zalman said as he stood up and unkinked his knees. "I love it."

After they left Caldwell's, Zalman and Earnest headed back toward Beverly Hills along the Coast Highway. It was a beautiful day; the air was only moderately unhealthy and the sky glimmered with a pale apricot sheen under a brilliant sun. It was the kind of day that made Zalman glad he was a Californian.

"Well," Earnest said happily as he lit one of Zalman's cigars, "we're ready to roll. I cased the joint."

"You did what?!" Zalman shouted in anguish, nearly sideswiping a prim elderly lady in a perfectly restored yellow Ford Fairlane as he turned up Sunset. "You cased the joint!"

"You bet I did, kiddo. Whaddaya think I was doing all that time you were listening to Caldwell tell you what a great guy he is—eating kreplach? Sure, sure, ol' eagle-eye Martha was in the dining room buried in papers, so I just nipped right around her, buzzed upstairs, and checked out the whole joint. Some setup Caldwell's got there, lemme tell you! He's got a study upstairs, so I took a look around in there and I figure I know exactly where the tapes and pics and stuff gotta be. He's got a safe, see, so it's a natural. Right? I'm not positive, of course, 'cause I couldn't get it open. Didn't have enough time."

"Let me get this straight," Zalman said as he stared at his hands white-knuckling the steering wheel. "Do you mean to say that you just tried to crack open Caldwell's safe? Just now? While I was downstairs talking to the man, you were upstairs trying to rob him?"

"Sure! Damn straight I was! You think I'm gonna let this guy blackmail Lydia, my lovely Lydia? Cause her all sorts of grief? No way," Earnest said, shaking his head. "He's not getting away with it, Jer, not while Earnest K. Zalman's got breath in his body. If you'da kept him busy a few minutes longer, I coulda had it, too!" Earnest grinned and wiggled his eyebrows like Groucho. "Fingers of gold," he said, shaking his hands in the air. "Deluxe digits."

"Dad," Zalman groaned, "didn't I tell you not to get out of line? Didn't I warn you? Beg? Plead?"

"Lighten up, will you, Jer? You're too young to be so nervous. Look, Caldwell's got Lydia's photos, right?" Earnest said, cigar firmly clamped between his teeth.

"Sure he's got 'em. But that doesn't mean you can just waltz in there and—"

"The hell I can't! Look, Caldwell's got the photos in the house somewhere, and I figure they're in the safe because that's the logical place you put something like that. You don't have to be a grade A certified detective to figure that out. So the pics are in the safe along with the tapes and probably a lotta other hot stuff as well! So that's where I look, get it? Listen, I got no scruples where this bozo is concerned! I'm gonna rob Roy! You wanna help me or not?" Earnest said pugnaciously. "I mean, we're talking about the woman I love here! Be reasonable, Jer—it's the only way we're going to get Lydia out of this mess, so don't gimme angina! Whose side are you on here? You're my son, aren't you? You're supposed to help me out! Christ, if I weren't such an honest guy, this would be a great scam! Lucky Tommy the Tyke doesn't know about this. He was here, he'd rip all the stuff off and go into business for himself. Great guy, Tommy, but a little drifty. . . ."

Zalman felt the walls beginning to shrink in on him, the world crushing him with the sheer weight of its insanity. Smaller, even smaller. . . . "Dad, I'm begging you to pay attention to me! First of all, you can't just breeze into a guy's house and start scuffling through his sock drawer! It's not legal! Besides, it's not nice!"

"Jer, you sound just like your mother—"

"Dad, I'm warning you, lay off about Mom!"

Earnest ignored his son's outburst and stared out the window at the sky. "So, way I figure it, we slip into the joint during the party, you keep him busy with some legal-ese, and I zip upstairs and—"

"Not another word, I don't want to hear another word! I'm a lawyer! An officer of the court!" Zalman protested hollowly.

"Yeah. Sure." Earnest grinned. "And I'm Strawberry Shortcake."

AFTER THEY HIT BEVERLY HILLS, ZALMAN AND EARNEST went over to Nate 'n' Al's—Earnest had the smoked whitefish—and then picked up Rutherford at Doggie Do-in's. The Doberman was very pleased with himself, posing artistically in the back seat of the Mercedes in case there were any photo hounds cruising Rodeo Drive, and Zalman gave him the remains of his pastrami sandwich.

Then Zalman dropped Earnest off at the Chateau Marmont and went home to call Marie. He needed to talk to her, to someone who wasn't involved, someone who could cut through the darkening gloom with a clear, perceptive shaft of light, a vision of reality untouched by a prior familial relationship with Earnest K. Zalman. More than that, he needed serious help.

Luckily, Marie was at home, watching the news with the Wishniaks. Mrs. Wishniak told him that the caterer was upping the price on the Thai chicken salad they'd decided on, and then she wanted to know did Zalman, as a lawyer, think that was fair? Especially because it was at the last minute and they really didn't have any choice and had to go with the Thai salad and felt taken advantage of by the caterer, whom they used to think of as a friend. Zalman said he'd consider the matter, and finally Marie picked up the phone.

"Jerry! I missed you last night! Where were you? I called and called but you weren't home! Were you and Rutherford out tomcatting?" she asked suspiciously, then added in a puzzled tone, "I guess he can't tomcat, though, can he? He's a dog, so I guess he has to tomdog."

"I miss you too, baby," Zalman told her. He felt better just hearing her voice on the phone. Funny, he'd always laughed off those dumb expressions, about how you felt better when you heard the other person's voice, but it was true. "I realize that I hate it when you go away."

"Oh, I'm so glad," Marie said happily. "Last night when you weren't home I almost had a panic attack and thought, oh, maybe he's run off to Rio with a blond bombshell. After all, I know your taste runs to platinum. . . ."

"Not since I met you, sweetheart," Zalman said. "Let me tell you something: it's you and you only. Other girls may have the hair, but in the long run, it's a sense of humor that counts. When we're sixty-four and huddled around the campfire 'cause the greenhouse effect has turned the whole damn world into a microwave and the polar ice caps are melting and there's water lapping at our ankles, it'll be your sense of humor that keeps me home those long summer nights. And don't ever forget it. Okay, enough lovey-dovey, I got some serious business to discuss with you."

"Uh-oh," Marie said succinctly.

"You ain't kidding it's uh-oh. A big, bad uh-oh. Now attend to my words, precious." Zalman proceeded to tell her every detail of every horrible event that had occurred since Earnest K. Zalman came tap-dancing into L.A. "So then the assistant falls out of the iron maiden and she's dead! Then your dad shows up and grills me and my dad for about three centuries, then finally he lets us go. Of course, he only let us go because he didn't have any other choice. If he thought he could get away with it, he'd have strung us both up and taken a chain saw to our toes."

Zalman continued his tale of woe with an account of his

visits with Bland and Lenny Dunn, his encounter with Roy the psychic, and Earnest's loco plan to knock over the safe. "So now he wants to rob Roy," Zalman concluded. "You gotta understand, I love my old man, but Earnest K. Zalman is not exactly concerned with the letter of the law. It's not that he's a crook," he added hurriedly, just in case Marie got the wrong idea, "it's just that he's a man in love. He doesn't want Lydia to be hurt."

"Boy, what a mess!" Marie said. "I can see you can't take care of yourself, Jerry. I go out of town for three seconds and look what happens! Besides which, I'm missing all the fun and I think it's a gyp! Well, the first thing you have to do is keep track of your father. Don't let him out of your sight, not for a moment. *But,* and here's the tricky part, you also have to go to the party and snoop around."

"What? What do you mean, Marie?"

"Now look, don't let him rob Roy, that would be insane. But is there some way you can, ummm, get ahold of the papers and things without actually robbing him?" she asked slowly.

"What are you saying?" Zalman said. He didn't like the sound of this. Not at all.

"Well, see, Earnest is right. Not completely right!" she said hurriedly. "Just a little bit right. He can't actually rob Roy, that would be illegal and you don't want to do anything illegal—"

"Damn right I don't!" Zalman said.

"—but if you and Earnest don't put a stop to Caldwell, who will? Not the police," she said. "My father's a cop and I should know. Lydia can't go to the police because she doesn't want bad publicity, and neither does Tom Kellar from what you've said, and so there's nothing the police can do! You have to be creative!"

"What kind of creative?"

"Well, what if Earnest was hanging around when Roy got the papers and tapes out of the safe and then the lights went out and when Roy turned around the papers were gone? . . . What if that happened?"

"Marie, how would the lights go out?!"

"I bet McCoy knows how to make lights go out," Marie said confidently. "That's just the kind of thing he knows all about! How to slash tires, get fake ID, make lights go out when you want them to. McCoy knows all about that stuff!"

"Marie, darling! What are you saying! You can't rob the guy!"

"I know that, silly! I'm not saying rob him, I'm saying what if the lights go out and Caldwell drops the stuff and Earnest just happens to pick it up? Or what if Caldwell got scared?"

Zalman was silent.

"See," Marie said thoughtfully, "McCoy's a very scary guy when he wants to be. Of course, I'm not scared of him because I know what a sweet, gentle person he really is underneath that tough exterior, but if Roy saw McCoy looming over him, he might be scared and drop the papers and then Earnest could pick them up. See?" she asked.

Zalman didn't know what to do. Only a day ago he'd felt like the Alexander Haig of Beverly Hills, completely in control of his own private universe, but now he saw a sea of madness washing it all away from him. He'd have to change his name, start over again in Montevideo. . . . "In other words," he said slowly, "you think Earnest is right."

"Not right. Oh, no, no, no, not right at all. Just . . . not wrong either," Marie said. "If only I was there, I'm sure I could explain it to you and you'd see it all my way! I wish I could come home tonight, darling, I really do. I can see you need me. But the wedding isn't till Saturday and I just can't leave! Sally and Norman—that's her fiancé, Norman —are driving everybody crazy! Or everybody's driving them crazy. Sally told me she hates the whole thing and wants to elope to Hawaii. . . . Boy, there's nothing like a full-scale wedding to put you off marriage. I wish you could see this place," she whispered conspiratorially. "Sally's dad has this fabulous neon clock downstairs in the rumpus room? It's just beautiful and it has two different colors of neon wheels whirling around in two different directions. I've got to have it!" she said hungrily. "I've admired it about thirty times and I'm hoping he'll pick up on my subtle hints and give it to me. Besides," she added thoughtfully, "it would look just perfect in your living room. . . ."

"Marie, darling," Zalman begged. "I just redecorated the living room and I love it just the way it is. Honestly I do. And I get more compliments on the salt and pepper sets than you can possibly imagine! But please, no neon clocks!"

"And here's another thing," Marie added, changing the subject in midstream, "I could call my dad and see if he knows anything he's not telling you, but my best judgment is that if I call him and try to wheedle some info out of him, it'll just make him more crazy than he already is. I wish I knew why he doesn't like you," she mused. "I mean, just because he used to hate you years ago when you were a kid, that's no reason for him to hate you now. Fathers are so silly about their daughters. . . . Now, here's what I think you should do. Go to the party, nose around, but for God's sake keep an eye on your father! Don't let him get caught trying to rob this guy! It would be sheer disaster! But think about what I said, will you? See if McCoy knows how to make lights go out on cue. Oh, and let's get some background on Roy, hmmm? We ought to know if he's got a record. Is he a professional blackmailer? Or is he just a Hollywood sleazeball trying to cash in on a good thing? As soon as McCoy has anything, call me and let me know. Now look, I'll be back as soon as I can, okay? I'm going to call the airline right this minute and bump my flight forward a little. Murder or no murder, I'm outta here right after the rubber chicken and the shrimp boats. Okay? Call me. . . ."

Marie hung up and Zalman sat quietly and stared at the telephone for a minute or two, his mind in a terrible state of chaos. Then he lit a cigar, went for a quick swim, and had a lovely long soak in the Jacuzzi until the ringing in his head stopped.

THE NEXT MORNING ZALMAN WENT IN TO THE OFFICE early. He felt a lot better after a night's sleep, back on top of the world, in control again, and he hoped he'd be able to put a dent in the papers on his desk before the tidal wave of the bright new day engulfed him and swept him kicking and screaming out to sea. Zalman had a suite in a small building on Beverly Drive, and one reason he enjoyed going to his office was that it reminded him of an English movie, or maybe something with George Arliss playing Disraeli, or at least a Rothschild. The office was filled with expensive furniture, thick oriental rugs, and a beautiful Victorian partner's desk that Zalman had accepted in lieu of an extremely fat fee once upon a time, and when he sat behind his desk he always felt a peaceful sense of accomplishment.

Another thing he liked about his office, it was never boring. Whenever he was on the phone and the conversation was droning on and on and on, he could always swing around in his chair and watch the foot traffic on Beverly Drive spread out below him like the little plastic ranch set he used to play with when he was a kid, except that this time, the little people weren't plastic but flesh and blood, with flesh-and-blood problems that all too often required them to seek out the services of a high-priced Beverly Hill lawyer.

He'd left Earnest back at the house, still lazing around the kitchen in his dice dressing gown. Earnest claimed he was going to make a few calls, watch a race or two on TV, then connect with Tommy the Tyke to make plans for the upcoming week's work on the tip sheet they owned together, but Zalman wasn't sure he believed his father's story. What if he got any more weird ideas? What if he decided to drive out to Malibu by himself and take another crack at Caldwell's safe? Was Marie right? Should he rob Roy? Was McCoy right? Was he getting too paranoid? Could you get too paranoid in this situation? Zalman shook these troublesome ideas out of his mind.

Then, Earnest said, he planned to run down to the Magic Cavern and spend the afternoon with Lydia as she rehearsed the changes for her new solo act. Even though Simone was dead, the show had to go on, and Lydia was planning to drop the fatal Metamorphosis routine and build up Sergeant Pepper's part of the performance so she'd have a big wow finish.

Esther Wong wasn't in yet—she'd left a note saying she had an early appointment for a manicure—so Zalman called up the lady agent he'd seen with Tom Kellar at the

Magic Cavern on the night of the murder. For a small, one-woman office, Annie Pepper had done very well for herself. She had started out as one of many secretaries to a big Italian producer who lost his shirt making gladiator epics in the late seventies. Luigi Renaldo never figured out that tastes had changed and Italian audiences wouldn't flock to see has-been American actors lip-sync lines like "Tonight we march on Rome!" while wearing polyester togas with zippers down the back. But Annie Pepper had learned a lot down on the spaghetti farm, and she managed to persuade those same actors that American TV was waiting breathlessly for their return to the States and quickly plugged her clients into series after series. Then she branched out and began to handle the behind-the-camera talent as well. While Zalman didn't exactly like her, they'd known each other a long time and had engaged in several reasonably amicable sparring matches in the course of business. So far, they were more or less even.

"One reason I should even talk to you, Jerry," Annie Pepper snorted as she picked up the phone. "Just gimme one reason after the screwing you gave me over that deal for Bland's picture score."

"You love me, Annie, that's why."

"I hate your guts, Jerry, but give my love to Lucille. So what do you want at ten in the morning?"

"Tom Kellar—" Zalman began.

"Believe me, darling, him you don't want. Besides, what does he need you for? He's got lawyers already and he's got representation up the botty. Sid Rosen handles him, and believe me, when Sid's got his teeth in, he don't let go. You wanna hear a funny story I heard about Sid? Say yes, Jerry. It's funny."

"Sure, Annie," Zalman said as he swung around in his chair and stared down at the street. He knew that Annie

Pepper would be in a more receptive mood if she started out the conversation by trashing Kellar's agent, Sid Rosen, a very famous guy around town. "Tell me a funny story about Sid."

"Sid's second wife, Miranda, told me this story herself, so I know it's true, okay? So you know what a liar Sid is, I mean, he's so Hollywood, he says yes to everything. So even if the guy swears up and down six ways from Sunday that you've got a rock-solid deal, you can never believe him unless you've got the thing notarized by the pope and hewn in granite in front of the White House, right?"

"Right, Annie. I heard this about Sid."

"So Miranda says one day she's in the house, she hasn't been out all day because she has a wicked head cold, right?"

"Right, Annie," Zalman said.

"So Sid comes in from the office, she says to him. 'Sid, what's the weather like outside, I haven't been out all day,' and Sid says, 'Darling, believe me, it's gorgeous outside, sunny, blue sky, simply gorgeous,' and Miranda tells me she looks him straight in the eye and says to him, 'Sid, swear to me on your mother's life.'" Annie Pepper waited expectantly for Zalman to laugh. "Don't you get it, Jerry?" she asked. "See, Sid's such a liar and so when Miranda asks him about the weather and he tells her it's gorgeous out, she says to him, 'Swear to me on your mother's life.' Don't you think that's a funny story about Sid?"

"Very funny, Annie. I like it."

"You're not laughing, Jerry! Whatsamatter, I told it wrong, didn't I?" Annie Pepper sighed. "I don't think I tell stories very well, y'know."

"You told it fine, Annie, it's very funny, and when I repeat it, I'll claim Miranda told it to me, okay? I'll tell it like it was my own. Now look, Annie—"

"Here it comes," Annie said. "You didn't call me up first thing in the morning just to hear my Sid Rosen story, I can see that!"

"Shut up, Annie, and listen to me a minute, will you?" Zalman barked as he punched his speakerphone and went to the bar for coffee. He'd had enough of humoring Annie Pepper. "This is serious. . . ."

Annie Pepper hacked out a thick cough over her morning cigarette. "In this town, darling, only a firm three-picture deal is serious."

"You two were at the Magic Cavern the other night. I saw you, remember, so don't think you can snake out of it."

"Sure, why would I lie? Was that a scene or what? I saw that girl come tumbling out of the iron whozis, I grabbed Tom and said, 'Let's beat it, babe, before the cops show up. . . .'"

"Right, Annie. You're a real concerned citizen. But here's what I want to know. You and Kellar, it's a business relationship?"

There was a prolonged silence, then the sound of smoke being exhaled.

"Annie? You there, doll?" Zalman asked. "Look, this ain't for *Showbiz Today,* got it?"

"None of your damn beeswax, Jerry damn Zalman, does that answer your damn question?"

Zalman laughed. "Yeah. I get the picture. But look, Annie, you and me, we go back a long way, right?"

"Too long, you ask me," she replied shortly.

"Annie! Don't give me trouble when I'm trying to save your fanny for you! I know all about Kellar's little habits, okay? Now, me, I'm broad-minded. A guy wants to make like he's the Lone Ranger, wear a cute little mask and pj's with a drop seat, do I care? But you and Kellar were there when the girl gets killed, and I need to know the answer to one question. Maybe I can keep your name out of it, you read me? Were you and Kellar together every minute you were at the Magic Cavern? Did he go to the gents', did you go to the ladies'? Go for a phone call, you know what I mean?"

"Sure. And the answer's no. We absolutely positively weren't out of each other's sight. I'll swear to it on the MGM production schedule."

"Nobody got up?"

"Nope." Annie Pepper giggled with evil-widdle-kid glee. "Kellar's a real weirdo, like he doesn't like to go pee-pee in a public place? It's hysterical, the guy's got a clean fetish along with all the rest. You get into the car with him, first he's got to wash off the steering wheel with those baby butt-wipe things?"

"Don't say *butt*, Annie, it doesn't become a swell dame like you."

"Listen, Jer, all kidding aside. You think this is going to be a problem? Kellar's really into his family image thing, so I don't want anything to get around. See—and this is strictly confidential—after we're through with the love in bloom, I'm hoping I can bump Sid Rosen out of the picture. It would be a real coup and I wouldn't mind having Kellar for a client, you want to know the truth. Love passes, but a solid business relationship lasts like real estate in Bel-Air. So if you tell him I told you about the baby butt-wipes, I'll swear you're a lying weasel!"

"Won't breathe a word, doll. Trust me. Look, one more thing. I need to talk to him, so front me in, okay? Set up an appointment for us this afternoon, maybe at Le Croque if he wants to do it at lunch."

Annie Pepper giggled. "He doesn't eat in public either, just swigs Tab."

"A fourteen-karat obsessive, huh? Well, it's important, so tell him to break whatever he has to break and then you call me back."

"Now I'm your secretary? Jeez, Jerry, you're a pushy sonofabitch!"

"Annie! I'm trying to help you out here! Don't gimme heartburn so early in the morning!"

"Call you back," Annie Pepper said as she hung up.

Half an hour later, just as Esther Wong breezed in, waggling her fingers because her nails were still wet, Annie Pepper called back.

"Could you get that, Mr. Z.?" Esther called plaintively. "I'm still wet. . . ."

"Terrific," Zalman growled. "I pay you a fortune, Esther!" he yelled into the outer office. "Can't you get your nails done on Saturday? Hello! Zalman here!"

"Calm down, will you, Jerry?" Annie Pepper snapped. "You and Tom Kellar, one-thirty at Le Croque."

"Thanks, doll," Zalman said. "I owe you one."

"Ha!" Annie Pepper said, and hung up.

ZALMAN ALWAYS LIKED TO EAT AT LE CROQUE BECAUSE the joint's oily owner, Pierre, a.k.a. Pete Marchetti from Cleveland, owed him a lot of money from a legal bill he'd never paid, so Zalman always took his fee out in trade. Le Croque was very chic and very expensive and Zalman went there often just to remind Pierre who was the boss.

"Ahhhh, M'sieu Zallllmannnn, eet eez zee plaisair to zee you again zo zoon!" Pierre said as Zalman walked in.

"You're getting your accents mixed up again, Pete," Zalman said as they shook hands. "You're doing Werner Klemperer and you're supposed to be doing Charles Boyer."

Pierre laughed nervously and looked around to see if anyone had overheard. "Cool it, will ya, Jer?" he said under his breath. "I'm trying to make a living here! M'sieu Zallmannn veal be so good to follow me to zee table?"

"Tom Kellar here yet?" Zalman asked as they worked their way through the crowded dining room where a raft of Hollywood hopefuls were gnawing away at their overpriced food. "We're having lunch together."

"You're having the lunch," Pierre mumbled over his shoulder. "Kellar just sits there takin' up the space and swigging Tab. God, I hate that guy!" he said. "Never eats a thing, just drinks a Tab. He's taking up the space, I could squeeze another body in there, know what I mean? I figure he should be eating. . . . What a stiff! He ain't here yet. He's one of them types is always late, thinks it makes him a big man. Oohhhh, 'allo, 'allo, I deed not zee you come in, mesdames, soo luffly today you look. . . ."

"That accent stinks, Pete. Honest to God, you ought to decide what country you're supposed to be from," Zalman said as he sat down at his favorite table in a little gazebo ringed with ferns. "Get me a Bullshot, will you? It's only one-thirty and already it's been a long day."

Tom Kellar showed up twenty minutes later. Not late enough for Zalman to punch him in the mouth, but late enough to make his point and late enough to be a pain. He was a six-footer with broad shoulders, a roll of flab around his gut, and a shock of thick white hair falling across his forehead that he kept brushing back boyishly. Another pain.

As Zalman watched Pierre leading Kellar through the room and over to his table, he had a hard time thinking of the guy strapped to a lawn chair yelling, 'Oh, no, sire, anything but the cat-o'-nine-tails, please!' but that's the way it was. No accounting for bad taste, Zalman thought as he and Kellar shook hands.

Kellar had his sunglasses on and he was wearing black satin sweatpants, an aqua and black "Win, Lose or Draw" windbreaker, and no shirt underneath. He pushed his sunglasses back on his head, gave Zalman a big smile filled with white teeth, and ordered a Tab. "Jerry," he breathed, leaning forward across the table with a great show of friendliness, "I've been looking forward to meeting you for a long time, but we can talk friendship later. Annie Pepper —a wonderful human being—says you can help me out here. . . ." Kellar fumbled in his pocket, took out a pristine white silk hankie, and began to polish the silverware. "Hey, we both know I got a problem, and Annie says you can keep my name out of this thing," he said as he folded the handkerchief into the smallest possible square and returned it to the pocket of his windbreaker. Kellar shook his head seriously, then brushed back the white forelock. "A man with my reputation, well, you can understand why I don't want to get involved. My people, the people who depend on me for their family entertainment concepts, they think I'm right up there with Walt Disney, a regular humanitarian! I don't want to disabuse them of this nutty notion!" He laughed heartily, shaking his head. "Disabuse, is that a great word? I just got it off one of my writers. Disabuse . . ."

"Are we talking about the same thing, Tom?" Zalman asked casually, resisting the urge to fork the producer in the eyeballs. "Are we talking about you and Annie at the

Magic Cavern when the girl gets killed, or are we talking about some . . . shall we call them 'candid photographs' of you and Lydia Devanti? Or are we talking about some tapes that Roy Caldwell's got of Lydia talking about your personal habits and now Caldwell's using them to blackmail you? Which is it, Tom?"

Kellar looked horrified and nausea swept over his big face like a wave destroying a kid's sandcastle at the beach. "Oh, shit, you know about everything! That's it, I'm screwed!" he said, his voice choking up. "My entire career is gone, gone, gone—there'll be nothing left but the residuals! Oh, God, how could I have been such a fool!" He pushed his sunglasses over his eyes, glanced around the room nervously, then leaned closer to Zalman, panting in short little bursts like a dog on a hot summer afternoon. "Jerry, Jerry, you gotta help me! I'm still working on my house! I've got an image to protect! People depend on me for wholesome entertainment, for television the entire family can enjoy as a unit! You and me, Jerry, we're sophisticated, we're experienced. You and me, we know a man needs a change, some diversion once in a while . . ."

Zalman sipped his Bullshot and nodded with priestly understanding as he watched Kellar wriggle. He figured he wouldn't get any lunch unless he could get Kellar to wind up his pathetic spiel, so he decided to give the screw a quarter turn. "Look, Tom," he said quietly, "you don't have to explain anything to me; believe me, I don't care." Kellar opened his yap but Zalman cut him off. "Listen to me a minute. The police don't know you were at the Magic Cavern, and as far as I know, nobody else does either. Nobody cares if you were there. That's not the point. The point is, you heard from Caldwell?"

"Yeah," Kellar said moodily as he took out his handkerchief and started in on the rim of his glass. "See, he doesn't exactly say pay up or else. He says, 'You need to talk to Mr. MacTavish about your aura.' He says, 'Let's talk about doing my life story as a Movie of the Week.' He wants to produce, he wants me to help him get a book deal, he wants, he wants, he wants! What am I? The guy's agent? Now he calls me this morning, tells me he's having this party, he wants me to come. . . . I hate parties," Kellar groaned. "People breathe on you and they're always trying to sell you a screenplay. . . ."

"And you and Annie were together the whole time you were at the Magic Cavern?" Zalman asked, watching Kellar closely. "You understand, I have to know. You were there, you got the motive. . . ."

"Never left the table," Kellar said piously. "We were sitting there watching the show and when the girl falls out of the thingamajig, Annie says, 'Let's beat it before the cops show up.' Her very words, I swear it! Look, I didn't do anything, Jerry, honest! Can't you keep my name out of this? I need you to handle this for me, Jerry. I need representation. And I need it from you. You're the best in town for this sort of problem, everybody says so."

"Yeah?" Zalman said. "Who told you that?"

"My agent, Sid Rosen. He says he doesn't know you personally but you have a very major rep. And Annie Pepper told me all about the kind of weird stuff you handle. Hey, buddy, no offense, you got me? It's just that Annie says you're a specialist. You handle stuff other guys don't touch. Look, be my lawyer on this," Kellar begged. "It means a lot to me. A *lot*," he repeated with heavy emphasis. "You won't be sorry for it, I promise. I'll messenger over a retainer to you first thing I get back to the office. Okay? Do we have a deal?"

Zalman didn't like Kellar, but he thought the producer was telling the truth. Simone had stepped into the iron maiden alive and she fell out of it three seconds later, dead as yesterday's *New York Post*. Kellar and Annie Pepper were in the audience the whole time; Kellar said so and Annie backed him up. Unless Kellar knew how to kill by telepathy, he was in the clear. "I'll see what I can do," Zalman said shortly. "I don't promise anything, but I'll see what I can do, okay?"

Kellar leapt from his chair and pumped Zalman's hand. "Should I go to Caldwell's party?" he asked anxiously. "Whaddaya think?"

"Do what you want! No reason not to go. You gonna go for the Movie of the Week, or talk to the cops about it?" Zalman asked curiously. He wondered which way Kellar was going to jump.

Kellar pushed his white hair off his forehead and frowned. "I can't go to the cops," he said slowly. "Maybe I can sidetrack Caldwell with a book. . . . Who knows? All this meditation stuff is big, maybe it'll sell. One thing I'll tell you, sincerely. I can't afford to have my personal life exposed, so if it comes to it, I'll have to pay. But I'd sure like to get those tapes back." He sighed. "Not to mention the photos."

"Like I said, I'll see what I can do." Zalman smiled thinly, leaning back in his chair.

Kellar grabbed for Zalman's hand. "Help me, Jerry! I'm begging you. I gotta have those tapes! Hey! Look at the time! I gotta big meeting at Paramount. . . . Be in touch, hey, Jer?"

"What a jerk," Zalman mumbled as he watched Kellar working the room on his way out. "Pierre! Zee menu!"

WHEN ZALMAN RETURNED TO THE OFFICE, HE FOUND Lydia Devanti and Esther Wong knee to knee on the couch in his office, having a serious conversation about the men in their lives.

"I don't know," Esther was saying as he came in. "Am I a woman who loves too much? Why am I always getting involved with men who aren't serious! All the men I meet are so shallow," she sighed sadly. "They only care about cars. That's all they talk about. Cars. Whether they should get a BMW or a Mercedes and how big the engine on the silly thing is! I'm bright, I'm attractive, why don't they talk about me? No. Cars. Just cars," Esther said, twirling a strand of her long black hair around her finger. "It's very discouraging."

Zalman tossed his car keys on the desk and sat down in his chair. "Am I interrupting a deeply feminine moment of communication?" he asked. "If so, I hate to break up this intense woman-talk, but I have an office to run. Esther, are there any messages for me? Anything to do with business? I just thought I'd ask," Zalman added. "I don't want to press you."

"I have to tell Esther one little thing," Lydia said. "Don't make the same mistake I did! So many times I settled for second best, and now I wish I'd been more careful. Hold out until you find someone wonderful! Don't take anything less than real love, that's what I think. If only I'd thought more highly of myself when I was younger, had a better sense of self-worth. I wouldn't be in the trouble I'm in if I'd followed my own advice."

"Thanks, Lydia," Esther said, "I appreciate everything you've shared with me. And don't worry about the office, Mr. Z. I had the machine on while Lydia and I were talking. I'll just run and see if there's any messages on it. Everything's taken care of that needs to be taken care of."

She and Lydia kissed cheeks, and then Lydia took Esther's hand in hers. "Promise me you'll think over what I said, won't you?" she asked. "If I'd been smarter about the men in my life, I wouldn't be here now, asking Jerry to help me." She sighed.

Esther squeezed her hand. "Don't worry, Lydia. Mr. Z. can take care of anything. He always does." And with that she went back to her desk to peruse the new copy of *Elle* that had come in the morning mail.

Zalman put his feet up on his desk. "This is unexpected, Lydia," he said. "What can I do for you?"

Lydia sat down in the armchair opposite Zalman's partner's desk, leaned forward, and looked searchingly into his eyes. She was wearing a beige wool suit, a cream silk blouse, and a long strand of pearls and looked every inch the lady. "I thought I'd better drop in, Jerry, just to tell you something. Under the circumstances . . ."

"Go ahead, Lydia. Shoot."

"I just wanted to tell you that I love Ernie." She smiled, toying with her pearls. "Very much. He's a wonderful man and I hope that he decides he wants to get married, because that would be much easier on my mother and the tax returns and boring things like that. But if he doesn't, we'll go right on the way we are. It won't change my feelings one iota. I know you probably think I've messed up Ernie's life, what with Roy and the blackmailing and Simone . . ." she trailed off. "I care very deeply for Ernie."

"I can see that, Lydia," Zalman told her.

"And I'm sorry that I've caused all this trouble. Poor Simone! And the pictures! Not to mention those terrible tapes Roy's got! I never would have told him those things about those men if I'd had any idea! If I'd thought he was going to—oh, it just makes me furious! I hate to say this, but I wish it'd been Roy in that iron maiden! I could have slammed the door on him myself!" Lydia shook her blond head angrily. "I shouldn't say things like that, it's very bad karmic practice," she said, sighing, "but I can't help it! I feel taken advantage of! So used!"

"So why are you going to Caldwell's party, then? Why don't you just tell the guy to bugger off?" Zalman asked, making a steeple with his fingers.

Lydia sighed. "It's my mother."

"Dad told me she was a missionary? Okay, I understand you don't want to hurt her, but you should take Caldwell seriously. Don't think you can make an end run around him. He's smart and he's ruthless where money is concerned. Everybody is, these days."

"It's just that my mother's so churchy! She and my father were saving souls before I was born! In Africa. That's how they met. But then after they got married they stayed here. But he died when I was twelve, and then my mother and I were awfully poor. I had to take care of her, there wasn't anybody else, and she's so wrapped up in her church work. . . . She never even knew I was a performer until a few years ago. If Roy does sell those icky pictures, it'll just break her heart! It will, Jerry, I know it will. So I have to do everything I can to stop him, you see? If going to his silly party will help, well, off I'll go. I made a big mistake with him and I may have to pay the price," Lydia said, her eyes determined. "But I'm going to pay as little as I have to. I mean it!"

"I can see that, Lydia," Zalman said. "Okay, you don't want to antagonize Caldwell. Makes sense. Just . . . keep an eye on my dad tonight, will you? He's got some funny ideas about handling Caldwell, and I don't want to see either one of you end up in the soup."

Lydia stood up, smoothing her suit over her knees. "I love Ernie," she said. "I wouldn't let him do anything that would get him in trouble. Anything. I hope you believe that, Jerry."

"I believe you," Zalman said as he walked her to his outer office door. "Trouble is, you and I may not be able to stop him."

ZALMAN, EARNEST, AND LYDIA ARRIVED AT ROY CALD-well's house at nine o'clock. At first, Zalman wasn't going to wear black-tie, but Earnest insisted. "See," he explained to his recalcitrant son, "Lydia's gonna be all dolled up 'cause she's gonna do a song, a few tricks. Now, me," he added moodily, "I wouldn't roll Caldwell over if he was drowning in the gutter, but she thinks maybe it'll oil the troubled waters if she does her routine. So that means you and I gotta wear black-tie because if we don't she's gonna pout and say she's overdressed and feel nervous. This kinda stuff, it's important to women, Jer, you oughta know that by now," Earnest said as he inserted his gold horseshoe cuff links into his cuffs.

So Zalman had put on his dinner jacket and chauffeured Earnest, Lydia, and Sergeant Pepper, who was also wearing a dinner jacket, out to Caldwell's place. The white house was glowing in the golden light cast off by the huge torch embedded in the front lawn, and the Pacific beat out a dark samba in the night. The front door was standing open and laughter, clinking glasses, and the sounds of a piano tinkling "Diamonds Are a Girl's Best Friend" drifted out.

"Doesn't this look pretty!" Lydia said happily. She was wearing a long green silk dress with a big lavender sequined flower draped over one shoulder, and she looked lovely. Maybe it was her heart-to-heart with Zalman, maybe the prospect of a party, but she seemed to have eliminated any ugly thoughts of the recent unpleasantness from her mind. "I just love to see people enjoying themselves, don't you, pookie?"

"Knocks me out," Earnest said, tickling Sergeant Pepper under his brown chin. The Sarge chattered fiercely and adjusted his satin lapels. In his well-cut suit and tiny top hat, he was clearly going to be the best-dressed monkey in the joint.

"If only Simone could have been here." Lydia said, sighing. "She did love a party. . . . But I'm not going to dwell on the past! I've made a personal commitment to myself to live in the moment, be here now. But she was a good friend and she had a real future in the business. . . . Do you think that nice police captain will ever find out what happened, Jerry?" she said as she inspected her makeup in her compact, then settled Sergeant Pepper on her shoulder. The monkey wrapped his tail around her throat like a living scarf.

"No doubt about it," Zalman lied as he grabbed Lydia's music case and tossed the car keys to one of Caldwell's caftan-clad minions. "Arnie Thrasher's got the fangs of a terrier."

Inside, the party was in full swing, and as Zalman

scanned the room he saw Martha glowering at Cueball Caldwell, who was standing by the piano, his arm around an adoring girl in red. Caldwell was wearing a blue caftan shot with gold thread and he'd painted his bald head in a pattern of gold ringlets so that he looked like he was wearing a smooth, shining cap of hair.

"I have to get ready to do my number," Lydia said. "Pookie, could you hang on to Sergeant Pepper while I talk to the piano man?" She handed the monkey to Earnest and was about to go over to the piano when Caldwell joined them, a smile on his face as slippery as Crisco.

"Mr. Zalman, how nice," the psychic said. "And Mr. Zalman Senior, of course," he added pointedly. "You've come at last. Both of you. And my darling Lydia," he said in a silky, possessive voice. "I've missed you so." He gave her a light kiss on the cheek and ran his hand up and down her bare arm as if he were stroking a pony's warm flank. "Now that you're here at last, I hope you'll stay. You know, darling," he said, leaning toward her, his hand still on her arm, "I have everything you'll ever need here. Everything," he added suggestively. "Do join me. . . ."

"Let me ask you something, Caldwell," Earnest said, scowling up at him. "How'd you like a nice bop on the beezer? Huh? How'd you like me to rearrange your entire face? You might like it better when I'm done, it's not so hot now."

"You remember what I told you," Zalman warned his father.

"Forget it, Jer," Earnest said, brushing Zalman aside. "This is war! Huh, Caldwell?" he went on, his voice rising. "Howsaboutit?"

"Now, pookie," Lydia said uncomfortably, shivering under Caldwell's touch, "Roy doesn't mean anything. . . ."

Caldwell took his hand off Lydia. But he did it very, very slowly. "No offense, Mr. Zalman." He smiled. "No offense, I'm sure."

"Are you sure you're sure?" Earnest said, still combative. "Be sure, Caldwell, I'm telling you."

Caldwell continued to smile, but said nothing more.

"Where's my music case?" Lydia said, obviously trying to break up the pair before Earnest decided to throw a punch at Caldwell. "I just had it. . . ."

"Here it is," Zalman said, handing her the flat black leather case.

"Oh, good—I'm glad I didn't lose it. Now, pookie," she said, casting a nervous eye at Caldwell, "you and Sergeant Pepper come over here with me. . . ." Lydia grabbed Earnest's hand and led him over to the piano, away from Caldwell.

"Very cute," Zalman told the smiling psychic. "You know, he's got a mean right for a guy his age. I'd watch it, I was you."

Caldwell shrugged. "He doesn't bother me," he said. "Now, if you'll excuse me, I have other guests."

Zalman went over to the piano. "What did I tell you, huh?" he said to Earnest. "I told you to keep an eye on Lydia and stay away from Caldwell!"

"Right. You said that," Earnest snapped. "Your very words. But is it okay if me and the Sarge have a drink? Just one? Huh, Jer? Huh? Is it?"

Zalman glowered at his father. When had they changed places? For years, his father had had all the answers, the keys to life's many mysteries, and Zalman had always believed that Earnest had a lock on the truth. What had happened, and how had it happened so quickly? How come he was giving the orders all of a sudden? "Dad—"

"Just kidding! Me and the Sarge, we'll do anything you

want. It's a promise. Whatsamatter, don't you trust your old man?"

Zalman was cornered. "Of course I trust you, Dad. You're family, right?"

"You think I'm not, look in the mirror," Earnest advised. "C'mon, Sarge, let's go get us a drink."

Zalman took a look around, trying to get the lay of the land. The room was filled with well-dressed folks glugging down the domestic champagne, lounging around on the multicolored pillows scattered over the floor, and gazing out the big windows at the view. Several of Caldwell's glassy-eyed sisters were serving drinks and veggie snacks, and Zalman grabbed a glass of champagne as a girl with a shaved head sailed by.

Lenny Dunn, wearing a white dinner jacket, a white sequined cowboy hat, and some very butch boots, had his arm around a baby-faced blonde and they were staring into each other's eyes like they were poleaxed with loved. Tom Kellar was over in the corner nodding absently as Annie Pepper yakked at him. Annie winked and waved Zalman over and Kellar gave him a cheerful grin. "Later," Zalman mouthed across the room.

"Zally, howyadoin'!" a voice breathed behind him.

"Not a cent, Phil," Zalman replied without turning around.

"You're making a big mistake," Phil Hanning said as he grabbed Zalman's hand and pumped it happily. "Me and Isobel are gangbusters with this Jack the Zipper deal. You don't get a piece of it, you'll be sorry. But that isn't what I wanted to talk to you about. You know Lenny Dunn?" he asked, jerking his head at Dunn and the little blonde.

"He's a client," Zalman said warily. "Where's Lucille?" He loved Phil—after all, a guy saves your life, you love him. But Hanning had a money problem: he didn't have any. And he had the bad habit of leeching dough off any damn fool dumb enough to lend it to him, so whenever Phil wanted an intro, Zalman always had to warn his friends and clients off before they got burned.

"She hadda go over to Bland's, pick him up. Oughta be here any minute," Hanning said, looking at his watch. "She's late already. See, I want to talk to Dunn about this Wild West Museum thing—an old cowpoke like him, he's gonna go crazy for it! Gonna make a fortune, Zally, a fortune! Did I tell you I gotta line on a guy who used to be a prop man out at Republic Studios in the old days, and he stole something from every picture he ever worked on? An incredible collection! Next best thing to the ruby slippers. . . ." Hanning ranted on, his natural huckster's desire to push his product getting the better of him. "Dunn's a natural for the deal, you don't get in on the ground floor, you'll be sorry about it later. You'll hate yourself. So whaddaya say, Jer?"

"Everybody! Everybody, please!" Zalman turned and saw Martha rapping on the piano with her knuckles. "Could we all gather around, please?" she said. "Roy has a special treat for you. We weren't expecting this, but he's received a communication from Mr. MacTavish, and Mr. MacTavish has agreed to speak through Roy for us this evening, isn't that special?"

The audience oohed and aahed like they were looking at a cuddly litter of puppies. "Let's talk about it later, okay, Phil?" Zalman said. "I want to watch this."

"You'll be sorry, you don't get in on it, Jer," Hanning said, a little miffed that Zalman wasn't leaping at the glorious business opportunity he was offering. The thing about Hanning was, he never learned.

"So if we'd all just take our seats, pull up a pillow, we'll just settle down now and give Roy a few peaceful minutes to get in touch with Mr. MacTavish. As some of you know," Martha went on, her voice now hushed with the beauty of the moment, "the channeling experience can be very trying for Roy. It drains a tremendous amount of his psychic energy, so it's important that we all be very, very quiet. Can we do that? Can we all be very, very quiet?" she asked in the dulcet tones of a preschool teacher with an unruly little flock. The crowd scurried to obey her, settling in a circle around a straight-backed chair with a purple velvet cushion that Martha placed in the center of the ring of pillows.

"That's very nice," Martha said, smiling. "Thank you very much. Now remember, quiet, please!" she said as she faded over to a corner of the room and dimmed the lights.

Roy Caldwell walked firmly to the center of the seated crowd and sat down on the chair, his gold cap of painted hair shining with an eerie glow in the dim lights of the big living room. Caldwell sighed deeply, inhaled several big gulps of air, and closed his eyes. Then he began to hum "Aum," and rock back and forth in his seat, his hands planted firmly on his knees.

Zalman watched skeptically, but he had to admit, he was impressed. Caldwell took his performance seriously; his sets and costumes were first-rate, his theatrical sense superb. Too bad he never made it as an actor, Zalman thought, the guy is big-time Oscar material.

Caldwell continued to drone, "Aum," then stopped suddenly, opened his eyes wide, and grinned like a lunatic who'd just found the keys to the asylum gate lying on top of his bowl of Froot Loops.

"Weeel, halloooo, evrabody!" he exclaimed with a chuckle. "Here's Mr. MacTavish talkin' to ye!"

The crowd oohed and aahed again, clearly impressed with the miracle of transformation they were witnessing.

"Mr. MacTavish, how are you this evening?" Martha called out softly. She spoke very slowly and deliberately, as if she were talking to a child. "Hello, Mr. MacTavish," she repeated. "Will you be able to answer a few questions for us this evening?"

"Questions, weeel, sartainly ah weell! Speech is the midwife o' the mind, d'ya ken?" Mr. MacTavish chortled heartily. "And as far you, Martha, it's weel yer thoughts are no written on yer forehead! Mr. MacTavish can see yer in deep spiritual distress! Wat's troublin' ye this evening, little hen?"

"I'm surprised you can see through my facade so clearly, Mr. MacTavish," Martha said. "Let's just say I have money troubles, a problem many people in this room probably share."

The crowd murmured its agreement and Martha put her finger to her lips. "Quiet," she mouthed. "Ssshhhhh."

"Money! Filthy lucre!" Mr. MacTavish sighed. "As sure as Nessie swims in the loch, weel all have money troubles someday. . . ."

Zalman continued to watch curiously as Caldwell played out the scene. Caldwell's concentration rivaled that of Pee Wee Herman. He didn't break character for a minute, there was no telltale flicker of laughter behind his eyes, no twitch coming through from his Roy Caldwell persona to spoil the show. The stage had lost a genius when Caldwell decided to go into the spirituality racket.

As Mr. MacTavish was talking, Zalman slipped over next to Martha. "Can I ask him a question?" he whispered to her.

Martha looked at him with suspicion written in caps all over her face. "This is serious business," she said under her breath. "Dry up."

Zalman laughed despite himself. "Hey, really, no kidding, I want to ask him a question, okay?"

"I'm warning you," she said, "you screw this up and I'll punch your eyes right out of their sockets. Get it?"

"Hey, it's not gonna be a problem," Zalman said. "Mr. MacTavish, it's Jerry Zalman speaking. I met Roy Caldwell the other day—remember me?"

"Roy tollld me alll aboot ye, laddie," Mr. MacTavish said. "D'ye have a question for me?"

"I do. A friend of mine has lost something that's very important to her. Some photographs and tapes," Zalman said, glancing over at Lydia. She made a little round O with her mouth and widened her blue eyes. "She thinks perhaps these papers might have been stolen. Can you tell me anything about where they might be?"

"Stolen, eh? Weeell, it's opportunities that make a thief, d'ye ken?" Mr. MacTavish said, his bright eyes glittering. "Can ye tellll me more?"

"Do you think she can get her things back?" Zalman asked.

"Oh, there's verra few things ye canna get back, laddie!" Mr. MacTavish laughed. "If ye be willin' to pay the prrrice. There's few things lost that canna be found. Few things in this worrrld!"

"Heeeey, just hold on here a minute!" a voice called out. Zalman looked across the room and saw Lenny Dunn jump up off his pillow. "I've had enough of this!" Dunn said as he worked his way forward through the seated audience.

"Mr. Dunn, please!" Martha called out, desperation in her voice. "This is all your fault, you!" she snarled at Zalman under her breath.

"What're you two guys really talking about, huh?" Dunn demanded. "I got the feeling you're a damn faker, Caldwell! Making out like you're some kinda weird Scot! What the hell is this, some crazy kid's game? You've got that junk of Lydia's and you're gonna mess up my whole life! I'm an artist! I got a future in front of me! You can't do this to me! You're a thief and a blackmailer and I don't wanna listen to any more of this crap!" Dunn's big shoulders were hunched over, his hands clenched at his sides.

The crowd mumbled hungrily to itself. With any luck there'd be a fight, some blood on the saddle, maybe a knockout punch. Something to talk about later, when life got a little dull at dinner parties.

Martha twitched frantically at Zalman's side. "Do something!" she begged Zalman. "If he gets hurt . . ."

"I get the feeling Caldwell can take care of himself," Zalman told her. "He's been doing okay so far."

"Weeeel, ye dinna need to get so excited, laddie," Mr. MacTavish said in a smooth, unruffled voice. "No need at all. Ye take things too seriously. Too much ta heartt."

Zalman thought he saw faint traces of Roy Caldwell oozing to the surface, but then Mr. MacTavish took firm control once again and the fleeting flash of Roy Caldwell disappeared.

"I'm not kidding, Caldwell, I've had enough of this crap! You're a damn liar, is what you are!" Dunn wasn't about to let anything slide by him, Zalman could see that. "I'm warning you, there's gonna be trouble if you don't give that crap back to Lydia!"

"A liar is just an economist of the truth, laddie," Mr. MacTavish said sharply. "And now ay think ye best whist yer mouth. Yer too violent fer ma peaceful naturre. Ye be a wolf, a bloodthirsty wolf, and a wolf may lose his teeth, d'ye ken, but never his nature. . . . Ay'm feelin' tired now, Martha, ay think that'll be aboot all ay can say tonight. . . ." Mr. MacTavish passed his hand over his eyes, and when he took his hand away his eyes were closed once again and he began to intone "Aum" in the same droning hum.

"It's not fair!" Dunn yelped. "He don't wanta fight fair!" He threw his glass in the fireplace—a nice, stagy effect—and stalked over to the corner, where the little blonde threw her arms around him and nuzzled at his handsome face.

"Hey, Zally! Some show, huh?" It was Phil Hanning. "So what about you gimme an intro to Dunn, huh?" he pressed. "I hate to go up to a guy and just start pitching, it makes a bad impression. So what about it, huh?"

"Bad timing, Phil," Zalman said. "Trust me."

"Well, maybe later then, huh?" Hanning said, undaunted. "Hey, where's Ernie? Maybe he'd like to get in on this deal."

"See the dame with the monkey?" Zalman said, still watching Dunn closely. The guy was red in the face and he was talking a mile a minute at the little blonde, who was nodding her head up and down, agreeing with everything he said.

"Yeah," Hanning said.

"Right over there."

"Where?"

As he turned around, Zalman had a bad feeling. Again. "Right over th— Oh, damn it to hell, he's gone!"

"HEY, LOOKIT THE MONKEY!" PHIL HANNING EXCLAIMED, his handsome face lighting up with pleasure. "Cute little guy, isn't he? Zally, you think the kids would go for a thing like that?"

"Forget it, Phil," Zalman said as he scanned the room, vainly looking for Earnest. Trust me, he thought. I'm family, he thought. "Monkeys are dirty. They rip up the drapes and they gotta wear diapers. No sense of personal hygiene."

"Whatsamatter," Phil teased, "you lose Ernie?"

"This is serious, Phil!" Zalman told his brother-in-law. "Where is he?"

"Lemme help you look for him," Hanning said happily. Lucille claimed he couldn't handle responsibility, so poor Phil was always trying to prove he was on the case.

"Yeah, great, Phil," Zalman said. "I came in with him and last I saw he was with Lydia, at the— Aww, cripes, and Caldwell's not here either!" Zalman moaned as his stomach took that mile-a-minute elevator ride to the ground floor. "I gotta find him, Phil. Fast. I gotta bad feeling. . . ."

The pianist swung into Lydia's intro and one of Caldwell's dippy sisters motioned for everyone in the living room to clear a space around the Steinway. Lydia hitched up on top of the piano with Sergeant Pepper on her lap and went into her "Lovey Dovey" number, but Zalman couldn't see his dad anywhere in the room. Earnest K. Zalman had disappeared.

"Damn," Zalman muttered, the bad feeling in his stomach getting worse by the second. "He's gone. Now I *know* I'm in top trouble." Why did he think he could trust his own father? Where was he? What was he doing? Zalman was disgusted with himself. It was his own fault that Earnest was gone, and he knew exactly where Earnest was and he knew precisely what he was doing, no doubt about it. Earnest was upstairs in Caldwell's study trying to crack the safe. He was going to rob Roy.

Very casually, Zalman slipped to the back of the group

clustered around Lydia and Sergeant Pepper, who was now twirling a tiny ebony baton in one paw and waving a multicolored handkerchief in the other while Lydia pulled silver dollars out of his ears.

Zalman made a quick check of the downstairs just to keep himself honest, but it was hopeless. Then, when he was sure nobody was watching, he slipped up the carpeted stairway to the second floor. Upstairs, Caldwell's house was quiet, and although several bedroom doors were standing open along the hallway, revealing monastic white rooms, there was nobody in sight.

"Jerry!" Earnest called out softly.

Zalman turned around; Earnest was poking his head out of an open doorway at the end of the hall, an unlit cigar jammed in his mouth. Father and son looked at each other wordlessly as a brief, silent second ticked by. "In here," Earnest said quietly, stepping back to let Zalman into the library.

Zalman looked around. It was floor-to-ceiling books and hunting prints on the wall, big leather sofas, and a shining collection of horse brasses; obviously Caldwell's private hideaway. No plants, no pillows, no crystals; this was the regular guy room. Roy Caldwell was lying on the floor, crumpled up in front of an open wall safe, with his mouth a bruised wound of surprise, the back of his head blown off, and his brains smeared all over the cobalt blue oriental rug like a peanut-butter-and-jelly sandwich that had fallen face up. If he wasn't dead, he knew a lot more magic than Lydia, Zalman thought as he bent over the body and felt for a pulse. He knew it was useless. Nobody with a head like that could possibly have a pulse.

The library window was open, the blue taffeta drapes rustling in the damp night air like silk on silk. Zalman went to the window and looked up and down the broad, flat beach. The tide was way out and the moon's reflection was skittering across the breaking waves like a flat silver stone. As he squinted in the brilliant moonlight, he could barely make out a figure darting down the beach in the distance. A familiar tune echoed across the empty sand and for a moment, Zalman couldn't quite place it. Then he realized that the scurrying figure was whistling "Here Comes Peter Cottontail."

"What happened?" he asked as he turned away from the window and looked back at Earnest. "Make it fast, Dad, we don't have much time."

Earnest nodded, all business. "I came up here, I was gonna take a crack at the safe. Wasn't sure I could do it, but I figured, hey, take a crack," he said. "But it looks like somebody beat me to it. I almost had it before. Too damn bad I didn't make it." He shifted the unlit cigar to the other side of his mouth, looked around the room and then back at his son, his eyes flat and hard behind his bifocals. "I came in here and saw he was dead. Then I was going to go get you. That's it."

"You touch anything?" Zalman asked sharply. "You look in the safe? The truth."

"Took a peek inside. No photos, though. No tapes either," Earnest said, "but I didn't leave any prints, if that's what you're worried about. Didn't touch a thing except to feel for a pulse just like you did. . . . What do we do now, Jerry?" he asked. The sound of Lydia's lighthearted music drifted upstairs over the beat of the waves outside.

Zalman shrugged. "Personally, I always call the cops when I find a stiff," he said as he moved toward the telephone. "What do you do?"

L.A. COUNTY DEPUTY SHERIFF DEREK ANTHONY WAS happier than any human being had a right to be. "Boy, this is dynamite," he said. "My first big case since I got my promotion, and it's a murder! Full on! Totally cool! How lucky can you get?"

"I don't think Caldwell would've agreed with you," Zalman said mildly. "I bet right now he's thinking he wasn't so lucky. Getting his brains blown out and all." It had been a long night and Zalman's sense of humor was getting ragged around the edges.

Anthony stared at Zalman for a long minute, uncomprehending. "Well, sure, yeah," he said as the light bulb finally went on over his head. "But, like, he's dead! Okay, not so lucky for him, but for me, wow! Dynamite! And almost in the Colony, too. Man, I'd love to live in a house like this. I grew up right around the corner in Santa Monica, but I've never been inside a fancy place like this before. Gotta tell you, it's kinda out of my league," he said, looking around Caldwell's living room apprehensively.

"Don't let it bother you, Sheriff," Zalman said, trying to put the big kid at ease. "You're a cop, and when you wear a badge, you're even with the world."

"I never thought of it like that, Mr. Zalman, but I guess that's right." Anthony smiled. "But it sure is a cool house, doncha think?" he said, his khaki uniform straining over his Stallone chest. "But answer me this, hey? Wouldn't you think if a guy has enough money he can afford to live in a fancy place like this, he could afford some furniture to put in it? Hey, I've got furniture," Anthony said proudly. "Okay, so it's rented! But it's furniture! This joint's almost empty. Doncha think it's kinda strange?" Anthony wondered. He was a big, happy kid, a local surf god gone legit, with blond hair, crinkly blue eyes, and a muscular body that showed the effects of endless exercise, dieting, and iron-pumping.

"Caldwell was trying to create an effect so his clients would feel at ease," Zalman explained. "He wanted the room to look meditative. He was after ambience."

"That's what it's called, ambience? Damn, rich people have weird ideas, doncha think? Look, can I just ask you a couple questions, Mr. Zalman?" he asked hopefully. "You could really help me out. This isn't like official, and you're the only guy around here seems to know anything. I just don't want to go back to the office and not have anything to tell 'em. Nobody else'll talk to me," he complained. "I'm not gonna arrest anybody! Hell, I don't know anything yet, how can I arrest anybody?"

"I'll be glad to help if I can, Sheriff. . . ." Zalman said. With any luck at all, he could placate Anthony and then he could take Earnest home and murder him personally.

"Like what's the real deal here, Mr. Zalman? I wanted to talk to Lenny Dunn—man, I really dug 'Gunshy' when I was a kid, didn't you?—and he says to talk to you, you're his lawyer. Like it's no big deal, I just wanted to find out what went down," Anthony said, a little sadly.

"Yes, I'm representing him. What do you need to know?" Zalman asked. Dunn's public screaming match with Caldwell did put the cowboy at a disadvantage, especially when Caldwell was murdered only a few minutes later.

"I dunno," Anthony said miserably. "This lady Martha? You know who she is?"

"Caldwell's factotum."

"Huh? Fack-what?"

"She works for him. Worked."

"Yeah, right. So she says that Dunn and Caldwell have this big fight, there's screaming and yelling . . ."

"What can I tell you? A difference of opinion," Zalman said blandly.

"Well, Dunn accuses Caldwell of being a liar and a blackmailer and all sorts of no-good stuff, so I'd call it more than a difference of opinion. I mean, Dunn was flipped out over all this junk, and as soon as I hear about that, I think, hey, great suspect! But here's the problem— this guy Hanning I talked to?"

Hanning. Always Hanning. Everywhere, it's Hanning grinning like a damn monkey, Zalman thought. "My brother-in-law," Zalman put in, just in case Phil the mental giant had conveniently forgotten to mention it.

Anthony smiled and gave him a sidelong glance. "Yeah, he told me he's married to your sister. So this guy Hanning says he and Dunn were standing next to each other right about the time we figure Caldwell got shot. Which sorta puts Dunn in the clear, if it's true. Not that I think your brother-in-law is a liar, Mr. Zalman. But I gotta ask around. Caldwell was right there in the room, in plain sight and all, and then like ten minutes later, he's dead. So then you and your dad find the body. Is that the way it comes down, Mr. Zalman?"

"Pretty much. Actually, my dad found the body, and then I found him."

Anthony looked confused. The kid wasn't exactly a Nobel Prize winner. "He found it, then you found it?"

"He found it, then I found him, finding it. Right after he found it, I found him. He found it first."

"Yeah. I get it. Kinda," Anthony said. "Like I understand that your dad and Caldwell were kinda uptight with each other, too? Like there was a hassle between them, too? And then your dad finds the body and then you walked in? Is that the real deal? Gotta tell you, I'm a little confused here. . . ."

"Can't imagine why," Zalman said, looking over at Earnest. Earnest, Lydia, and Sergeant Pepper were nestled in a corner of the living room, sprawled on a Romanesque assortment of colored pillows. The Sergeant was napping in Lydia's arms, his tiny top hat cocked over his eyes like a sleep mask.

Anthony had released the rest of the partygoers, including Phil Hanning and Lenny Dunn, and all of them were too worldly-wise to spill any information. The few who'd deigned to give the surfin' sheriff the time of day claimed they'd been downstairs watching Lydia perform when the body was found and knew nothing about Caldwell's death.

Zalman was relieved that at least Phil Hanning had a solid alibi. He'd told Anthony that he'd been standing next to Lenny Dunn, making a furious pitch for his Wild West Museum throughout Lydia's number, and that put Dunn in the clear as well since Phil swore Dunn had never left his side. "Hey," Phil had whispered to Zalman as he sidled out of the house, "I got a real shot with the museum! You think I'm letting Dunn get away from me?"

But there was an unexpected problem and it was making Zalman a little nervous. Lucille and Bland had never showed up at the party, and Zalman was hoping that they could account for their whereabouts, if it came to that. Meanwhile, he wasn't going to mention his sister or Bland to the sheriff, and he'd managed to gloss over Simone's death and given Sheriff Anthony Arnie Thrasher's phone number. For the first time in living memory, Zalman had lucked out; Thrasher was off duty and the laconic desk sergeant at the Hollywood station simply grunted that he'd "tell 'im when he seed 'im."

"It's pretty gross upstairs, boy, like I almost up-chucked," Anthony said. "But don't tell anybody, okay? Gotta tell you, you barf around these guys, they never let you forget it. So could you just explain it all one more time? This deal's really weird. . . ."

"I went upstairs, looking for my dad," Zalman began again.

"And why was he upstairs? The party was downstairs."

"Looking for the men's room, I think," Zalman said casually, wondering if Anthony would go for it. The kid didn't say anything, so he plunged onward. "And there's my dad and he tells me to come in, and there's Caldwell and he's lying on the floor and he looks like he's pretty well dead."

"You touch him? You touch anything?"

"Both my dad and I checked for a pulse, that's all."

"Yuck! Messed up as he was, I wonder you had the guts. Now, me, gotta tell you, I wouldna touched him. Guy's got his brains splattered all over the rug like that, you figure, hey, he isn't dead, he's the next best thing to it. . . ."

"I thought it was my duty," Zalman said piously.

"You hear a shot or any stuff like that? Yelling? Anybody else hear a shot?"

"Not a thing," Zalman said honestly. "Miss Devanti was singing and there was a piano backing her up right about the time I went to look for my dad, so . . ." He shrugged. "I don't think anybody downstairs could've heard anything." It was a relief to tell the truth once in a while. He figured "Here Comes Peter Cottontail" didn't count. After all, whistling wasn't yelling, it was whistling. "Besides, I thought probably the killer used a silencer?"

"Wouldn't surprise me one damn bit. I figure with that

much mess and blood and yuck all over, it was a pretty big-caliber gun, maybe like a forty-five or something. I dunno. With a Dirty Harry forty-four Mag, there wouldn't even be that much head left, just like watermelon mush all over. . . ." Anthony shivered.

"Listen, Sheriff, I believe you! There's no need to be so graphic! I didn't see a gun. . . . Your guys find anything?" Zalman said, trolling for info.

"Nah, not a thing. If I had a gun, we could try for prints. . . . Guess he took it with him."

"The killer? Yeah, probably so. Say," Zalman said, trying to be helpful, "Caldwell's library looks out over the ocean, maybe the guy tried to toss it out the window or something. The window was open, like I said."

"Boy, that's a good idea! Thanks, Mr. Zalman! Hey, Billy?" he called to a uniformed deputy. "Cruise outside, man, like see if you can find a gun or anything like that. Y'know, like some evidence? Like on the beach under the window of the room where we found the dead guy? Okay? Know what I mean?"

"Sure, Derek," the deputy called. "No prob. Say, you got any flip-flops? I don't want to get my shoes all wet and sanded out."

"On the floor of my car, man," Anthony called. "Me and Billy surf on the weekends," he said, turning back to Zalman. "Bitchin' waves last Saturday on the Rincon. You shoulda been there."

SEVEN-THIRTY THE NEXT MORNING, ZALMAN CALLED McCoy and told him to get on it, fast. "Look, Dean, when this gets back to Arnie Thrasher, probably in a microsecond or two, I'm going to be in jail if I'm not dead! Got it? Thrasher will personally slaughter me! Anything to get Marie away from me! Dean, you gotta turn something up, okay? Dean? How many guys are bopping down the beach whistling 'Here Comes Peter Cottontail,' huh? You listening to me, Dean?"

McCoy was giggling like a stoned teenager. "Jerry, I love ya, pal, but this is a crack-up! It just kills me to see you sweat once in a while."

"Dean, I want that guy found! I want your ass in every lowlife dive, every hockshop, every scummy bar between here and Trancas! C'mon, Dean, it'll be like a vacation for you! Look, a guy doesn't get snuffed like this without somebody on the street knowing something, right?"

"Generally right, yeah . . ."

"So get on it!"

"Jer?"

"Yeah?"

"I'm a little short till payday, you take my meaning. . . ."

"Double scale, Dean—and don't say short!" Zalman hung up and thought about taking it on the lam to Tasmania, changing his name, growing a beard. . . . There was a knock on the front door. "Not already," Zalman said, burying his head under the covers. "Not so soon, God, I haven't even had a shower. . . ." The pounding grew in volume, heavy whacking thuds that echoed through the house with fee-fi-fo-fum intensity. Slowly, Zalman got out of bed. Rutherford, the fearsome watchdog, was cowering under a chair.

Zalman opened the front door without even bothering to look out the peephole. He knew damn well who it was, and he was right. "Arnie!" he said with a thick layer of false jollity. "What a surprise! How are ya? How's every little thing? How's—"

"Shut up, you shrimp sonofabitch!" Thrasher trumpeted. "Soon as I come in this morning, the boys tell me you found another body! You must be getting used to it by now, huh? Kind of taking it all in stride, are you?" Thrasher barged in and crashed down on the couch, glaring at Zalman. His huge bulk loomed over the living room like King Kong on top of the Empire State Building. "Listen up, Zalman. I'm not here officially as a cop! I'm here officially as a father! Where's your father, by the way?"

"Probably sleeping," Zalman lied. Anybody who could sleep through all that pounding was either dead or in a coma.

"I want to talk to him," Thrasher said ominously, "when I'm through with you. . . ."

"He'll be thrilled," Zalman said. "No kidding, it'll put the cap on his morning. But since I'm his son and his lawyer, why don't you talk to me first? You're not here officially, remember?" Even though it was only eight o'clock in the morning, well before the crack of dawn, Zalman time, he wasn't about to let Arnie Thrasher get the better of him.

Thrasher looked around Zalman's living room and started to laugh, big, Jackie Gleason har-de-har-hars booming off the walls. He pointed at the shelf of salt and pepper shakers. "I told you she'd redecorate," he said. "One thing I'll say for you, Zalman, this place usta look pretty normal; now that my Marie's been through here, it looks just as nutty as her house! Kinda warms my heart," he added sentimentally. "Don't these silver walls give you a headache?"

"You give me a headache, Arnie!" Zalman exploded. "Lay off about the decor, okay? I love Marie, I've asked her to marry me—"

"God forbid!" Thrasher said, making a cross with his fingers like he was warding off Dracula.

"—so gimme a break! I'm crazy about her and anytime she's ready, we'll get married, okay? What don't you like about me, anyway? I'm a nice guy, I make a good living—"

"Marie's got her own money, she's got a good business, she don't need your dough, you squirt!"

"Damn right she's got her own money! After the pile she made on that World O' Yip deal, she can buy and sell Donald Trump, lemme tell you!" Zalman was getting a little hot.

"Thing I don't like about you, Zalman, you keep falling over dead bodies! I spend my whole life trying to make that little girl happy, trying to keep her sheltered so she don't have any bad experiences and get traumatized, and now she gets involved with you, Mr. Beverly Hills Highlife, and you keep finding these stiffs all the time and I don't goddamn like it!" Thrasher said, raising a bulbous finger. "First there's the deal with Sticky Al Hix, right?" he ticked off. "Then you take her away for a weekend at your ex-wife's house—a situation an unsophisticated guy like me don't quite understand—and two or three people get killed! And then it's this looney-toons magician gets herself stabbed to death, and now a psychic! Go ahead, Zalman, explain it to me! What's the deal with you and the dead bodies, huh?" Thrasher glowered at Zalman, went to the bar, and poured himself a stiff scotch, then looked at his glass in surprise. "I don't want this!" he said. "It's nine o'clock in the morning!"

"Eight o'clock."

"You see what you do to me? You make me crazy, Zalman!" Thrasher tossed the scotch down the bar sink and stood there, staring at Zalman defiantly.

The sound of two hands clapping put a period to Thrasher's tirade. Earnest, wearing his dice dressing gown and his royal flush slippers, was standing in the doorway, applauding. "You're absolutely right, Captain Thrasher," he said.

"Huh?" Zalman couldn't believe it. His own father was turning traitor on him!

"Quiet, Jerry, I'll handle this. You know, Arnold—by the way, may I call you Arnold? You know, I've talked to my son about this on more than one occasion and told him that he's got to settle down, try to make some sense out of this tangled web we weave. . . . Arnold, Jerry's a good boy but he needs direction, a purpose in life to make it all worthwhile. And even though I haven't met your daughter, I have the feeling she's the woman to give it to him."

Zalman sank down on the couch and curled up in a fetal position.

"Man needs a woman to make sure he's on track," Thrasher said gruffly, eyeing Earnest with amorphous suspicion.

"Truer words were never spoken, Arnold. Now, these two kids, they're modern, and a pair of old-timers like us, we try our best to give them solid advice, but do they listen? I ask you, Arnold, do they listen?" Earnest had one hand over his heart like William Jennings Bryan doing the Cross of Gold shtick.

"Why should they listen?" Thrasher said moodily. "Just because we've had experience, because we've seen every difficulty life has to offer. They're kids, what do they know?"

Zalman put a pillow over his head.

"Say," Earnest said brightly, "you had breakfast yet? I was just gonna make some eggs, howsabout you and me see if we can rustle up some eats." He gave Thrasher a friendly whack on the back and led the big cop toward the kitchen. "Now, Arnold, these two kids of ours, they're good kids . . ."

Zalman peeked out from under his pillow, and when he was sure they were gone he jumped up, ran into his bedroom, and locked the door behind him.

ZALMAN WENT INTO THE OFFICE AND PERSUADED ESTHER Wong to do a little work, though she wasn't happy about it. "I have a hair appointment at three, Mr. Z.," she warned. "That nice young lawyer you introduced me to, Ed Robin? He's taking me to the Forum to see the Lakers."

"You don't have to get your hair done for the Lakers, Esther," Zalman told her. "I swear it."

But Esther left early, so Zalman was alone in the office when McCoy finally called in with the good news. "Zally!" he said cheerfully. "We're in clover! I got the poop you wanted, and you ask me, we got the bad guy nailed! It's a wrap on this crime."

"Talk to me, Dean," Zalman said, swinging around in his chair so he could admire the shopaholics along Beverly Drive.

"I ask a few questions, I go a few places, and guess what I find out!" McCoy was pleased with himself and there was the muted sound of barking in the background.

"What, Dean," Zalman said patiently. "Just tell me what you found out, okay?"

"I'm getting to it, I'm getting to it! So I put out a few calls and then I decide to call Wacky Winger? Of Wacky Winger's Wanch?"

"The pawnshop guy?"

"That's him! Yeah, and it turns out there's a nasty ol' forty-five got pawned in Wacky's West Hollywood store—you know Wacky's expanded since you knew him. He's got five or six shops now, he's doing pretty good. Gun came in this very morning, and said gun is registered to Lenny Dunn, the ol' velour cowboy himself! That's number one. And you're gonna love this: it turns out Wacky Winger knows the guy who hocked the gun, 'cause as soon as I mentioned you heard the guy whistling 'Here Comes Peter Cottontail,' Wacky knows just who I'm talking about! The guy hocks stuff all the time, stuff he, uh, finds on the beach. Guy's a hobo, an ex-script doctor or something, and I'm on the sucker's trail! He won't escape ol' Eagle-Eye Doyle Dean McCoy, lemme tell you!"

"That's great, Dean. Look, let's you and me run over to Dunn's and see if we can nail him to the wall before Thrasher gets to him."

"You bet! Where is ol' pus-brain Arnie?"

Zalman sighed. "Last I saw, he and my dad were having eggs over easy and bemoaning their fate as parents."

"Are you kidding me?" McCoy hooted. "I'd give anything to see that duo in action."

"Meet me at the corner of Woodman and Ventura in an hour, okay, Dean? We'll shoot out to the beach."

"Yowsah, Mr. Zalman." McCoy laughed as he hung up.

"YEAH, IT'S MY GUN," LENNY DUNN SAID, HIS VOICE cracking with fear as he stared at the .45 McCoy had picked up at Wacky Winger's Wanch. "But look, Mr. Zalman, it was stolen last week, I sweartagod! I wouldn't lie to you, Mr. Zalman, you're my attorney, right? So anything I say is privileged communication, right? Anyway, I wouldn't have to lie 'cause even if the cops were after me and I did have to lie, you'd do it for me, right?"

"The hell I would!" Zalman snapped. "You think because I'm your attorney, I'm gonna lie to the cops for you? Get straight, Dunn. You're not worth it."

"Okay, okay," Dunn moaned as he yanked off his bucking bronco bolo tie and threw it on the boulder coffee table. He looked terrible and he was beginning to sweat circles in his aqua cowboy shirt. "But I didn't kill Caldwell, I sweartagod! This lunatic Hanning was standing right next to me the whole time, driving me crazy about some Wild West Museum he's starting up way the hell out in Saugus or someplace. Hey," Dunn said slowly, the bright gleam of self-interest beginning to sparkle in his blue eyes. "Now that I think about it, maybe it's not such a dumb idea at that. Ever since 'Gunshy' went into syndication, people call me up all the time, wanting me to appear at supermarket openings, zucchini festivals, stuff like that. Maybe a Wild West Museum isn't such a bad idea. . . ."

"You got bigger problems than a zucchini festival, Dunn!" Zalman told the cowboy.

"I'm telling the truth, I'm telling the truth!" Dunn howled. "Please, Mr. Zalman, you gotta believe me! I didn't kill Caldwell! Somebody stole the gun from me! I don't know who did it! Please, you gotta help me!"

"Okay, Lenny," Zalman said finally. "Relax, will you? I believe you. But look, after you found out the gun was missing, you reported it to the police, right?"

Dunn looked at him, his mouth slack, his eyes dull with fear. "Huh?" he said.

"The theft?" Zalman explained patiently. "I mean, right after you found out the gun was gone, you reported the burglary to the cops and then you called up your insurance company so you could collect, right?"

"Wrong," Dunn said miserably, running his hands through his thick brown hair. "It's got a silencer on it so it's not legal. It was just a part of my collection—beefs up the old image for the ladies. They go for all this rough-and-tumble stuff, knives, guns—why do you think I got this junk around? Rich dames I hang around with, they don't know the difference between life and TV. I didn't think it was a good idea to call the cops. Besides, it was the only thing gone, and you make a small claim like that, your insurance company jacks up your rates! Zoom! Right through the sky! It just ain't worth it, Mr. Zalman!" Dunn whined. "You know what my flood insurance is out here! Between that and the damn taxes, I'm just about making it! A hardworking guy like me! It's a crime!"

"You have any idea when the gun was stolen?" Zalman asked, ignoring Dunn's pathetic mewling.

Dunn shook his head. "Last week sometime. So many people in and out of here all day, you live right on the beach, people like to drop by, soak up some rays. See, one of the advantages of the Colony is the casual atmosphere, but the problem is that even though we've got a guard at the front gate, the beach is public. Sometimes you get a low-class crowd. . . ."

"You're breaking my heart, Lenny."

Dunn looked at Zalman anxiously. "You think there'll be any trouble about this, Mr. Zalman?"

"I'm sure of it." Zalman laughed. "What with the Malibu sheriff *and* the LAPD on the case, one of 'em is bound to talk to Wacky Winger. Technically, even the fact that I sent McCoy over to pick up this gun from Wacky isn't so smart, but I'm beginning to think I can talk my way out of anything. I oughta go into politics where this kind of skill can make you some real dough," he said ruefully. "But my trouble is I'm too honest for public office. You're just lucky I'm on your side, Dunn, that's all I got to tell you."

"And I'm grateful, Mr. Zalman. You gotta help me! But look, there's something else worrying me. Now that Caldwell's dead, what do you think's happened to Lydia's tapes?"

"Ahh, well," Zalman said. "That's another unpleasanat subject, but at least it's not life or death—"

"It is to me!" Dunn cried. "It's not my fault all these rich wives follow me around like lost puppies and I take pity on 'em! I just want to make my furniture! Contribute artistically to the community!"

Zalman stared at the big cowboy as a sudden flash of inspiration hit him. "You know, Dunn, my advice to you is to get involved with Phil Hanning. Go on, call him up, see if you can get the Wild West Museum off the ground. I think you two could be one of the great teams of all time —like Abbott and Costello, Starsky and Hutch, Spin and Marty. Look, Lenny, I have the feeling that you'll hear from somebody about the tapes in the next day or so. Call me whimsical, call me irresponsible, but it wouldn't surprise me if the guy who dropped Caldwell and cleaned out his safe decides to take over the blackmail end of the business, too. It's a natural, right? So if you hear from anybody, let me know. Day or night," Zalman said as he walked out the door. "Talk to me later."

ZALMAN GOT BACK IN THE MERCEDES AND TURNED TO McCoy, who was fiddling with the radio trying to find a golden oldies station. "Dean, I'm taking you back to your car and then I want you to hit the beach, just like it was D day. I want to find this bum who hocked Lenny's gun and I want him now! What the hell's his name, anyway?"

"No name," McCoy said mildly, settling on "Wooly Bully." "Guys on the street, they don't part with their names so easy, Jer. But Wacky told me what he looks like and I'm gonna find him. Relax on it, will ya? Wacky told me he used to be a script doctor but now he's on the skids, lives on the beach under the Santa Monica pier mostly. He was doin' okay, cranking down big bucks in the studio wordmills, but then he gets into a money squeeze so he sells this idea to one of the studio bigwigs, see, but it turns out the bigwig didn't want a movie, he wanted to work out his personal problems. So he stole the plot and used it for a blueprint. Tried to kill his wife. . . . Is that a howl? So the studio guy gets five to ten in—"

"Dean, I don't need the guy's entire bio, I just want to talk to him! Please, help me out here." Zalman felt his exasperation level beginning to climb as he zipped back onto the highway. Cars were stopped up and down 101, Fellini-esque families staring out the windows at the distant water, their tongues out with longing. "But he's got no name? For some reason, that makes me nervous. What kind of guy doesn't have a name? Can't you find out his name?"

"I don't need a name, Jer," McCoy said as he fired up a Lucky and blew a long, thin stream of cancerous smoke out the car window. "Damn, a Lucky is a great American cigarette," he said blissfully. "Camel ain't bad either. You gotta understand, a guy drops out these days, goes on the streets, he don't want to be found under normal conditions. Now, this situation we got here, a stolen gun, a murder or two, all of a sudden this guy realizes he's hooked into a major mess, now he seriously don't want to be found! It may take some time, but I'll find him. All I need to do is turn over the right rock."

"Terrific," Zalman said. "I love this soooooo much!"

"Don't hassle your brainpan, Jer. I'll find the guy. Just gimme a minute or three. Listen, when's Marie coming back? I get the feeling you're overdrawn at the mental bank."

"Couple days. After her cousin's wedding."

"I hate weddings." McCoy retuned the radio and got "Poison Ivy."

"That's only because you never had one."

"How right you are, Jer. And it's gonna stay that way. I'm better off. So what's with the suburban cowboy in

168

there?" McCoy asked, jerking a thumb in Lenny's direction. "You think he's the baddie in this little playlet?"

Zalman shook his head. "Dunn couldn't shoot a fish in a barrel at a small-town carnival. Besides, he and Phil were talking when Caldwell bought it—"

"Phil can talk?"

"He can beg for money, does that count? Yeah, well, Dunn's story about the gun's pretty weak. He says it was stolen. Okay, let's say we believe that. Then it turns up in Wacky Winger's hockshop and Wacky says this script doctor turned street freak hocked it. That doesn't mean the street freak did the crime. It could, but we don't know yet and I doubt it. Personally, I think our killer disposed of Caldwell, then ditched the gun out the window; the street freak found it lying there while he's on his rounds underneath rich windows, hocked it, and is now enjoying an unpretentious little bottle of Ripple with the proceeds."

"But maybe he saw something," McCoy pointed out. "Something we can use."

"Exactly. Maybe he did," Zalman agreed. "So that's why I'd like to have a little chat with him."

"Trust me, Jer." McCoy grinned.

"That's my line, Dean."

AFTER HE DROPPED MCCOY AT HIS PICKUP ON VENTURA Boulevard, Zalman drove over to the Burbank Studios to see Tom Kellar. Kellar's production company, TotFlicks, rented space there, so Zalman pulled into the circle in front of the Warner Brothers entrance and went inside.

"Can't park there," the guard at the desk said. He had the droopy eyes of a basset hound and he was wearing a plastic name tag that said "Happy" on it.

"Buzz Tom Kellar, will you, Hap?" Zalman said, ignoring his protests.

Happy put down his copy of *Variety* and picked up the phone. "They'll be steamed," he said, shaking his head. He pointed overhead toward the executive offices on the second floor. "They come back from lunch, you're in their space, they'll be steamed and I'll catch it. An executive over in the bungalows? He slashed a guy's tires who was in his space— Yeah, Dolores, it's Happy over at the Warner entrance? Saw you at the screening last night at Paramount. . . . Yeah, that's what I thought. A dog. Listen, dear, there's someone here wants to talk to Mr. Kellar. . . ." He handed the phone to Zalman and went back to *Variety*.

Zalman took the phone. "Jerry Zalman to see Tom Kellar. He around? Tell him I need to see him. . . . Where's your office? I need a drive-on pass, too." The secretary gave him directions and Zalman handed the phone back to Happy. "See?" Zalman told the guard. "Now they won't be steamed."

He went back outside, drove around to the Barham gate and onto the lot, then parked in front of Kellar's offices. Kellar had a nice location, a suite of onetime dressing rooms that had been refurbished and now offered an expansive view of the workaday activity on the sound stages lining the back lot as well as the beehive condos that laced the low brown hills beyond.

"I'm Jerry Zalman," he told the secretary. "Where's Tom?"

"He's on the phone," the girl said. She was about twenty, with the longest, blondest hair Zalman had ever seen on anybody who wasn't a Barbie doll. She was wearing a skintight fifties-style black-and-white polka-dot sheath with a sweetheart neckline, seamed fishnet stockings, and black patent leather ankle-strap heels, and she had a big gold padlock on a thick gold chain around her neck. She looked like the centerfold for *Whip 'n' Chain Weekly*. She got up, undulated over to the connecting door, opened it, and peeked through the doorway into Kellar's office, kicking up one bondage bootie as she posed there. "He's almost off," she said as she bent down to straighten her seams. "You want anything? Anything to drink?"

"Not a thing," Zalman said, admiring the girl's act. Even in L.A., so few people had the pizzazz to take it to the limit. Despite the great view, Zalman didn't like to waste time waiting for a sleaze like Tom Kellar, so he brushed past Dolores and barged into Kellar's office.

"Hey, wait a minute," she said nervously. "He's on the phone. . . ." She followed Zalman into the office and gave Kellar an "it's not my fault, boss" shrug.

Kellar waved her away, smiled broadly at Zalman, and pointed to a zebra-striped butterfly chair across from his big glass-topped desk. Like Dolores, the office was done up in refurbished fifties drag with shiny rubber plants, a ziggurat wrought iron bookcase filled with videotapes, and a hideous orange and green assemblage behind Kellar's desk that looked like a family photo of ten midgets wearing bowling shirts. The other walls were lined with photos of Tom Kellar with his arm around celebrities like Pat Sajak and Robin Leach, everybody smirking broadly at the camera.

"Forget it!" Kellar shrieked into the phone. "I'm not giving up one point! You listening to me, Sid? I been in this business too long to give it away for free!" He looked at Zalman, winked, and gave the phone the finger. "Same to you, Sid. But just remember who's got the talent here. You listening, Sid? This is the guy who makes the money talking to you!" Kellar slammed the phone down, grinning happily, and ran his hand through his thicket of white hair. This time, he was wearing red satin sweatpants and a yellow satin jacket with red piping and a "New Dating Game" emblem on it. "Dolores!" he yelled. "Get me a Tab, honey. You, Jerry?"

"Nothing," Zalman said as the girl ankled in and set a Tab down on a black rubber coaster in front of Kellar. She sashayed out again, very slowly, and closed the connecting door behind her.

"I didn't really want this," Kellar said as he whipped out his handkerchief and began to polish the rim of his glass furiously. "I just dig her hair so much I can't stand it—I only hired her 'cause she went with the furniture. . . .So what can I do you for, Jer?"

"I was wondering if you'd heard from anybody. Anybody like a blackmailer or maybe the police," Zalman asked casually. "And I thought we ought to talk about the late Roy Caldwell."

"I'm in the crapper, aren't I, Jer?" Kellar said sadly. "First Simone, then Caldwell. But I was with Annie both times! I swear it! But if the papers find out . . . Nobody knows yet, do they, Jer? Any reporters been around to see you? I can take reality, give it to me straight. Now that Caldwell's dead, I'm right down the old dumperoonie. Jeez," he said, a look of sharp gastrointestinal pain flashing over his face. "I shouldn'ta leaned on Sid so hard, maybe I'll need him if the bottom drops out. . . . Dolores! Honey, get me Sid Rosen back again, pronto!" he yelled, a tinge of hysteria creeping into his voice. "Way I see it, at least Caldwell was a professional," Kellar moaned in agony. "At least he was in the blackmail business as a long-term proposition. He was a crook, but him you could trust. Now maybe some amateur comes in, takes over the business, and I'm down the tube-o-matic. That's what you mean, isn't it, Jer? Dolores! Honey, where's Sid, get me Sid!"

"He's on another line, Tommykins!" the girl's voice singsonged through the closed door. "Honestly! He'll get right back to you!"

"Oh, God!" Kellar said as he put his head in his hands and flopped down on his desk. Zalman could see his hot breath frosting the glass in short little thirsty-dog bursts. "You know what it means in this town when somebody says they'll get right back to you, don't you, Jerry?" Kellar said hollowly, his voice thick with terror. "I'm through, I'm trashed, everybody's got a line on my personal code of ethics! Just 'cause I like it a little unusual! Now I'm gonna hafta teach a film-writing course or something! How can I support my family!" he moaned, beating his fists on his glass-topped desk.

Kellar's endless bitching and moaning really jerked Zalman's chain. The guy was a whiner, a whimperer of the first water and Zalman had heard enough yap-yap from the guy. "I've had it with you, Kellar!" Zalman snapped as he jumped up out of the butterfly chair. "You think when you're hungry, the world eats lunch, don't you? Lemme clue you, Tommykins, nobody cares if you want to play pony ride with some dame, for Pete's sake! But you think you're front-page news, don't you? You got an ego as big as the Ritz and you're a jerk. Understand me, friend, generally jerks don't bother me. It's an occupational hazard in my racket. I see plenty of jerks, all day long, nothing but jerks, rich and poor, I'll point out. But you're the worst kind, a jerk with an ego. I've had it with you. You're no longer my client."

Kellar gave Zalman a hyperthyroid stare. "Jer, what are you saying here? Be reasonable—"

"Reasonable? I'm an attorney, I don't have to be reasonable! I'd blackmail you myself if my dad wasn't involved in this garbage dump you've created! I hope your photos turn up on the front page of the *New York Post,* Kellar. I'd love to see you squirm like a worm!"

Kellar shot out of his chair like he was wearing Slinkies on the bottoms of his shoes. "You can't do this to me! Nobody talks to me like this! You're fired! I'll have you disbarred!"

"Pipe down, you geek," Zalman shot back. "You never even gave me a retainer, you cheap sonofabitch! And let me tell you another thing." Zalman was beginning to enjoy himself; torturing Kellar was a lot of fun and it was turning out to be the best part of the day. "I don't have to like you. That's one of the big advantages of being a lone wolf, Tommykins, I don't have to suck up to geeks just in case I need 'em on the way down." Zalman smiled broadly and rocked back and forth on his heels. "Not that I'm ever gonna be on the way down, Tommykins, but you take my point, I trust."

Kellar stood behind his desk and glared at Zalman furiously, clenching and unclenching his hands, his white forelock hanging down over his eyes. Zalman had the weird feeling Larry Talbot was about to change into the Wolfman and start slavering and growing hair on his palms.

"Sid's on the line, Tommykins." Dolores's lilting Valley whimper echoed through the door.

Kellar leapt on the phone like it was hot meat. "Sid, doll, I been thinking over what you said and hey, maybe you've got something. . . ."

Zalman saw his opportunity and split, blowing Dolores a kiss on the way out. "Why do I hate that guy?" he wondered aloud as he peeled out of his space in front of Kellar's office. He headed off the lot toward Barham, but just as he pulled up to the gate he realized he was still mad so he circled the long studio block, drove around the looming sound stages, and went back to Kellar's office.

Zalman got out of his car, went over to Kellar's red Mercedes, and ripped Kellar's nameplate off his parking space. Then he broke it in half and threw it on the ground right by the driver's door, where Kellar was sure to see it. He felt a lot better. "That was a childish thing to do," he muttered, grinning to himself as he lit a cigar, pulled away from the studio, and headed for the freeway. "But, hey, I'm just a big kid at heart. . . ."

NOW THAT HE'D HAD HIS REVENGE ON TOM KELLAR, ZALman felt contented with his estate in life, so he went back to Beverly Hills and got Esther to call up Lucille, which took a while since all three of her home office lines were busy. Finally, the phone rang through. It was time to find out where Bland and Lucille had been last night during Caldwell's fatal soiree.

"Luce?" Zalman said when she picked up the phone.

"Oh, Jerrrrrrryyyyy . . . whaddamygonnado . . . whaddamygonna dooooooo . . ."

"Tell me, Luce," he cajoled. "Just tell ol' Jer what happened."

"It's Bland. . . . Whaddamygon—"

"Lucille!" Zalman said sharply. "Let's not waste time here! What about Bland? Never mind the rending of garments, okay? There's always time for that later. What happened?"

"Jerry, he's disappeared!" she said, lowering her voice to a hoarse whisper for dramatic emphasis. "Last night I go over to his house to pick him up and take him to the party with us and he's *not there!* So then when I get over to Caldwell's there's Phil outside, heading me off. He tells me about what's happened and we split. . . ."

"Very smart, you missed a wonderfully entertaining evening."

"I didn't think Blandie was involved, Jerry, honest!" Lucille cried. "Then this morning I schlep all the way back out to Malibu for this interview he's got? Only the cover of *Rolling Stone!* Only the cover! And he's *not there!* Where is he, Jerry? Whaddamygonnadoooo!!!!"

Zalman stared down at Beverly Drive and wished he had an Uzi. Just to throw a scare into 'em. . . . He shook his head briskly, trying to clear away the cobwebs. "You haven't any idea where he is? No idea? You call all his girlfriends?"

"Of course I have!" Lucille shrieked. "I am not a complete idiot, Jerry! I've been on the phone all day, looking for him!"

"Try to be calm, Lucille," Zalman advised his sister. "Hysteria is not the answer here."

"What is the answer?!" she moaned. "He's gone, there's people dropping like flies! The reporter from *Rolling Stone* was sooooo pissed! You know how those little twerps are, twenty minutes out of journalism school and they think they're God! Where is he!"

"Lucille, I'm going to come over in a few minutes. I'll bring Dad, we'll have a nice dinner—"

"I'll put Phil on. Tell him what you want to eat," she said, her voice dispirited. "At least with Phil around, we don't starve. . . .*Oh, God, whaddamygonna-dooooooo. . . .*"

Phil Hanning came on the line. "Hey, Jer! You and Ernie're coming over? That's great. The kids want to see him. I'll do Chinese, okay? Gee, if you'd told me yesterday, we coulda had the whole steamed fish. The one I do with my special hot boss sauce? Can't do it now, though, it takes too much time. Everything really good takes too much time," Hanning pouted. "It's Lucille's favorite, too. But whole steamed fish isn't a last-minute thing, it's a preparation thing."

"Phil, whatever you do, we'll love. Your Chinese is the best thing in the world. My stomach is in your hands," Zalman told his brother-in-law. "See you in about an hour. Esther!" he yelled into the other office as he hung up. "See if you can find my father. Try my place, the Chateau Marmont. . . ."

Zalman went to the bar and made himself a Bullshot. Another damn problem, he thought as he stirred his drink thoughtfully. Where the hell was Bland? This was an unexpected and highly unpleasant development. Where was the rock 'n' roll rebel? And when had he disappeared? Did he know about Caldwell's murder? Zalman didn't like to think about the possibility that Horace Edward Albert Bland had killed the psychic. It would be bad for Lucille, and besides, it didn't seem possible. Bland was such a simp. But yet . . . Zalman looked at himself in the mirror. "You know, Jerry," he said to his reflection, "if Thrasher finds out Bland's disappeared, he'll nail him for both the killings and Dad and I'll wiggle right off the hook. Lucille will probably fall on her sword—but on the other hand, if Bland takes the rap, there'll be two happy Zalmans trotting the highways and byways of Beverly Hills. Damn," he

177

muttered as he went back to his desk. "I hate ethical problems. . . ."

Esther buzzed him. "It's your dad, Mr. Z." she said. "He's over at the Magic Cavern."

Zalman punched the speaker. "Hey! Mr. Showbiz! What's going on?" He decided not to mention Bland's disappearance to his father. Not yet, anyway.

"Things are great! There's nothing like a murder to beef up the old box-office, I'll tell you that! Mitzi and Marty are going nuts! Lydia's booked solid for the rest of her run. Joy everlasting is what we got here," Earnest said, chugging right along. "Lydia and I have been going over the changes in her act all afternoon. She had to drop Simone's part, of course, but we've put in some stuff. . . . Only great! Only fabulous! But I'll give you the lowdown later on."

"Great. Meet me at Lucille's in about an hour, okay? We're having dinner there. Phil's making Chinese."

"Phil makes great Chinese," Earnest mused. "But I was hoping for brisket. I haven't had a good brisket since your mother, God bless—"

"Dad . . . I'm telling you . . ."

"—but Phil's Chinese is a little bit of heaven sliding right down tummy avenue. You know, Jer, we oughta set that schmuck up in a restaurant sometime, the guy's a fabulous cook."

"Don't give him any ideas, Dad, and while you're at it, don't give him any money either. Especially if he puts the bite on you for this Wild West Museum thing he's hot about. Trouble with Phil is, he's got the reverse Midas touch. Everything he touches turns to ratbait."

Earnest laughed. "Sad but trueski, my son."

ON THE WAY OVER LAUREL CANYON TO THE VALLEY, ZAL-
man called Marie in the wilds of Eugene, Oregon, but Mrs.
Wishniak said she and Sally had gone over to the new
house to look at wallpaper samples for the dining room.
Mrs. Wishniak said that the wedding preparations were
getting awfully hectic and there'd been a big fight about
the flowers, but Marie had managed to smooth everything
over. Mrs. Wishniak thought Sally was being rather trying
and ungrateful, especially if you considered everything that
was being done for her, but that's the way children were
nowadays. Then Mrs. Wishniak said Marie was a wonderful person, so helpful, and didn't Zalman just miss her
terribly? Zalman sighed and said he did and Mrs. Wishniak
laughed and said that absence really did make the heart
grow fonder in her personal opinion and Zalman said he
agreed. After he hung up, Zalman realized that he and
Sally's mom were evolving a nice phone relationship, so he
called Esther and asked her to send Mrs. Wishniak some
flowers and a scarf from Gucci, just to cheer her up.

Zalman pulled up in front of the Hannings' big house in
Toluca Lake and went inside. The house was quiet, so he
poked his head into the TV room to see where everybody
was. The three Hanning kids, Jason, Jennifer, and Sean,
were lying on the floor in front of the big-screen TV, eating
popcorn.

"What're you guys watching?" Zalman asked. On-
screen, a rubbery monster with about eighty tentacles drip-

179

ping slimy goo was attacking a scantily clad Polynesian lass.

Jason Hanning looked up. "Hey, Uncle Jerry! It's *Bloodsucking Beast*, a real exploitation classic. Wanna watch?"

"I'll pass," Zalman said. "Where's your mom?"

"Lying down in her room with an ice bag on her head," Jason said as he followed Zalman out into the Hannings' white living room. "She's having a fit about Bland. The guy's disappeared, huh? It doesn't surprise me. He's pretty loose," Jason said, tapping his head. "I think he's having an anxiety attack about his image, and Mom's really freaked. I can tell. The ice bag's a sure sign." The kid sighed. Jason was thirteen, and already it was clear he was going to be good-looking. He had his mother's thick dark hair and wise-child eyes and his father's handsome features. He was also developing a very smart mouth. "Ernie here yet?"

"Your grandfather Earnest?" Zalman said. "Shouldn't you call him Grandpop or something respectful?"

Jason shook his head and sat down on the edge of an overstuffed white armchair. "Nah," he said, swinging his leg nervously. "He told us to call him Ernie. He says when we call him Granddad, it makes him feel like Methuselah. Who the hell is Methuselah anyway? You wanna drink or what?"

Zalman stared at his nephew. "You got a bad mouth, kid."

Jason Hanning grinned happily. "Yeah, but I come by it honestly. That's what Mom says. So, you want a drink? I can make anything and tonic, anything and soda, or a Bloody Mary."

Zalman sat down on the white couch in the middle of Lucille's all-white living room and shielded his eyes with his hand. The sharp late-afternoon sun was glinting off the pool like a knife and the white room always gave him a headache. "Who taught you that trick, Jason?"

"Ernie, who else? When he was here last year. Mom didn't like it at first, but last time she had a big bash I saved her five hundred bucks. See, an extra bartender woulda cost her seven and I only charged her two, so we both did okay out of the deal."

"You're too young to drink, Jason, what the hell's the matter with you?" Zalman asked his nephew.

"I don't drink, think I'm stupid? Drinking's for dimbos," Jason said with the world-weary disdain achieved by a thirteen-year-old kid who's spent his entire life within the boundaries of greater Toluca Lake. "It messes with your wind and I'm going out for track next year. But"—Jason narrowed his eyes as a serious, thoughtful look came over his face—"I plan to go into the diplomatic corps and I think that bartending skills will be an important social asset when I'm a big-time Washington host. I'm also learning to play the piano, wanna hear me do 'Stormy Weather?' I plan to be a Renaissance man—think it's a good idea, Uncle Jerry?"

Zalman looked carefully at Jason, realizing he'd never taken the kid seriously before. "Yeah, Jason, I think it's a good idea," he said slowly. "You know, law school is pretty good groundwork for a diplomatic career, you thought about that?"

"You bet I have." Jason nodded as he jumped up, went behind the bar, and poured himself a Diet Coke. "I've got it all doped out, Uncle Jerry. I'm going to Harvard, then take a year in France to brush up my language skills, then maybe take a few months off, travel around, see Europe if it's still standing when I grow up."

"You're an interesting kid, Jason. Remind me to take you to lunch in a few weeks."

"That's a great idea, Uncle Jerry," Jason said, nodding. "I think we should get to know each other better, too."

Phil Hanning came into the room. "Hey, Jer, you hungry? Jason fix you up?" he asked, ruffling his son's hair.

"Daa-ad! Quit it!" the kid said, finally sounding like a kid.

Phil ignored him. "If I say so myself, Jer, I made a great dinner. Wanna come smell something great, huh? It's the carp—boy, I invented a swell variation on a classic red sauce. You're gonna love it."

"Phil, no offense, but you mind if I jump in the pool, then take a nap for ten minutes?" Zalman asked. "I think it might save my life." Zalman firmly believed there were few situations in contemporary life that a nap couldn't improve.

"Sure, Jer. Just lie down in the guest room. I'll call you when dinner's ready."

"Don't forget lunch," Jason called out as Zalman left the room. "I'll set it up with Esther."

Zalman conked out in the guest room and didn't wake up until Phil announced dinner. Just as they were sitting down at the table Earnest arrived with a load of presents for Jason and Jennifer and Sean, so Phil was a little ticked off because he'd made an extra effort and prepared Velvet Shrimp, Juicy Fried Squab, and Roof-Brick Carp and he didn't want the food to get cold. "It's no good unless you can see the steam coming off it," he said anxiously. "Visuals count in food!"

But Phil's dinner was great, and afterward, while Earnest took the kids outside on the patio because Jason wanted to learn how to do a time step and Phil popped back into the kitchen to whip up a fast mousse, Lucille took Zalman aside.

"Have you found him yet, Jer?" she asked, her voice ringing with high anxiety. Zalman could see that Lucille was in bad shape. Her eyes were puffy and she'd completely gnawed off her manicure. "Is Bland gonna get nailed for this? Where is he? I'm dying, Jer, dying!"

Zalman didn't answer her at first. If things got ugly, would Thrasher be willing to swap one Bland for two Zalmans? And then there were those troublesome ethics. . . . "Give me a break, Lucille!" he said finally, figuring he'd cross that burning bridge when he came to it. "You just told me he was gone twenty minutes ago!"

"Longer than that . . . " Lucille grumbled at her brother.

Zalman ignored her. "Nobody knows he's disappeared, right?"

"Nobody but us. I didn't tell anybody in the office, if that's what you mean."

"That's what I mean, and let's keep it that way, yes? What about the interview with *Rolling Stone?* After all, Bland's a big star. If word leaks out to the press that he's disappeared, they'll be on us like rats on Swiss! We don't want one of these journalism school wonders playing Woodward and Bernstein."

Lucille tore at the remainder of her nails. "You're not kidding. I faked it. Told the guy Blandie had to fly back to London 'cause his sister was in the hospital."

Zalman laughed. "And he believed that?"

Lucille managed a smile. "It's ingenuous. Of course he believed it. Oh, God, tell me straight. Do you think Blandie—"

Zalman laid a hand over his sister's mouth. "I don't think he anything. Don't say the word. You don't think, I don't think, we don't talk about it. That way we don't have to lie about it later, if Thrasher or Sheriff Surfgod comes nosing around. They been around, by the way?"

Lucille shook her head, still nibbling at her nails. "I would of told you first thing. But okay," she said slowly. "Hypothetically speaking. Purely as a matter of you and me playing Let's Pretend, right?"

"Right, right," Zalman said, lighting a cigar. He looked through the sliding glass door at Earnest, who was demonstrating a buck-and-wing for the kids.

"Suppose Bland did kill the guy, can you get him off? Like, uh, what do you call it, diminished capacity or something?"

"The Twinkie defense? You know I don't do criminal law, Lucille, I hate going to court. I don't even go to court for a no-contest divorce, if there is such a thing in Beverly Hills anymore. Look, if it comes to that, we'll get him somebody, but the results aren't in yet. C'mon, trust me, I'm working on a few angles. Besides, it's our honorable father we've got to worry about, not that dope Bland." He poked his cigar toward Earnest, now showing Jason how to windmill. "That Jason's gonna be nothing but trouble, if you let him grow up. You heard it here first."

"Dad wants to take him to Santa Anita on Saturday."

"Craziness always skips a generation, I hope I hope?" Zalman laughed, then kissed his sister on top of her head. "Look, Lucille. Don't worry about it. Trust me, I'll tell you when to start worrying."

Zalman took the remains of his cigar out to the car and called Marie again. He had to tell her about Caldwell's murder, and besides, he thought as he sat behind the wheel staring up at the stars twinkling over Toluca Lake, he missed her.

"Hello?" Marie whispered softly.

"Doll, it's me," Zalman said with relief. He enjoyed talking to Mrs. Wishniak, but it wasn't the same as fone fun with Marie.

"Jerry," she whispered, "I can't talk! Call me later!"

"I can't call you later! This is important! Caldwell's been killed!"

Marie sucked in her breath. "Oh, no!" she whispered. "How did it happen!"

"He was shot."

"Who shot him?"

"We don't know yet," Zalman said patiently. "If we knew that, all the fun would be over."

"I can't talk now! I've got to go," she said. There were terrible shrieks in the background, then the sound of breaking glass. "Oh, no," Marie moaned. "The Baccarat wineglasses!"

"What's going on?!" Zalman asked. "Anybody being shot?"

"This is serious!" Marie said. "Look, they need me! I'll call you later!"

"But, Marie—" Zalman said, but it was too late. She'd hung up.

After they left Lucille's, Earnest wanted to run by the Magic Cavern and see Lydia break in the new act. "C'mon, Jer, it's the shank of the evening. You gotta see the new routine she's doing. She was going to do it with Simone, poor kid, but we've worked out a few changes, added some great new props. . . ."

"We?" Zalman laughed. "Now you're a director? What's next, Mr. Spielberg?"

"Hey, hey, I got taste! Anybody says different, pow! Right in the beezer." Earnest grinned, waving a mocking fist in the night air. "C'mon, Jer, it'll be fun! You won't believe the wow finish with the monkey. That Sergeant Pepper is a cute little guy! Everybody loves him."

"Not me. I hate monkeys. I hate *that* monkey. His nasty little paws give me the creeps." Zalman frowned. "But, sure, I'll keep you company. I had a great nap, I could go a couple more rounds tonight."

As soon as they pulled up in front of the Magic Cavern, they could see that the joint was jumping. The parking lot was almost full, the caped attendants rushing back and forth like rats in a Skinner box. Inside, Mitzi Melbourne was sitting at her usual table at the back of the house with a sky-high plate of potato latkes in front of her. She was wearing an orange velvet dress and matching orange glasses and an absurd orange bow in her Halloween hairdo.

Zalman and Earnest stopped at her table to say hello. "Big night, huh, Ernie?" she said as they shook hands. "Business is great! Great! You know, first thing I think when Simone dies, I think it's gonna be bad for business, but it turns out just the opposite!" She beamed, pushing the latkes around with her fork. "Couldn't be better! Customers want to know all the gory details, where it happened, how it happened. . . . I tell them everything I know, and what I don't know, I make up!" Mitzi chortled, her chins trembling. She was obviously pleased with her new notoriety.

Sweating profusely, Marty Melbourne ran up to them and grabbed Earnest's hand. "Ernie," the magician breathed. "Gonna be a great night. Lydia's gonna knock 'em out, I believe it sincerely. This new routine is a beauty! And she's such a wonderful person," he said, turning to Zalman. "You know she's given me a spot in her act? A nice featured spot! Wonderful woman, Lydia. Truly, a woman with the potential to be at the top of her profession."

"Yeah, you're right, Marty. She's a great human being and a credit to the entire show business community," Zalman said. "Now, how about a table down front, okay? Sammy!" he called to the maître d'.

ZALMAN AND EARNEST SAT DOWN AT THEIR TABLE AND ordered a pair of Courvoisiers. Earnest went back and forth about the sour cream cheesecake, but Sammy finally persuaded him that life was short and it would be foolish to pass up a nice slice of cheesecake simply because of the specter of future arterial blockages.

He was working on his second order when the house lights dimmed and the combo struck up a jazzy version of "I Heard It Through the Grapevine," heavy on the drumbeats. "Here we go, Jer," Earnest said excitedly. "You're gonna love this!"

The curtain opened slowly to reveal a fanciful jungle set. Tall neon palm trees looped generously with thick green vines stood at either side of the stage while lush silk ferns waved in a fanned breeze. A flickering jungle moon hung in a starry backdrop sky, and outsize bunches of bananas festooned the arching proscenium like fat yellow teeth. The entire vision reminded Zalman of every Fox musical in which Carmen Miranda, Betty Grable, and Don Ameche had ever appeared. Once again, Zalman started to get that dreamy, soft-focus feeling. . . .

At the far corner of the stage a computerized model of a baby Tyrannosaurus that was easily six feet long flashed its nasty red eyes and snapped a hungry little snout, while an equally ugly junior Dimetrodon peeked out from behind a small palm and wagged its tail back and forth in time with the drumbeats.

"Awwwwwww . . . aren't they cute!" a skinny lady at the next table said, clanking her charm bracelet. She was wearing cat's-eye glasses and a bright purple dress, and she had carefully frizzed gray hair.

"How 'bout those dinos, huh?" Earnest stage-whispered with evident pride. "Saw 'em on 'Eyewitness News,' some science fair thing that was closing down at the museum. Knew they'd be perfect for Lydia's act. Called the guy up, he let 'em go cheap! All computerized, y'know. Got a layer of latex spread over 'em give you the willies if you run your hand over it. Feels more like skin than skin—"

"Shhuuuush!" the skinny lady hissed violently. "I'm watching this!"

"Okay, okay," Earnest replied. Zalman turned his attention back to the stage. The pint-sized dinos continued their animated antics, and as the drumbeats increased in intensity, Lydia scampered onstage wearing a minuscule leopard-skin bikini and a frightened expression. Given the flawless condition of Lydia's figure, nothing else was necessary. Still, her acting ability was limited to excessive eye-rolling, and she reminded Zalman of Sheena of the jungle with a bad case of PMS. Two muscular young men wearing a lot of eyeliner, furry headdresses, and some plastic bones clipped on their noses ran after her, making threatening gestures with their spears. All three of them pranced around the stage, posturing and squealing, until the two young men grabbed Lydia and began to tie her to a stout palm tree in the center of the stage.

"You think that bikini's gonna hold?" Zalman whispered to Earnest. "Looks iffy to me . . ."

Earnest winked. "I give you eight to five," he said. "Whaddaya say?"

"*Shusssh!*" the skinny lady hissed again. "I mean it!"

Earnest cringed. "Yes, ma'am," he said, then stuck out his tongue behind her back.

The young men had Lydia secured, tugging at her bonds in pantomime so that the audience realized an escape would be tough going.

"Too bad Tom Kellar isn't here," Zalman muttered, grinning. "He'd love this!"

"I'm warning you two," the skinny lady said, rattling her bracelet threateningly. "One more time and I punch your lights out!"

Marty Melbourne ran onstage wearing an off-the-shoulder Tarzan outfit that sagged in all the wrong places. He was carrying a flaming torch in one hand and Sergeant Pepper in the other. The Sarge, who was holding a miniature bow and arrow, chattered angrily when he saw Lydia tied to the tree and began to wiggle in Marty's grasp. The monkey was wearing a furry little Tarzan suit that matched Marty's, and he looked like he'd be happy to bite anybody he could sink his fangs into.

Marty put Sergeant Pepper down on the floor and the monkey quickly darted up into the palm trees, then began to rip bananas off the set and toss them into the audience. The audience loved it, and the Sarge got a big round of applause.

Zalman bolted his Courvoisier and signaled to Sammy to keep 'em coming. "Show business is my life," he said to Earnest.

Onstage, Marty drove off the two young men like an elderly lion protecting his pride, then fixed Lydia's bound body with an evil leer. Zalman covered his eyes. "I can't bear to watch this," he groaned. The Sarge plunked a miniature arrow across the stage, the drumbeats increased, Lydia wiggled in a vain effort to escape, and Marty moved closer, ever closer to the bound maiden.

Suddenly, there was a terrible scream from the rear of the restaurant, and as Zalman swiveled around in his seat, he saw porky Mitzi Melbourne standing up at her table, clutching her throat with both hands.

"Aaaaaaakkkkkk!!!" she croaked with the lonely resonance of a Canadian honker winging its way south for one final summer in Mexico. *"Aaaaaakkkkkkkk!!!"* Mitzi's eyes bugged out like Wile E. Coyote's and she clawed desperately at her throat, then pitched forward on the table and landed face down in her overflowing plate of potato latkes.

"Baby!" Marty Melbourne screamed as he saw his wife slump onto her table. "Baby, what's wrong! Daddy's coming!" He made a tremendous flying leap off the edge of the stage into the horrified audience and ran through the crowded dining room toward Mitzi, who was slowly sliding off her table and onto the floor, dragging her latkes with her. Her porcine body made a painful thump as she hit the ground, sending her chair tipping over backward into the next table. Through the noise and the gasps of the audience, Zalman heard a hollow, lonely quality in Mitzi's heavy landing that told him that she was dead and didn't care doodley-squat if Daddy was on his way or not. But Marty kept on coming, pushing and shoving his way through the excited crowd, which was making humma-humma noises and clattering its silverware.

"Say, doll," the skinny lady next to Zalman asked in a conversational tone, "this part of the act or what?" She leaned forward and took off her cat's-eye glasses, then stowed them carefully in her purse.

Zalman and Earnest turned toward her and stared. "No, it isn't," Zalman said, making a major effort to be civil.

"Oh, yeah?" she said in amazement as she jumped to her feet. "You mean this is for real? This isn't part of the magic show? Ohhhh boy, am I gonna be on TV?" she asked, patting her gray hair.

"That's right, lady," Earnest said sharply. "It's for real. Can't you tell the difference between truth and illusion, for Pete's sake?"

"Well, if you're so smart, buddy," she said, smirking as she smoothed her lurid dress, "and if this is for real, why don't you answer me one question? What happened to the blonde?"

Zalman and Earnest looked back at the stage. The lady was right. Lydia was gone; the ropes that had bound her to the palm tree in the center of the stage were dangling loosely to the floor. The two chorus boys had scampered away in terror and only Sergeant Pepper was left, disconsolately tossing bananas at the crowd from his perch high above the stage.

Zalman and Earnest looked at each other in surprise. "What the hell's going on here?" Earnest said, his voice rising. "Where's Lydia?" He was shaking as he stood up and looked vainly around the room. "Jerry, where is she!"

Lydia was nowhere in sight. "Hold on, Dad. She's around somewhere. She's backstage, probably in her dressing room," Zalman said, wishing he was as sure as he sounded. "Look, you go backstage, see if she's there. I'm gonna go check out Mitzi."

Earnest nodded, and Zalman watched as he began to fight his way through the crowd of anxious diners now making a lemminglike rush for the front door. One murder at the Magic Cavern was good box-office; two was bad karma, and nobody wanted to be around when the police showed up.

Zalman slipped through the crush to Mitzi's table. Marty Melbourne, his moth-eaten Tarzan suit hanging on him limply, was crouched over his wife's body. "Baby," he crooned, "honey . . ." Marty cradled her head in his hands, patting futilely at her pudgy cheeks, but it was no go. Mitzi Melbourne had the glassy-eyed stare of a three-day-old trout on a Styrofoam tray. "Mr. Zalman," Marty moaned, "you gotta do something for my little baby! Help me, please . . ."

"I am going to do something." Zalman sighed, absently feeling for Mitzi's nonexistent pulse. "I'm gonna call the cops."

CAPTAIN ARNOLD THRASHER GLOWERED DOWN AT ZALMAN, sarcasm in his voice and venom in his heart. "What is it with you, Zalman?" he demanded angrily. "Didn't I warn you, huh? When we had that little heart-to-heart the other day, didn't I warn you? Look, Ernie," he said, taking a softer tone, "you almost had me convinced about him"—here he jerked his head in Zalman's direction—"but this tears it. You're the guy's father, you have to stick up for him! But every time I turn around, there's a stiff on my turf and there's Jerry Zalman grinning at me like he's Smilin' Jack, and I'm telling you, I don't goddamn like it! The guys down at the precinct are startin' to talk!" Thrasher said moodily. "It's an embarrassment!"

"Look, Arnold," Earnest said quietly, "this is an emergency! My friend, my close personal friend Lydia Devanti has disappeared! Not only has poor Mitzi Melbourne died, but Lydia's gone! I've looked everywhere, her dressing room, searched the club, and I can't find her! You don't like my son, okay, that's a subject we can discuss at a more opportune moment. But a woman is in danger! Lydia needs our help. She's been kidnapped! I know it! I feel it in my heart! You're a police officer, do something! You gotta find her before she ends up on the side of a milk carton!"

"Dad," Zalman said, trying to be reasonable, "explain me this. Lydia was going to do a disappearing act, right?"

"Right." Earnest nodded brusquely.

"So where was she going to disappear to? I mean, Marty was going to go ooga-booga-boo for a few minutes, then what? Pull a string, she disappears in a puff of smoke?"

"Yeah, yeah," Earnest said impatiently. "There's a trap under the stage, first thing I thought of, Jer! Of course I looked down there! She's not there! She's gone! She's been kidnapped!"

"Well, that kills that idea. . . ." Zalman said. "Arnie, how do you think Mitzi was killed? Poison?"

"Probably. I figure the killer slipped it in her chow before the show, but we won't know until after the autopsy," Thrasher said impatiently. "Meanwhile, we gotta talk about the disappearing Miss Devanti. I don't think she's in danger at all!" the big cop hooted triumphantly. "Now, Ernie, I know this is gonna be tough for you, but after all, she had the opportunity, coulda slipped the poison in Mitzi's food when she came through the kitchen to go onstage. Sammy, the maître d', says Mitzi's orders were always kept in the same place, ready to go in the microwave. She didn't like to wait for her eats, which, considering the bulk of the lady, isn't surprising. So your Miss

Devanti figured Mitzi'd get it while she was onstage doing her act and—"

"What are you saying!" Earnest snapped. "Jerry, is he saying what I think he's saying?"

"Motive? How about a motive?" Zalman said angrily. "Thrasher, you really are a dork, you know that? Why would Lydia want to kill Mitzi, huh?"

"I've never heard such garbage!" Earnest was furious. "Garbage!"

"I got a motive! And it's a winner! She killed Mitzi so she could marry Marty Melbourne and get the Magic Cavern all to herself!" Thrasher said with pride. "That's why! How do you like that?"

"Marry Marty Melbourne? Are you kidding me?" Earnest said. "I resent the hell out of that comment, Arnold. That's really over the line! Lydia and I, we're just like that!" he said, shaking crossed fingers under Thrasher's nose. "We've talked about marriage! Making a serious lifetime commitment! Lydia and Marty, that's a joke and it's in very bad taste!"

"Yeah, well, they'd known each other a long time! Melbourne says so! He also says he taught her everything she knows, and you know what that means!" Thrasher grinned like a croc with a full tummy.

"Yeah? What does it mean? Huh! Go on, what do you think it means, you jerk!" Earnest was getting steamed.

Thrasher smiled with all the assurance of Napoleon ten minutes before he hit Waterloo. "Well, I think Devanti—"

"Miss Devanti, to you," Earnest huffed.

"Okay, then, I think Miss Devanti killed Mitzi and took it on the lam," Thrasher announced with stodgy certainty. "She ain't been kidnapped at all! That's what I think!"

"And I suppose you think she killed Simone, too?" Earnest said sarcastically. "And why, pray tell, did she do that?"

Thrasher grinned happily, his big face fat with pride. "Well, Melbourne says he and this Simone girl were fooling around, you know, clandestine meetings in seedy motels, all hot and heavy. Lydia was jealous. She found out and got mad."

"Garbage," Earnest said shortly. "Absolute garbage. Marty and Simone, I dunno, maybe yes, maybe no. Guy's married to a porker like Mitzi, you can't blame him if he wants a little action on the side. But I never noticed anything between 'em, tell you that. Hey, I wasn't exactly looking for it either. But Marty and Lydia? Garbage. Thrasher, think it over, will you? Melbourne's a fool, Lydia's a great dame, and besides, why would she want him when she's got me? I mean, hey, you think a great dame like Lydia would waste her time on a two-bit fool in a Tarzan suit? C'mon . . ." Earnest had cooled down a little bit, but he was still unhappy. "Marty was stuck with Mitzi, like it or not; Simone or no Simone, he was still stuck with Mitzi. She owned the Magic Cavern, y'know. Marty just followed orders. It's him you oughta be investigating, not Lydia."

"Lookit," Thrasher barked, "I'm gonna investigate everybody who needs investigating, okay? Starting here, starting now. But if Lydia Devanti isn't the killer, then where is she? Huh? Marty didn't have time to kidnap her. He was onstage the whole time, and she was gone in thirty seconds, just like a hot car. If she isn't guilty, why isn't she here? Answer me that, Mr. Earnest Zalman."

Earnest was silent. "I can't," he said finally. "She's disappeared and I think she's in danger! Somebody's bagged her, Arnold! She wouldn't leave of her own free will without telling me about it," Earnest said. "That much, I absolutely know. I'm telling you this, Thrasher, she didn't kill anybody and that's the end of it! I'll find her myself. Jerry'll find her!" Earnest announced, his voice rising as he turned to Zalman. "Won't you, Jer?"

Zalman looked at his father and Captain Arnold Thrasher, who were staring at each other in fury, two cantankerous, battle-wise pit bulls ready to boogie. "Huh, Jer?" Earnest demanded. "You'll find Lydia for me?" If anybody was backing down, it wasn't going to be Earnest K. Zalman.

"Okay," Zalman said with finality. "That's a wrap. You two guys break it up before you both get a stroke. Arnie—"

"Quit calling me Arnie, will ya?" Thrasher was feeling churlish.

Zalman ignored him. "My dad and I are going home. You got anything to say, talk to me later."

Thrasher nodded in serene contentment. "I'm through here. You two are free to go," he said magnanimously. "Boys! Lock this joint up, will ya!"

WHEN ZALMAN PULLED UP IN HIS DRIVEWAY HE COULD SEE that every light in his house was on. Inside, he found Marie Thrasher asleep on the couch, a two-foot neon clock and a huge pile of luggage by her side. Rutherford was lolling on the floor next to her, gnawing on her purse.

"Hi, baby!" she said sleepily, rubbing her eyes and fluffing up her curly auburn hair. "Where've you been! I called from the airport but— Oh, hi! You must be Earnest." She smiled as she got up and kissed him on the cheek. "I'm so happy to meet you after all this time. Jerry's told . . . Hey, what's the matter with you guys?" she asked suspiciously as she looked from Zalman to Earnest and back again. "You two look like you just lost the election."

Earnest sank down on the couch and put his head in his hands. "Marie," he said, "we're in the middle of a serious crisis. A crisis of mammoth proportions. And it involves your father. . . ."

"Oh, no," Marie moaned. "Earnest, this is terrible! What happened? What has he done this time! Jerry told me all about Simone and the iron maiden and Lydia and Roy Caldwell. . . ."

"There's been another murder," Zalman said quietly. "Mitzi Melbourne, the owner of the Magic Cavern. It was probably poison, but we won't know for sure until after the autopsy, and your dad has accused Lydia. And, to make it worse, Lydia's disappeared and we think she's been kidnapped, probably by the same person who killed Mitzi and Simone. But Thrasher Senior has some crackpot theory and he thinks she's taken it on the lam, that she was in love with Marty Melbourne and killed both Simone and Mitzi. He hasn't managed to tie Caldwell into it yet, but as soon as he finds out about the blackmailing, it'll be the last piece in his jigsaw puzzle."

"You're kidding moi!" Marie gasped, her brown eyes glistening with excitement. "But you think she's been kidnapped? By who? How? Who do you think killed Mitzi? What happened! Tell me all! Details! I want details!"

"Lydia isn't a killer," Earnest said, shaking his head sadly. "My Lydia! She couldn't kill anybody! She's too nice, that's Lydia's whole problem in life! Too sweet! Too giving! He thinks Lydia was in love with Marty Melbourne, which I swear is a complete crock, but the worst part is that she's gone, disappeared! She's been kidnapped! I know it in my heart!" Earnest slapped himself on the chest.

"Oooohhhhhh boy," Marie said. "This sounds bad. . . ."

"Hey, wait a minute, why are you here?" Zalman asked as he cuddled up next to her and knuckle-burned the top of her head. He couldn't believe it was possible to be so happy to see another living person, and made a mental note to propose to her again at the first auspicious moment. "What happened with the wedding?"

"Oh, I couldn't believe it." Marie squealed as she gave Zalman a kiss, then another one. "This afternoon, my cousin Sally and her fiancé Norman got so freaked out by all the wedding preparations and how everyone was fighting about money and how much the cake cost and what kind of flowers to have that they eloped to Hawaii! It was unbelievable! They didn't tell anybody, just left a note. My aunt was fit to be tied! I mean, she was so mad she was wriggling! Was it funny!" Marie started to laugh. "But by the time we found out, it was too late, they'd already left! So I just hopped on a plane and came back here, because I knew you'd need me. Hawaii . . . that's where I'd like to be," she told Zalman pointedly. "Ever since Jerry and I met, he's been promising to take me to Hawaii, but then something awful always happens so I never get to go," she said to Earnest. "It's a gyp."

"We'll go! We'll go!" Zalman said. "Anything you want, babe! I swear it on the head of this dog beside me!"

"Oooh, you must be serious." Marie laughed. "But we'd better do something about Lydia first. Now, Jerry darling, I want you to tell me everything that's happened. Somebody has to make some sense out of this situation, and I think it's going to be me."

So Zalman and Earnest gave Marie a detailed blow-by-blow synopsis of everything they'd seen and done since that first night only a few days ago when poor little Simone fell out of the iron maiden pricked full of holes like an old pincushion. They told her about the many loves of Lydia and Roy Caldwell's scheming plot to blackmail her and her ex-sweeties with the sleazoid tapes and nasty photos. Earnest shamefacedly recalled his plan to rob Roy and how it had backfired when he found Roy with his brains squished all over the carpet. Zalman explained his encounter with the Surfin' Sheriff and recounted the story of Lenny Dunn's stolen gun and the whimsical street freak who was whistling "Here Comes Peter Cottontail" as he hotfooted it down the beach. Finally, Zalman concluded with the tale of Mitzi's demise and Lydia's disappearance. "And that's the way it is," Zalman said in Walter Cronkite tones. "What do you think?"

Marie had listened to the entire story very quietly. She didn't interrupt once, which was quite unusual for Marie, simply sat on the couch scratching Rutherford's head and nodding at Zalman's long and involved account of the fun and frolic of the previous few days.

"Hmmm," she said slowly after Zalman had wrapped it up with a big red ribbon. "I see. I understand everything now." Marie jumped angrily to her feet, Rutherford panting at her side. "Well, I have only one question for you two and you'd better have a good answer!"

"Sure, honey. What do you want to know?"

"Where's the monkey?" she said, planting her hands on

her hips and glaring at Zalman and Earnest like a school-marm with a tough pop quiz in her pocket.

Zalman and Earnest looked at each other. "Huh?" Zalman said.

"You heard me, Jerry Zalman. Where . . . is . . . the . . . monkey?"

"I dunno . . ." Earnest said.

"Ahhh, well, I guess he's still at the Cavern, don't you think, Dad?" Zalman said, looking at his father for support.

"Sergeant Pepper? Yeah, last I saw him. . . ."

Marie glared at them both. "Do you mean to tell me that you two grown men left that poor defenseless monkey all alone? Does he have any water? What about food?"

"What does he eat, Purina Monkey Chow?" Zalman quipped.

"Got plenty of bananas," Earnest said brightly. "He was throwing 'em at the audience. He's okay, Marie, don't worry about Sergeant Pepper. He's a survivor. It's Lydia we ought to be worried about."

"Well, I like that! Honestly! Don't do that, ootsie-wootsie," Marie said, taking her chewed purse away from Rutherford. "Come on, both of you!"

"Come on where?" Zalman asked in horror.

"We have to go back to the Magic Cavern and get the monkey before something happens to the poor little thing!" Marie told him. "And I'm not kidding!"

"Marie, honey! Sweetheart! It's three o'clock in the morning! Can't we rescue the little ape tomorrow?"

Marie shook her head. "Not a chance in this lifetime, Jerry Zalman! How would you like to be a scared little monkey all alone in a big dark place with no food! No water! Honestly, if you two aren't coming with me, I'll do it alone! I'll call the S.P.C.A.! We're going to *go . . . get . . . the . . . monkey*. And I mean it!"

"She means it," Earnest told Zalman.

"I can see she means it," Zalman said as he got to his feet. "Well, back to the scene of the crime. . . ."

"CAN'T YOU GO ANY FASTER!" MARIE NUDGED EARNEST. She was so antsy she was hopping up and down from one foot to the other like a peewee Mount St. Helens as she hung over Earnest's shoulder with the flashlight. Earnest was hunkered down behind the Magic Cavern in a dark alleyway piled with smelly garbage and empty cardboard boxes, busily trying to pick the lock on the kitchen door, and Rutherford, who'd come along for the ride, was inspecting a trash can for goodies. Zalman was unhappily finishing a cigar.

"Hold the flashlight a little closer, Marie," Earnest whispered. "I almost got it. . . ."

Zalman looked around in horror and tossed the end of his Macanudo into a puddle of greasy water that reflected a pale silver slice of Hollywood moon. "What are we doing here! This is burglary!" he moaned. "I'm an attorney, I get caught I could get disbarred! . . . This is a felony!"

"We're just breaking and entering. I thought that was only a misdemeanor or trespassing or something, silly," Marie said absently as she stared intently at Earnest's tender hands tickling the lock.

"Steady with the light, will ya!" Earnest warned. "I almost got it!"

"Who's the lawyer here!" Zalman demanded sharply. "I'm telling you it's a felony! Robbery is when you steal from a person by force, I remember that much from law school. We're breaking and entering in the nighttime! It's burglary! It's a felony! You get sent to the big house! You get a roommate who was too tough for 'Wrestlemania'!"

"Relax, Jerry darling," Marie said, giggling. "With your legal expertise, it'll only be a few months at Club Fed, and I won't forget you. I swear it!"

"Ba-bing!!" Earnest said as the door clicked open. "That Marty's a cheap sonofabitch, he ain't even got a dead bolt and this electronic warning sticker he's got pasted on the door is a dime-store phony. . . . Jerry, you wanta go first?"

"I don't want to go first, you go first!"

"I'll go, I'll go," Marie said angrily. "Honestly, you two are such cowards! C'mon with me, ootsie," she called to Rutherford as she barged into the kitchen, wiggling the flashlight on the walls. "Ooooh, it's dark in here! We could do shadow hand puppets, like camp. . . ." She giggled. "Here, monkey monkey monkey. . . ."

Earnest looked skeptically at his son. "You're crazy about this dame, right?" he said as they followed Marie inside.

"Don't start with me, Dad! This isn't the time!" Zalman said in exasperation. "We can discuss my love life later, we'll have plenty of time while we're waiting for our case to come up in court. Of course I'm crazy about her! You think I'd put up with this lunacy if I weren't crazy about her?"

"Here, monkey monkey monkey. . . ." Marie's voice echoed softly through the dark kitchen. Hanging pots and pans were throwing weird, twisting shapes on the wall. "Here, monk!"

Earnest shook his head. "You sure can pick 'em. Hey, quiet down, Marie. I hear something out in the dining room. And there's lights on!"

Zalman, Earnest, and Marie crept slowly toward the twin circles of light shining through the pair of portholes in the double doors that led to the dining room of the Magic Cavern. Rutherford, no fool, had snagged some ribs out of the kitchen garbage and was hiding under a stainless steel worktable with his booty.

Zalman tiptoed up to the door and looked through one of the portholes. "Holy Toledo!" he said with a low whistle. "Dad, c'mere and check this out!"

"I want to see, too!" Marie said. "Whose idea was this!"

"Wow!" Earnest said in a hushed voice as he looked through the window.

"You're kidding!" Marie said in awe as she stood up on her tippy-toes and peeked through the porthole. "What do we do now, Jerry?"

"Oh, yeah, *now* I'm in charge! Now it's 'what do we do, Jerry'!" Zalman whispered. "Now all of a sudden you want to know what I think! Why didn't you listen to me before when I told you it was three in the morning and we shouldn't come down here with felonious intent!"

"Jerry darling, do belt up!" Marie said. "You want me to beg?"

"Yeah," Zalman said, "but not about this. . . ."

"You two might as well get married," Earnest remarked mildly. "You've already got the act down pat. Well, kids, I don't know about you, but I've got nothing to lose but my hide. . . ." And with that he stepped boldly through the swinging doors and into the Magic Cavern.

THE INTERIOR OF THE CAVERN WAS ABLAZE WITH LIGHTS: candles flickered on every table, and onstage, Lydia's jungle set shimmered in a halo of pale yellow spotlights. Lydia, still wearing her leopard-skin bikini, was once again tied to the palm tree in the center of the stage, but now her blond hair hung loose around her shoulders and she had a leopard-skin gag stuffed into her mouth. Her eyes flashed as she saw Zalman, Earnest, and Marie staring in through the door. "Urrrgh," she moaned, wriggling helplessly. *"Uuurrrgggghhhh!"*

"Boy, she sure has a fabulous figure," Marie said enviously. "I wish I could wear a bikini like that, but when you're short-waisted you look like a smoky link sausage!"

"Pipe down, doll," Zalman told her.

Marty Melbourne was seated at a table in the center of the audience, and all around him leered a group of ghoulish mannequins, decked out like dress extras for *Last Tango in Paris.* Marty was wearing a shining suit of white tie and tails and a white top hat encrusted with silver sequins. *"A-ha!"* the mediocre magician shrieked as he saw Zalman, Earnest, and Marie peeking out of the kitchen doorway.

Marty's eyes glittered wildly as he jumped up out of his seat. *"A-ha!"* he shrieked again. "Now, finally, my audience is complete! At last the show can begin! Now I will be recognized as the King of Magicians, a veritable Merlin, a necromancer of the first water, and Lydia Devanti will be crowned as my queen!!!" Marty cackled madly, tipping his top hat to the mannequins.

Zalman and Earnest looked at each other in horror. "It must be Christmas," Earnest whispered. "'Cause this sure looks like fruitcake to me. . . ."

"Now what?" Marie whispered.

"Play along," Zalman advised as he stepped out into the lighted dining room. "Yes, Marty—"

"You may address me as El Magnifico. I am Marty the Magnificent!"

"Ay-yi-yi!" Earnest moaned, conking his head with his palm. "El Magnifico? Marty the Magnificent we got here?"

Lydia struggled in her bonds and made wet snuffling sounds into her leopard-skin gag, the silken palm fronds rustling softly above her.

"Marty the Magnificent!" Zalman intoned. "The audience has arrived! Let the show begin!"

"Are you nuts?" Marie said from behind him. "If we go in there he's gonna try and kill us, and I'm not ready to be a two-line obit in the *Hollywood Reporter!*"

"We don't have a choice," Zalman said softly. "Marty's popped his cork. We have to try to rescue Lydia before he bubbles over completely. Play along and we'll watch for a chance and jump him. Besides, there's three of us and only one of him—"

"Wrong," Earnest said softly. "There's ten of him. He's got a nine-shot automatic in his hand."

"Sit down," Marty yelled, waving the bright, nickel-plated gun back and forth like a scepter. "At that table over there where I can see you!"

"Where'd he get the gun?" Marie asked. "He didn't have it when we came in, I swear it."

"He's a magician," Zalman told her as the three of them slowly walked into the dining room and sat down at the table Marty was pointing to. "A lousy magician, but a magician nonetheless. I made a big mistake when I didn't take him seriously. I thought he was just a pathetic loser, but he thinks he's Marty the Magnificent! But don't forget, the mouth is quicker than the eye, so you two keep quiet and let me handle this. . . . Marty the Magnificent!" he said loudly. "We, your humble audience—"

"Humble, my rear end," Earnest muttered.

"Quiet, Dad! El Magnifico! Your humble audience salutes you!"

Marty the Magnificent stood up and pushed a button on a small console in front of him. The room was filled with wave after wave of recorded applause, and Marty bowed with royal gravity, left, right, and center.

"El Magnifico! We have a request!" Zalman called.

"I don't usually do requests before the show," Marty the Magnificent said, puzzled. "I usually do requests as an encore. It would be a break with tradition. . . ."

"But your public demands it! We must know how you managed the illusions you performed so brilliantly in the last few days! El Magnifico, it is our humble request—"

"I'm gonna kill this guy!" Earnest said, starting up out of his seat. "No kidding, this guy is in for a serious punch in the beezer!"

"Put a lid on it, Dad! He's a wacko! We gotta get Lydia out of this before he flips completely!" Zalman mumbled under his breath. Earnest subsided, glowering.

"I will grant your request. Three wishes! Like in all the fairy tales! Three questions!" Marty pushed the button again, the recorded applause flooded the room, and he bowed happily to his nonexistent public.

"How did you kill Simone?" Zalman asked. "And why?"

"That's two, but I'll let it count as one," Marty said graciously. "El Magnifico will deign to answer your question. Simone stole those terrible photographs of Lydia and sold them to Roy Caldwell, that psychic faker," Marty the Magnificent said. "So I had to get even. Usually the spikes on the iron maiden fold inward when you pull a little lever inside, but I rigged it! The lever didn't work and Simone died horribly!" Marty howled with laughter; he pushed another button on the console and his phantom audience howled right along with him. "Next question!"

"Mitzi? Why did you kill Mitzi?" Zalman called.

"I had no choice! She made me kill her! She had a big offer for the Magic Cavern, because of all the publicity we'd had! She was going to sell out and retire to Miami Beach! I couldn't stand it! I hate the heat, and besides, I don't speak Spanish! One more question! Then it's on with the show!" Applause, applause from the audience. Marty bowed happily, a second-rater who'd finally gotten his big break.

"What about Roy Caldwell?" Zalman called out. "After you killed him, you stole the tapes and photographs from his safe. Where are they now?"

"Wrong!" Marty shrieked. "I didn't kill that phony! I would have killed him! I wanted to kill him! I was thinking about killing him! He was going to hurt Lydia! My Lydia! I had it all planned, but someone got there before me! Your questions are over, fools! Now, Marty the Magnificent will begin the last magic show!" Marty waved the nine-shot and plinked one off into the ceiling.

"Jerry, do something!" Marie said in terror. "He's got a gun!"

"I see he's got a gun, doll!" Zalman said, wondering how the hell he was going to get out of this impossible situation.

Marty rose from his table and ceremoniously cocked his silver-sequined top hat at a debonair angle on his head.

"Now, everybody dies!" he shrieked as he walked toward the stage. "You're doomed! Doomed! The world of magic will little note nor long remember what we say here. . . ." he cribbed. He ascended the stage and stood in the center in front of Lydia, who was still squirming madly in the ties that bound her. "Now! At last Lydia will be my queen!"

Marty turned and took a final step toward the Princess of Prestidigitation, waving the automatic over his head like a banner of victory, but as he took that one last step toward his helpless victim, there was a sudden *whoosh* in the air over Zalman's head.

Zalman looked up and saw Sergeant Pepper come swinging out of the flies above the stage, chattering fiercely like the tiny terror he was, clinging to his little prop vine with his nasty little paws. He was still wearing his Tarzan suit, and as he flew through the air he made a tremendous leap into the vines hanging directly over Lydia's head and landed in the palm tree.

"The act!" Earnest cried. "He thinks it's the act! What a trooper! That's his cue for the big wow finish!"

Marty took a potshot at the monkey, who scampered into the palm leaves and disappeared, then reappeared with a guy wire in his paw. With a simian grin, the Sarge gave it a solid tug, and a ring of gas jets set in the stage all around Lydia burst into flame, casting jagged shadows on the walls of the Cavern. Lydia collapsed with fear, hanging loosely in her ropes as the flames jumped up around her.

Marty fired again, but it was too late. Still grinning, the Sarge yanked again, and this time, the stage beneath El Magnifico's feet yawned open and the mediocre magician plummeted into the bowels of the Magic Cavern, howling like a maniac as he went. There was a heavy thunk as Marty hit the concrete twenty feet below; then there was nothing but silence from El Magnifico.

Quickly, the entire stage erupted in flames as the fire from the gas jets curled up the palm trees and torched the vines over Lydia's head. In just a few seconds the Magic Cavern was alive with dancing red flames and a sharp, threatening crackle cut through the air like a chain saw in the night. Zalman felt the heat lapping at his face as the fire chewed away at the jungle set.

Onstage, Lydia wiggled and made "urgh" sounds while Sergeant Pepper perched nonchalantly on the paw of the baby Tyrannosaurus and began to peel a captured banana.

"Dad, get Lydia, quick!" Zalman yelled to Earnest. "This joint's catching, and fast! If we don't get outta here, we'll be roasted like weenies!" He was right; the mannequins were already beginning to sweat hot wax, their red lips bleeding, their dolled-up faces collapsing inward like fallen souffles. Zalman and Earnest jumped up onstage, and as Earnest raced over to Lydia and began to untie her, Zalman ran to the yawning trapdoor and peered down into the depths of the Magic Cavern's basement. The crumpled body of Marty the Magnificent was lying sadly on the floor below, arms and legs akimbo. El Magnifico had performed his last two-bit trick. "At least he died with his tails on," Zalman said as he helped Earnest with Lydia's ropes.

Earnest ripped the gag from her mouth. "Oh, poookie," she whispered, "you saved me!" Sergeant Pepper ran down the tree and settled on her shoulder, snarling like a villain.

"C'mon, kids, you can snuggle later. Let's blow this pop stand. . . ." Zalman barked. The palm trees at the side of the stage were consumed with flame and the latex skins on the dinos were beginning to melt. "It's gonna look just like *House of Wax* in here in about thirty seconds. . . ." As he spoke, the flames reached higher and began to gnaw on the curtains above the stage and quickly traveled up into the flies.

"Marie, out the kitchen, fast!" Zalman yelled as he and Earnest helped Lydia off the stage and down to the floor. They were only a couple steps away when the entire stage went up with a terrific roar.

"Way ahead of you, honey!" Marie called as she ran for the door, Rutherford yelping in terror at her heels.

Outside, they all piled into the Mercedes and Zalman pulled the car around front to watch the show. "I'm gonna call your dad," Zalman said, grinning. "I'd hate for him to miss this. . . ." He picked up the car phone, called the Hollywood station, and left a message for Thrasher as the wail of oncoming fire engines howled louder and louder in the background in a plaintive urban serenade. Then he settled back to watch the last gasp of the Magic Cavern.

The old war-horse was putting on a terrific show, and a small gaggle of fire buffs quickly appeared from out of nowhere to enjoy the blaze, laughing and pointing and snapping their Instamatics at the blazing building. The heat was tremendous and Zalman decided he'd better move the Mercedes farther back so the paint wouldn't get blistered. Minutes later, three companies of fire engines roared up, casting up a small tsunami of gravel as they slid into the parking lot, horns blasting, Dalmations barking. Zalman and Marie got out of the car and leaned up against the hood of the Mercedes, and Zalman smoked a cigar while the firemen battled the intense blaze.

In the car, Earnest and Lydia were all cuddled up while Lydia whimpered and told Earnest every last detail of her capture by Marty the Magnificent and her subsequent ordeal at the stake.

"Just as Mitzi keeled over, he hoisted me up into the flies! He must have been planning it for ages! I could see everything but I was all tied up and I had this icky gag in my mouth and I tried to yell but nobody could hear me! It was awwwwwful! Then everybody went away and Marty let me down and tied me to the tree and he kept saying he loved me," she wailed. "He said he'd always loved me! He wanted to be the King and Queen of Magic and go on a U.S.O. tour with Bob Hope! He wanted to play an aircraft carrier! I tried to tell him his close-up magic wouldn't work with a big audience like that, but he wouldn't beleeeeeve me! And I couldn't get away because I was all tied up! It was awwwwwful!"

"There, there, pookie, everything's all right now! Ernie took care of everything just like he promised, didn't he?"

"Ummmm, yes . . ."

"Doesn't Erniekins always come through when you need him?"

"Ummmm, yesss . . ."

Zalman and Marie could hear every saccharine detail of the conversation from their perch on the hood of the car. Zalman gagged audibly and grabbed his throat. "Marie, doll, promise me something. If I ever, ever begin to sound like that, have me humanely destroyed, will you?" he asked.

Marie giggled and nodded as she snuggled up next to him on the hood of the car. "You darn betcha, pookie," she said with a laugh. "Oh, look, there's Daddy!" She hopped off the car and ran over to her father, who enfolded her in his gigantic arms, stroked her hair, and looked around at the mob scene.

"Now what!" Captain Arnold Thrasher roared as he caught sight of Zalman, blowing double smoke rings into the blaze. "Zalman! You monster! I'm gonna kill you! Now you're trying to set my little girl on fire! What's the matter with you? Have you lost your mind?!"

Zalman sighed and looked over at Sergeant Pepper and Rutherford, who seemed to have reached a détente hitherto unknown in the mammal kingdom. The Sergeant, perched on Rutherford's back, was having a doggy ride all around the fire scene, tipping his hat to the onlookers like a theatrical veteran and collecting a nice piece of change from the firebugs.

"Yes, Arnie, I have lost my mind," Zalman admitted as the Magic Cavern, now fully involved in fifty-foot flames, collapsed inward with tremendous intensity, spewing smoke and fire and sparks high into the torpid L.A. sky. "Say, you got any marshmallows?"

THE FOLLOWING MORNING, EVERYONE WAS RELAXING IN Zalman's living room enjoying a gigantic high-calorie feast that Marie had ordered in from Greenblatt's Deli down on Sunset.

Captain Arnold Thrasher sank his fangs into a bagel loaded with cream cheese and smiled happily. "Boy," he said, "I'm in solid with the chief. Wrapping up three murders in two different jurisdictions! I'm a damn hero is what I am. I'm up for a commendation," he said dreamily. "Ernie, thanks to you, things are going great. What a career move!"

"Terrific," Earnest said warily. "It's great things worked out so good for you, Arnie. But look—"

"Yeah," Thrasher went on as he speared a hunk of smoked halibut and positioned it carefully on top of his bagel. "First the magician girl, then the psychic, then the fat lady. Boy, I look great!"

"But, Daddy—" Marie said.

"I might make the five o'clock news! I could go on 'Geraldo'! 'Lifestyles,' maybe . . . nahhh, I guess maybe not 'Lifestyles.' "

"But Arnie," Zalman said, "I don't think Marty killed all three of—"

"Yeah. It's case closed," the big cop said, ignoring his critics. He waved his bagel in the air for dramatic emphasis, and Rutherford followed it longingly with his eyes. "Boy, that dumb Malibu sheriff is mad he didn't get there first! Dumb surfer. Where do they get those guys, anyway?"

"Marty said he didn't kill Roy, I heard him," Earnest said.

"Me, too," Marie stressed. "With my own ears."

"You couldn't hear anything with somebody else's ears, could you?" Lydia asked in a puzzled tone as she reached for another prune danish.

"Arnie," Zalman said patiently, "I hope you get to go on 'Oprah,' I honestly do. But just before he died, Marty Melbourne told me, told all of us, that he didn't kill Roy Caldwell. He said he *wanted* to kill him, he said he *would* have killed him, but he said he *didn't* kill him!"

"Killers lie all the time," Thrasher said indignantly. "You can't believe what a killer tells you!"

Zalman shrugged. "I can't speak for the veracity of murderers, it's out of my field. But I don't think Marty was lying. Why should he? There he was, he was about to kill all of us, he was an ego freak—"

"Ooooooohhhh," Lydia squealed as the ugly memories of the past few days swept over her pretty face. "It was sooo awfulllll . . . I was all tied up! I hate being tied up! I'll never let anyone tie me up again! Especially not a man!"

"That's the spirit," Marie said in a tone of fervent feminism. She reached out and patted Lydia on the back. "You have to draw the line somewhere, after all."

"Good decision, Lydia," Zalman said. "I applaud your personhood. But back to Marty. Look, Arnie, he was going to kill us, he'd admitted to two out of three killings, so why not cop to the third? If he'd killed Roy, what was the big deal about saying so?"

Thrasher helped himself to a slice of lox the size of a Pontiac's hood. "Well," he said with his mouth full, "like I said. Your killers, they can't be trusted. A guy'll knock off a whole raft of folks, but he won't want to say so in front of his mother. It's psychological, see," he said in a mysterious tone as he tapped his cranium wisely. "The human mind is very psychological."

Marie sighed and nibbled at her toast. "Daddy—" she began.

There was a pounding at the door, accompanied by the sound of a howling dog. Rutherford, who'd managed to beg a bit of prune danish from Lydia and was enjoying it on the rug under the coffee table, leapt to his feet and ran over to the door, yipping and barking hysterically.

"That's Dean," Marie said as she got up. "Ruthiewootsie loves to see hims baby brother, doesn't hims?" she asked Rutherford. She opened the front door and McCoy barged in, Rutherford's brother Chester at his heels. The two dogs began to sniff each other ceremoniously.

"Hey, everybody! How's it going! Arnie! How the hell are ya, you old badger! Jeez, I'm starved," McCoy said as he saw the spread on the dining room table.

"Help yourself, McCoy," Zalman told him.

McCoy, who was already loading up his plate, nodded happily and motioned to Zalman. "Zally, we gotta talk," he said, spearing a slab of lox. "Like, something crawled out from under the right rock, you catch my drift."

"Into the den," Zalman said. "Bring your plate."

"I wasn't going to leave it with Chester, he ain't trust-worthy." McCoy grinned as he followed Zalman.

"Back in a flash, folks," Zalman said. Once they were in the den he turned to McCoy. "What's up, Dean?" he asked. "What sort of slimy good news have you discovered?"

McCoy smiled, enjoying his little moment of triumph. "This took me a long time, Jerry. . . . I mean, this was not an easy gig."

"You're a brilliant man, Dean. Your mental prowess is akin to that of Barnaby Jones! What did you find out?"

"I had to go into a lot of sleazy bars," McCoy said, munching thoughtfully on a kosher dill. "You wouldn't be-lieve how many sleazy bars there are in North Hollywood, not to mention those toilets down around Vermont."

"You're a hero of Hollywood labor, Dean. Just tell me what you found out, will ya?" Zalman pressed.

"It was in one of those joints down by the V.A. Hospital on San Vicente? I got to talking to this old goofball name of Rusty, guy was in the big war—that's what they call it, the big war?—"

"Dean, I'm begging you—"

"—and he knew this guy who knew this funny story this other guy had told him only a few days before, about this third guy who lived on the beach up around the Malibu Colony?"

"Dean, I'm pleading with you, I'm down on my knees . . ."

"I'm getting to it, Zally!" McCoy said defensively. "So Rusty tells me this story about this guy, and it seems he used to live in the Malibu Colony, he was a screenwriter but things went bad on him and he went belly-up and ended up on the streets. So right away I know this is the guy we want, so I keep buying the drinks—by the way, I went a little over on the expenses—"

"Dean!!!"

"—but seeing as this guy was a writer and had a creative mind, he figured out a little racket for himself, keep himself in Night Train Express, Thunderbird, your heavy-duty wines."

Zalman sank down on an ottoman and put his head in his hands. "Anytime you're ready, Dean. I'll just sit here and wait for you, it's no problem, believe me."

"This is good, Jer! It's really good! So the guy lives out on the beach in the summer and he hangs out under the decks during parties, 'cause he knows that folks always get tanked up and start pitching stuff into the drink, 'cause like, he's been there, get it? Good stuff, splash, right in the ocean. TVs, mostly. That's what Rusty says. Radios, wedding rings, once some movie star's husband got pissed at her and pitched her whole Bob Mackie wardrobe out onto the sand. Luckily it was low tide, so Rusty's pal made out like a damn bandit. You know what a Bob Mackie original is worth these days?"

"Dean!" Zalman exploded. "You should be working for *Women's Wear Daily!* Where is this guy! Can we find this guy! What is this guy's name! Can you give me a name, Dean?! I'm pleading with you!"

"No problem." McCoy smiled. "So let's buzz out to the beach, hey?"

"Immediately, if not sooner," Zalman said as he jumped to his feet. "Let's hit the road."

"I'd take my shoes off, I was you, Zally," McCoy said as they got out of the car. "Roll up your pants, too, if you don't want to get 'em all full of sand."

"The things I do for my family," Zalman fumed. "God, I hate the beach! It's horrible here, why do people do this to themselves? You get sand all over you, it itches, you get sunburned, you look like a roasted pepper! For my money it's a disgusting way to enjoy yourself." Nevertheless, he slipped out of his Guccis, rolled up his pants, and stared around the huge parking lot. "Where are my sunglasses?" he mumbled as he rummaged in the glove compartment. "Ahhh, thank God!" he said as he grabbed an old pair of Ray-Bans he kept stashed for emergencies. "Okay, Dean, where is this guy?"

"I heard he was near the Santa Monica pier," McCoy said as he and Zalman got out of the car, walked to the end of the parking lot, and stared off at the hot Saharan sand. "So that's what I thought we'd try first."

Zalman and McCoy trudged along the beach admiring the peons at play for a quarter mile or so until McCoy spotted a small encampment of street folks barbecuing a chicken on a portable grill they'd set up amid a pile of rocks.

"Hang back a minute, will you, Jer?" McCoy said. "This isn't a job for an uptown guy like you. . . ." McCoy sauntered over to the little knot of people, and after several minutes of talk and an exchange of cash and three packs of

Luckies, he returned. "No prob," he said, grinning. "I got it nailed."

They doubled back, and after wending their way through miles of sun worshipers, McCoy spotted a large candy-striped beach umbrella under which a man of about fifty was morosely sucking on a bottle of Night Train Express. Zalman and McCoy sauntered over to him, casually.

"Your name Huston?" McCoy asked.

The man looked up at them. He was wearing mirrored sunglasses, a red tank top that said "I'd Rather Be Smashing Soviet Imperialism," and a pair of baggies decorated with red and green sailfish. He had a full white beard and a nimbus of white hair and he looked like a bargain-basement Santa Claus. "Nope," he said, shaking his head. "Name's Lanky Pete."

McCoy sighed and kicked some sand around with his bare toes. "Too bad," he said, squinting off down the beach. "Isn't that too damn bad, Jer?"

"Too damn bad," Zalman echoed as he took off his Ray-Bans and polished them carefully on his monogrammed hankie. "That's what I call too damn bad. Say, you don't know where this guy is, do you?" he said hopefully. "Me and my pal here, we need to get ahold of him. Real bad."

Lanky Pete stared into the surf and sipped thoughtfully from his bottle. "I know who he is," he said. "I mean, I don't know him, but I know who he is. Maybe I could get a message to him, you needed to see him that bad. Course, I'd need a little cash, if I was gonna go looking for him. But if I found him, then I could give him your message, see?"

"A message?" Zalman said as if the idea was so elegant that he was dazzled by its prosaic simplicity. "Wow. A message. I never thought of that. Whaddaya say, Dean?" he asked, turning to McCoy.

"A message. Hmmmm, gee, I dunno," McCoy said, shaking his head. "I don't think a message would get to him on time, do you, Jer? Well, thanks all the same, buddy," he told Lanky Pete. "It's too bad old Huston'll miss out on this deal, but you can't win 'em all. We'd better get back to the studio, Jer. Give 'em the bad news."

Lanky Pete stiffened as a tremor of excitement traveled up and down his body like he'd been belted by an electric eel. "The studio! What studio! You guys from a studio? What bad news?" Lanky Pete said, his voice rising with hysteria. "Like what kinda deal we talking about here? I'm still a member of the Writers Guild, y'know! In good standing!"

"You mean, you're Huston? What a piece of luck. I can't believe it, can you, Jer?" McCoy said. "We're from MGM."

Huston's eyes flashed fire and his lips peeled back to reveal a very expensive set of perfectly capped choppers. "MGM!" he breathed. "I can start tomorrow! I'm off the sauce, I swear it! Say, how much money we talking about here? You guys better call my agent, Sid Rosen. I may be down on my luck, but I don't work for peanuts, believe it. Wait a minute, wait a minute! Is this about that rewrite I did for Elliot Minkstein out there? That wasn't my fault! Minkstein screwed up, not me!" Huston's face turned dark and suspicious as a nervous cloud of thought hit him. "Okay, who are you guys? You guys vice-presidents? I only deal with guys who can close, believe it. Goddamn Minkstein couldn't close a door." He glanced at McCoy, then at Zalman. "You must be the vice-president," he said as he took off his mirrored glasses and looked Zalman over carefully. "You got the right clothes for it. And that makes you the stooge," he said to McCoy.

"I resent that!" McCoy said. "I'm no stooge! I'm the idea man."

Zalman reached into his pocket, took out his cigar case, and offered one of his Dunhill Macanudos to Huston, a.k.a. Lanky Pete. Huston took it and smelled the wrapper lovingly.

"You know," he said thoughtfully as he put the tip of the cigar to the flame of Zalman's gold lighter and puffed it slowly, "it's a cigar like this that makes me remember why people have money. Haven't had one of these since the bottom dropped out of my life about three years ago. Who the hell are you guys and what do you want?" he said suspiciously.

"Mind if we squat down?" McCoy said. "We've been looking for you, man. How come you're so hard to find, and what's this Lanky Pete business, anyway?"

"My street name," Huston said, blowing a cavalier stream of smoke into the afternoon sun. "Call it a nom de plume if you will, a nom de guerre if you must. It's a simple affectation, yet we hobos enjoy our little joke as well as the next man."

Zalman cleared a place on the sand, took out his hankie, and sat down on it. "Mr. Huston," he began, "I'm not from MGM."

"Damn," Huston said bitterly. "I thought for a minute there my star was in the ascendant again. Boy, you guys don't know how fleeting fame can be! Okay, so who the hell are you and what the hell do you want?"

"My name's Jerry Zalman, I'm an attorney, and this is my associate, Mr. McCoy. Now, look, all we need is a little information. I'm willing to compensate you, Mr. Huston. But, and let me make this perfectly clear, *only* if you tell me the truth. If you tell me a lie, I may not find out about it right away, but rest assured, I will find out eventually, and when I do I will send Mr. McCoy after you and he will rip out your guts with a pair of rusty barbecue tongs. Is my position in this matter crystal clear to you, Mr. Huston?"

"Just like Waterford, pally. How much you payin' and what do you want to know?"

Zalman pulled out his gold money clip, selected two crisp one-hundred-dollar bills, and set them on the sand in front of Huston. "But remember," he said, holding up a warning finger. "The truth."

Huston took the bills and rustled them between his fingers, then folded them and slipped them into the pocket of his baggies. "Nice to have fresh bills," he said wistfully. "Always used to get fresh bills from the bank back in the bad old days. Jeez, I remember one time I was doing a rewrite over at Paramount, musta been the late seventies or so, some damn spy picture. I forget who was in it. One of those guys with a cartoon jaw. . . . Anyway, they called me in at the last minute because they were stuck for a second act, so me and this other writer were over at Nickodell's, tanking up so's we could be brilliant after lunch, and this waitress I was friendly with at the time says to me, 'I bet I could do what you're doing, if I had the chance.' Well, me and this other guy, we were just drunk enough to go for it, so's we took her back over to the studio, gave her the script, and asked her how she'd fix it, and she gave us her ideas. Then we sorta fooled with it, made it play a little better, and the next morning, we shoveled it at the studio brass and they went for it! Damn, we thought that was funny! Gave her a third of the take, too, just to show we were right guys. Think she opened up a doggy beauty parlor with the dough. Did okay for herself out of the deal. . . ."

"Mr. Huston," Zalman said patiently, "last Wednesday

night there was a party in the Malibu Colony. There was an altercation and a man was killed. Now, Mr. McCoy here has it on very good authority that you pawned a gun that you found on the beach in front of that very house. Is this true?"

"Sure," Huston said. He sipped from his bottle, wiped the neck, and offered it to Zalman, who shook his head in horror. Huston held it out to McCoy.

McCoy reached out for the bottle, took a hit, and shuddered. "Little thick for my taste," he said as he handed the bottle back to Huston.

"You saw the guy who threw the gun?" Zalman asked.

Huston grinned and combed his beard with his fingers. "You know, this reminds me of a script I was working on over at Fox in about 1972. It's a fascinating story and I'm sure you'll enjoy hearing it in explicit detail. See, me and this agent I had at the time were having lunch over at Hillcrest. . . ."

Zalman sighed and reached into his pocket for his money clip.

ZALMAN PARKED THE CAR UNDER A SCRAGGLY WELLINGton palm around the corner from the big Beverly Hills house and turned to McCoy. "Now look, Dean, we're not kidding around, right? You scoot around the rear of the joint and back me up. I wanta get a confession here! Signed, sealed, and delivered, you understand me? And I want Lydia's tapes and photos so Dad doesn't yammer at me for the rest of my life about how I failed his true love and broke the heart of her missionary mother. But remember, this guy's a menace! He's killed once and I figure he'd love to kill again. Especially me. . . ."

"Yeah." McCoy laughed evilly. "First thing we do, let's kill all the lawyers, right?"

"Wrong! Shakespeare can get away with that, Dean; you can't, and don't forget it! I want to know you're right behind me, okay? Dean? You receiving me, Dean? I want a strong yes answer here or no bonus. Dean? Got it?"

McCoy wasn't impressed with Zalman's ranting. "Chill out, Jer, it's a cakewalk. I'll slip around back while you're yakking it up, then jump him when you give me the high sign. What is the high sign, by the way?"

"Dean—"

"Just kidding, Jer. Don't get nervous in the service, okay?"

Zalman got out of the car and slammed the door behind him. He bent down and peered in the window at McCoy, who was scrabbling around in his pockets, searching for his Luckies. "You gotta quit smoking, man!" Zalman snapped. "Here we are, in mortal peril of life and limb, and you're goofing around looking for your smokes! My life is in your hands! How did this happen to me? When did my life start to cave in? Everyone around me is insane, I'm convinced of it!"

Finally McCoy found his smokes and fired one up, inhaling half an unfiltered Lucky in one long, blissful suck. Then he grinned like Ming on Mongo. "C'mon, he's gonna fold the first time I lay a glove on him, Jer. You think I'd be doing this if I thought he'd put up a fight? It's no prob, man. We'll be heroes, Arnie Thrasher'll love you to death especially since he'll get all the credit for the bust, so relax. Go with the flow."

"Go with the flow! Go with the flow! You better start

rethinking your vocabulary, Dean! You could stand some verbal updating! 'Go with the flow' is in the same category as 'far out.' It's simply not trendy," Zalman said. "I wish I had another jacket. I just got this a few weeks ago and I don't want to rip it in a fight here. Ahhh, the hell with it. Just be right behind me, okay, Dean?"

"No prob, Zally."

Zalman walked around the corner and up the terraced flagstone steps to the big white house and knocked on the door with a huge brass knocker in the shape of an exclamation point. To his surprise, Tom Kellar himself answered the door.

"Jerry!" the producer said, breathing heavily as he took a sneak peek up and down the street. He was wearing a purple "Hollywood Squares" T-shirt and matching satin sweatpants. "Is this synchronicity or is this synchronicity? C'mon out on the lanai, I'm doing my creative shtick. Nice jacket, by the way." Kellar turned and led the way toward the back of the house to a large room furnished in bamboo and glass furniture and a gaggle of plants that looked like outtakes from *Little Shop of Horrors*. "I just got off the phone with Sid Rosen, my agent. You know Sid, don't you, Jer? Helluva guy and a major piece of artillery in the agenting line, I might add." He motioned to a deep sofa covered with a lurid banana-plant motif and strolled over to the bamboo bar, still talking it up. "So Sid—he sends his warmest regards by the way, his warmest, personal regards —so Sid thinks this deal I've been working on over at Metro is gonna be a go project and I want you to produce, Jer. Sincerely. I sincerely want you to produce. Hey, I know we had a little problem yesterday, but that was yesterday. Right? Like Tom Wolfe says, 'Fuhgedaboudit.' Right, Jer?"

Zalman sat down in the sofa and put his feet up on the

glass-topped coffee table. "Mind if I smoke a cigar?" he asked. He knew it would annoy Kellar if he blew smoke all around the house; that's why he wanted to do it.

"N-noooo," Kellar hedged, eyeing the length of Zalman's Macanudo uneasily. "That a good cigar? I don't smoke, myself, I just wanted to know. Case I got a character who smokes a cigar. Research, see?"

Zalman lit up and blew a thick cloud of smoke in Kellar's direction, then stared out the sliding glass door, hoping he'd see McCoy lurking behind an azalea. No McCoy. "Produce, huh?" he stalled. "I could consider it. But there's something else we need to discuss first. Very important. Very serious."

Kellar poured himself a glass of Tab, then wiped off the glass with a bar napkin with a TK monogram. "You want?" he asked, motioning to the bottle. Zalman shook his head and blew some more smoke at him. Kellar was twitching visibly as he went over to a six-foot-square ottoman in an ugly leaf motif that clashed with the sofa and perched uneasily on the edge, clutching his glass. "I know, I know," he said, laughing painfully. "You want to talk money. As Sid would say, 'Believe me, you won't go hungry out of the deal.' Is that enough for you, Jer? Can you live with that?"

Zalman leaned back in the deep sofa and smiled, shaking his head. He took a look out the back window again, but McCoy wasn't there yet. Still, he didn't mind. He was really enjoying torturing Kellar, who was beginning to sweat visibly. Why did he hate this guy so much? he wondered. He wasn't half as phony as some other guys who frequented the posh dives of L.A. and Beverly Hills. Hell, his own schmuck brother-in-law Phil Hanning was phonier than Kellar. Maybe it was Kellar's faintly slimy quality, his constant weepy apprehension, that gave him all the savoir

faire of a slug on a pizza. Maybe it was because he pol-
luted America's airwaves with his sugar-shock sitcoms.
"You know that Marty Melbourne was killed last night?"
Zalman asked slowly, enjoying every dull twist of the but-
ter knife. "Turns out he killed Simone and Mitzi. He con-
fessed. Then he kidnapped Lydia. Had some idea they
were going to be the King and Queen of Magic. He was in
love with her," Zalman told Kellar. "He was nuts, by the
way."

Kellar shook his head sadly and peered into his Tab as if
it spelled out his future in Day-Glo letters a mile high. "My
God!" he said, his voice radiating fear. "There's an *ant* in
my glass! How did an *ant* get in here! Yeecccch! An *ant*!
That's disgusting!" He got up, scurried over to the bar, and
dumped the contents out in the bar sink, then threw the
glass in the trash can. "I hate ants," he said, shivering. "I
heard about it on the news. A terrible thing. How could he
murder his own wife?" he said in amazement. "Weeeeell,
okay, maybe I can understand that. Mitzi was a fine person, but whew! Stop a clock and all. Now, Simone, she
was sincerely a nice human being. And even Roy, okay, a
blackmailer, a sleazeball of the first water, but murder! A
terrible thing! Poor Roy. We coulda done business together,
me and Roy. We were in the process of working it
out. . . ."

"Melbourne said he didn't kill Roy," Zalman said
slowly. "Oh, right before he died he admitted he killed
Simone and Mitzi, but he said he didn't kill Roy Caldwell.
And the thing is, Tom, his story makes a lot of sense, if
you wrap your brain around it for a minute. Think about it.
Both Simone and Mitzi were killed at the Magic Cavern,
and they were killed by someone who knew their habits.
Marty rigged the iron maiden so that the poor kid would
get stabbed to death when she stepped inside. It wasn't an

easy thing to do, and other than Lydia, he was the only person involved who knew how to do it—plus, he had access to the maiden just before showtime. With Mitzi, he just slipped the poison in her food, it was easy for him. Her plate was always kept in the same place in the kitchen, so he just sprinkled it on like parsley and waited for one of the waiters to trot it out to her when she got hungry. And knowing his wife, he knew that she'd get hungry sometime during the evening. He was lucky there, too, because she died while he was onstage and he got a great chance to play the frantic husband. But Caldwell, that looks to me like a straightforward case of murder. Bang-bang in the head, nothing tricky about it. Very messy but very basic. Completely different style, you see? I'm a modern guy and I think that style makes all the difference, especially in a murder. Besides, I was there last night just before Marty died, I heard him say he didn't do it, and you know what?" Zalman said. "I believe him. Whaddaya think of that?"

"Killers lie," Kellar said with concrete certainty. "Lie all the time. Can't trust a killer."

"Funny, that's just what Captain Thrasher, the cop in charge, told me only an hour ago." Zalman smiled, wafting another gigantic cloud of smoke in Kellar's direction. "And I thought he was full of shit, too. Marty was going to kill us all, he was nuts, he didn't care. He had a gun, had the bullets, had Lydia tied up—"

"How'd she look?" Kellar blurted out.

Zalman frowned. "Give it a rest, will you, Tom? Anyway, there he was, he was going to kill some or all of us, and so I ask him about the killings and he says he didn't kill Caldwell." Zalman shrugged philosophically. "And I believe him. You see, Tom, I listen to people telling me ridiculous stories all day long, it's what I do for a living. You hear enough stories, after a while you learn how to sort out the truth from the jive. And if I'm right—and I usually am—and Marty didn't kill Caldwell, then somebody else did. Now," Zalman said in tones reminiscent of the Church Lady, "I wonder who that person could be?"

Kellar sighed and raised his hands palms up in a 'who, me?' pose. Slowly, he went over to the bar and poured himself another Tab. He swigged it defiantly, and this time he didn't even bother to clean off the rim of the glass first. Zalman took this mental slippage as a bad sign.

"I guess there's just no use trying to lie to you, is there, Jerry?" Kellar said sadly, as if he'd been nailed skipping Sunday school. "Try to see things my way, will ya, Jer? I had to do it. I didn't have a choice," he said, gazing at Zalman with trustful, warm puppy eyes. "Lots of people in this town would like to see me take a fall. I've been flying high in this crazy business we call show and, hey, when a guy has the kind of series luck I've had, when a guy just might be first in line for a humanitarian award one of these happy days, lots of folks would love to go tramp-tramp-tramp all over his broken show-business bones. What I'm saying here, Jer, is that an image problem isn't exactly first choice on my menu. Do I make myself clear?"

"Just like Waterford, pally," Zalman said, stealing Huston's line. He took another peek through the sliding door. Where the hell was McCoy anyway? He decided he'd play for time, torture Kellar a little more, give him a chance to hang himself high.

"Can I tell you my story?" Kellar said thoughtfully. "Can I trust you, tell you just how tough it can get in this town?"

"Oh, please do," Zalman said, trying to sound sincere. It was not an easy line to read.

"I came here, a kid, what did I know? Fresh out of my high-school drama class with a dream in my heart," Kellar said. "I went to work in the mailroom of a big agency, call it dumb luck, but hey, fortune favors some of us, am I right, Jer?"

"Yeah, you're right, Tom."

"Well, I was working there, hating it, wondering if the sun was ever gonna shine on little ol' me, and one day this other kid in the mailroom tells me about this idea he's got for a play. Not a great idea, but an idea. But this kid, he sees it all serious, like it's from, what's that depressing guy's name? Writes plays about sick families . . . O'Neill, that guy! Just like that! But I knew this kid had a comedy. I knew that it could go for TV, half hour, syndication forever, and this schmuck kid's telling me it's serious high artsy-fartsy stuff. What can I tell you, Jer?" Kellar said slowly, rumpling his white hair. "I killed him."

"You killed him?" Zalman said. This was getting strange.

"Yep. Pushed him off the top of a parking structure in Century City. What else could I do? It was a shot, a chance, a big, fat picture window of opportunity. And it worked for me, Jer. Nobody missed him, hell, he was just a kid in the mailroom. And here I am at the top of the Hollywood heap, career-wise, so I'm obviously doing something right!"

"That's a very interesting story, Tom," Zalman said, wishing he had a roll of Tums in his pocket. "How does it relate to Lydia?"

"Well, that's the thing. When Caldwell got in my way, murder was the obvious solution to my problem. Hey, they never got me on the other one, so I figured I could do it again," he said, smiling. "Now, look, man to man, we both know that Lydia is a lovely woman and she and I had a lot in common, and like I said to you once before, Jer, a man in my position, grinding out these half-hour sitcoms week after week after week, well, I need a little relaxation every so often. Change of pace. Hey, this town can be Tough-town, right? She and I had a good thing going, a sincere thing, an honest, open thing. And when it ended, I knew I had a friend for life in Lydia Devanti. But then Roy Cald-well enters the picture." Kellar sighed. "Now, strictly be-tween us, Jer, not for publication. Lydia is naive, I've found that many women are, and often it takes men like us, men of perception and integrity, to relate to a woman's warmth and candor on an honest, open basis, don't you think, Jer? Hey, I wasn't trying to exploit her or anything!" Kellar protested. "Women are the mainstay of my audi-ence! I respect women! As humans!" Kellar shot Zalman a hopeful, sidelong glance. "You gotta believe that, Jer."

"I do, Tom. I sincerely know what you mean," Zalman told him. This guy is completely bonkers, and I'm gonna kill McCoy, Zalman thought as he casually looked out the window, if Kellar doesn't get me first. I'm gonna rip that big lug limb from useless limb. Where the hell is he?

"Lydia had the pictures—say, Jer, can I get you any-thing, a Tab? All this talk can make you thirsty. . . ."

"No, I'm fine, Tom." Zalman smiled. "Go on."

"And then Roy bought the pictures from Simone, that little slut! She stole 'em from Lydia, figuring she'd pile up a little egg money on the side. This was bad for me, Jer. Very bad. Roy comes to me, he hits me up for dough, then for a spot on one of my shows, like associate producer. Something. Anything. Then he decides he wants more. Okay, I'm trying to be a reasonable man, so I offered to set him up to produce a Movie of the Week, but then he starts talking about his autobiography! He thinks he's Shirley MacLaine! Then he decides he wants to get into features! Can you believe it! Features, he wants! That crook wants me to step aside on this Metro deal Sid Rosen's setting up. A wonderful human being, Sid. Never holds a grudge either. But when Caldwell comes up with that, I knew I had to do something, Jer. When I realized Caldwell was going to get in the way of my career, I knew I had to kill him. I didn't see that I had another choice. I mean, what would you have done, Jer? You'd have killed the guy, too, wouldn't you? It's taken me a long time to attain the position of respect and trust I've achieved in the television community, and I can't let those kids down, Jer! Those kids are depending on me, on Tom Kellar, on TotFlicks, to provide them with the kind of wholesome prime-time family fare this country was founded on! I couldn't let Caldwell sell those cheap pictures of me and Lydia to the *National Peeper*, could I? I had to kill him, don't you see that, Jer?" Kellar said, begging for Zalman's understanding. "Just like I had to kill the kid in the mailroom."

Zalman looked out the sliding glass door again. Zip. No McCoy. Oh, God, Zalman thought, when will I be able to get out of this meeting? "How'd you get the gun?" he asked.

"I stole it from Lenny Dunn, that Virginia ham! I told Dolores—my secretary, Dolores? She thought very highly of you, by the way. I told Dolores to have him in for a casting interview and when he came in with the eight-by-ten glossies, I nipped out to his place and ripped off a piece out of a drawer. The guy's got so much hardware in his house I was kinda hoping he wouldn't miss it for a while. . . . I don't know from guns, so I grabbed the first one I saw, it kinda looked like the gun Robert De Niro used when he played Travis Bickle? Nasty things, guns. I guess you got the gun now, Jer?"

"Yup. I got it."

"How'd you get it? If you don't mind my asking . . ."

"Guy on the beach saw you throw it into the drink. Guy used to be in the industry, so he recognized you."

"You forget what a small town this is," Kellar said ruefully. "Actually, sometimes I think there's only a few hundred folks here. . . . So who found it?"

"Ex-screenwriter name of Huston?"

"That no-talent!" Kellar screeched. "I ran into him in Sid's office a few months ago, the guy was stinking! And he was drunk, too! He's a lush! It'll never hold up in court!"

"Perhaps yes, perhaps no. But you shouldn't throw guns out windows after you kill a guy, Tom. Wasteful."

"Damn. I shoulda kept it, I guess. But I was standing there, I heard the ocean roaring, and I thought, hey, the ocean is the source of all life, huh? Maybe it'll cleanse this weapon of its pain. . . ."

Kellar got up and went to the bar for another Tab. "Now look, Jer. The thing I want you to hear is this. Hear me, Jer. I'm begging you. You're the only guy who knows about my little problem, and I think you and I get along pretty good, we've both been around the industry a long time and we oughta think about doing this picture together. You and me. Partners. You'd be completely involved in the new organization I'm setting up, TKO? Stands for the Tom Kellar Organization. You like? Tell me you like. . . . This'll be a big job, a tough job, but you're the guy for it. Money isn't a problem. We'll leave Sid to work out that end of the deal, but I'm telling you here and now, it's not a problem. It's your expertise I'm after, Jer. Your acumen. Your know-how."

"My silence?"

"No, no, no, it's your friendship I want, Jerry." Kellar laughed, his voice filled with agonized enthusiasm. "That's what I'm after. Your friendship and your legal expertise."

"It's a great offer," Zalman said thoughtfully, wishing like hell he could see McCoy outside. Zalman didn't want to get too close to Kellar; Kellar was a lot bigger than he was, especially if you included his spare tire. Seriously bigger. I'm surrounded by idiots, Zalman thought; just when I need McCoy most, the big lummox disappears. He smiled up at Kellar, just a happy-go-lucky guy, as it hit him he'd better keep right on stalling until McCoy showed up. "A great offer. What do you figure it's worth, ballpark?"

"I gotta tell you, Jerry. Only my accountant knows for sure. And he keeps telling me, 'Mr. Kellar, you look great on paper, but you got a cash flow problem!'" Kellar laughed heartily at his accountant's waggish ways, then frowned as if he were adding up a column of figures in his head. After all, money lives a lot longer than murder. "Like I said, you and Sid can work it out, but hey, we gotta be talking at least a mil a year—just as a retainer, you understand," he added hurriedly. "That doesn't include the profit sharing, the stock options, pension. I take care of my own." He laughed heartily. "I like to combine good citizenship with good television," he said as he polished off another Tab.

Zalman saw the bushes rustle outside. McCoy, he thought happily, at last, thank God, it's McCoy. Finally I can get out of this meeting. He shook his head grimly. "It's tough to say no, Tom, but I just can't do it."

"Jer, we can talk!" Kellar pushed, his voice rising. "More than a mil? Hey, we can talk!"

"I don't know why everybody thinks I can be bought so easily," Zalman said sadly. "Okay, I gotta swim in the sea same as the rest of the sharks, but fundamentally, I'm an honest guy. Look, Tom, hear me out. I understand your problem, believe me. If I were you, I'd get me a good trial lawyer and see what can be done. But me, I just can't countenance murder. What can I tell you? Call it a character flaw, call me an integrity kind of guy. But you killed a man! Two men, now that I think of it!"

"One of 'em was a long time ago," Kellar sulked. "It doesn't count."

Zalman didn't know what to say to that, so he plunged on. "Never mind that Roy Caldwell was a crook, he was a man! That poor slob will breathe no more the smog-filled air of Baghdad by the Pacific! No more will he eat expensive dinners he doesn't appreciate! Send back great wine in top flight restaurants because he thinks it'll impress some lame like you. Okay, he was a crook, a blackmailer, a user, and in the end, a loser. But he was a citizen of Hollywood! A regular Lotusland type of guy! One of our own, so to speak. And me, I can't go for it. Part of me wants to do it, Tom. A mil a year, two mil a year." Zalman shook his head. "Lots of expenses, huh?"

"Jer, anything you want!" Kellar said frantically, clawing at his palm-frond chair with pleading fingers.

"Yeah." Zalman sighed, glancing over at the window again. The bushes rustled comfortingly, and Zalman moved in for the kill. "It sounds great, Tom, and I'm sure Sid and I could get together on the financial end. But the trouble is, if I go for it, I won't be able to sleep nights. And eventually, neither will you. Didn't you ever see *The Maltese Falcon*, for Chrissake? You'll get nervous and come after me. You know you will, Tom. Murder is starting to come natural to you, I can see that. You'll start to think maybe you can't trust me to keep my yap shut, you'll start to lie awake nights and as you stare up at yourself in the old mirror on the ceiling you'll think, hey, I got away with it before, I can get away with it again. I'll just push old Jer over a cliff, or slip a little salmonella in his sushi, or maybe I'll just hire it done. . . . Hell, in this town you can get a real guy killed for a guest shot on 'Thicker 'n Water,' right? See what I mean, Tom?" Zalman said, leaning back in his chair and spreading his hands wide. "It's a great offer, but I'll have to pass."

"Damn," Kellar said as he reached under the cushion of his chair and pulled out a blue steel .25 Browning automatic. "Damn, Jerry this is no time to go moral on me! One more time, how about it? I do not want to kill you," Kellar said strongly. "I sincerely do not want to kill you."

Zalman smiled as he got up and went over to the sliding glass door. "Hey, Dean!" he called as he pulled it open. "In here, man."

There was no one there. Only a large black standard poodle with a cheery red bow in its topknot. The dog snouted him in the legs and growled fiercely.

Zalman patted the dog on the head and the dog slobbered all over his hand. Zalman carefully closed the screen and wiped his hand off on his jacket. All of a sudden, he realized, that familiar bad feeling was knotting up his stomach again. He didn't see McCoy anywhere. Why didn't the idiot come out? Zalman looked at the bush he'd seen moving, but it was only a playful California breeze tickling the green leaves. "Dean!" he called, wondering if Kellar could hear the strain in his voice. "Come on out!"

Kellar laughed sardonically, blew on the Browning, and polished it on his sleeve. "There's nobody out there, Jer. Good dog, Inky," he said to the poodle. Inky ignored him and lay down on the patio outside, panting and staring in through the screen door. "It's just you, me, and this little puppy right here." Kellar smiled as he waggled the Browning playfully in the air.

Zalman turned and faced him. When in doubt, wing it, he thought. "It's no good, Tommykins," he said. "Take a look out the window and you'll see this huge, hulking guy lurking in your garden. My pal McCoy. He'll rip your ears off with his teeth. He's that mean."

Kellar laughed again and pointed the Browning at Zalman in a two-handed cop stance he'd probably learned from a Chuck Norris movie. "You think I'm listening to you? No more, Jerry. You had your chance and you blew it! I wanted to make a deal! But you turned me down and now I'm not listening to you anymore! I give a guy one chance, that's it! No more!" Kellar's eyes shot past Zalman and out the window. "There's nobody out there but my dog, Jerry! We're all alone! Just you, me, and Mr. Browning here. I'm going to kill you, I'm serious! This is a gun I got here!" Kellar fired a shot into the ceiling.

"I can see it's a gun, Tom!" Zalman said, and hoped he sounded brave. He exhaled more smoke in Kellar's direction. "C'mon, Dean, let's go!" he called out. What was the matter with that guy? Zalman wondered. He was out there. Wasn't he? Somewhere?

"You turned me down, I can't believe you turned me down," Kellar said miserably. "Now I've got to kill you! I hate it when I have to kill people! I made you a great offer. A lotta guys would kill for this offer. I killed for this offer, matter of fact."

"I just can't do it, Tom," Zalman said, sighing. "Is it my fault I'm honest? Is it my fault I'm the last honest guy in Hollywood? C'mon, give me the gun. My pal's outside, take a look, will you?"

"Forget it! There's nobody there!" Kellar yelled. He blasted off another shot and made Zalman jump. "This is it, shorty!"

"Shorty! That's a low goddamn blow, Kellar! If I weren't such a nice fellow, I'd be inclined to give you a punch on the snout for that crack!" Zalman tossed his glowing cigar on an end table and glared at Kellar angrily.

"Hey!" Kellar shouted, pointing at the cigar with the barrel of the Browning. "That's a genuine lacquer finish! That's about eighty million coats there! Pick up that cigar!"

"The hell I will!" Zalman yelled back. "You called me shorty! I hope it burns right through to the carpet, you murdering geek!" The cigar was smoking along nicely on the table, and it was going to leave a big ugly scar unless somebody picked it up fast.

"Pick it up! I'm telling you, pick up that cigar!" Kellar hollered.

Zalman shook his head and stood there, rocking back and forth on his heels and grinning. Gun or no gun, Kellar wasn't getting the better of him. Not a chance in this lifetime.

Kellar couldn't stand it. The damage to his decor pushed him right over the edge. He lunged forward and made a grab for the cigar. As he did, Zalman took his best shot and made an identical grab for the Browning. The two men collided in midair with a heavy thunk and fell sideways onto the coffee table, which collapsed in a crack of broken glass.

"I cut myself!" Kellar yowled, dropping the gun amid the shards of glass littering the carpet. *Damn*, that hurts! I'm bleeding!"

Zalman rolled away from him, over the crunching glass, and as he did, he tried to give Kellar a short chop to the jaw, but Kellar twisted away from him so that the blow glanced off his ear. Outside on the patio, Inky whimpered at all the action in the room and began to leap around on the cement, barking and ripping at the screen with his paws.

Kellar was crawling around on the floor, moaning and looking for the gun, and Zalman popped him again, behind the right ear this time.

"Owwww-wow-wow," Kellar yelped. He sounded a lot like a dog in pain. Inky didn't like it and began to mimic his master's voice.

"Shorty, huh!" Zalman said. He was really steamed. It didn't bother him that he was short, lots of important guys were short. Napoleon was short, Billy Rose was short, Paul Simon was short, Billy Joel was short, it didn't bother him. But he hated it when a tall guy made a crack about it. It didn't show class. He'd had enough from Kellar. If only he could get the guy to shut up! Zalman jumped to his feet and tried to give Kellar another quick jab, but the blow didn't land hard enough to do any damage. Kellar got a grip on the gun and stared madly around the room, looking for Zalman. He popped off another shot, but it went wild and whizzed out the screen door, scaring the socks off Inky.

Zalman ducked behind the couch to regroup. Matter of fact, he thought, he'd damn well had enough from everybody. Why should he take all this abuse? He was the guy in control, wasn't he? Didn't Jerry Zalman have his entire life completely under control? His newly redecorated house, his never-boring legal practice, his nice, peaceful office . . . he'd worked hard for everything he had. So what had gone wrong, he thought as he looked futilely for McCoy. His girlfriend kept loading him up with salt and pepper shakers, his father had moved in with him and was smoking all his cigars, his sister was driving him crazy because she'd misplaced her rock 'n' roll meal ticket, and now all of a sudden he was fighting for his life with a deranged TV producer! And on top of it all, Doyle Dean McCoy, his best buddy, his pal McCoy, had vanished on him! McCoy was supposed to ride in at the end like the cavalry in a B Western on Saturday afternoon, and where was he? What had happened?

And now Kellar was yowling about his interior design quotient! Now this! It was too much. Jerry Zalman was mad as hell and he wasn't going to take it one single minute longer.

"I'm gonna bust your skull open, you sleazoid worm!" Zalman yelled, poking his hand up from behind the couch.

Kellar took a shot at him, but Zalman knew it was coming and ducked. Was that three shots or four? "You and your sitcoms! You think you're the tastemeister to the masses, don't you? I'm telling you, that junk makes me puke! It makes everybody puke!"

"How dare you malign my product!" Kellar screeched. Blam blam.

Four and five? Zalman wondered. Or was it five and six? Did an automatic have eight shots? Nine? He wished he'd listened more carefully to McCoy's boring speeches about his weaponry and the sanctity of the National Rifle Association. "It's gonna be worth putting you in jail just so's I don't have to see that crap on my TV screen when I zap through the channels! You're polluting the video waves, Kellar! Somebody's gotta put a stop to you, and I'm glad it's gonna be me! Dean!" Zalman shrieked, "Dean! Get in here, you idiot!"

"You're gonna die, Zalman!" Kellar snarled. "Nobody maligns my product and lives!" He stood in the center of the room, the gun in his hand, shaking his head like a mastiff, his white hair hanging down over his eyes.

Even in the midst of his fury, Zalman knew that the only way he was going to survive until that idiot McCoy showed up was to sting like a bee. He had to dance, stay out of the producer's clutches, not get pinned down. If he did, it would be all over. In his anger, Zalman grabbed a lamp and heaved it across the room at Kellar.

"My lamp!" Kellar shrieked in anguish as it shattered at

his feet. "It's Neo-geo! Now I *am* gonna kill you!" He aimed at Zalman and squeezed off another shot with the Browning, but he fumbled the trigger and the bullet plunked right into the center of a large painting of a smiling eggplant on the far wall. *"Nooooo!"* Kellar howled. "That's a genuine Bibinski! His airbrush period! Look what you made me do!"

Zalman ducked behind the couch again. He was beginning to get a great idea. "Look what you made me do! Look what you made me do!" he mimicked. "You mental sixth-grader! Dean!" he yelled in desperation. "Where are you!"

"My painting!" Kellar mewled pitifully. "My beautiful Bibinski! It's worth a fortune! It's a masterpiece! You're gonna die!" Kellar took another shot at Zalman; this one went whizzing by his head and shattered a large vase. Kellar howled again, a man in the kind of investment-quality agony only Sotheby's could understand. "My artwork!" he shrieked. "You little monster!"

"Cut out that 'little' crap!" Zalman yelled, looking around him for more ammunition. He'd lost count. Eight shots? Seven? He picked up a small crystal figurine that had fallen off the end table and pitched it over the couch at Kellar like a hand grenade. He heard the crash of shattering glass and smiled, the taste of victory in his mouth. Kellar howled again.

"Whatever that was, I hope it was expensive!" Zalman called. He snaked along the floor behind the couch. Where was McCoy? He looked out the window again, but the garden was still empty. No one was there but Inky, lying on his back with all four paws in the air, scratching his thick pelt on the sunny cement patio.

"What did I do to deserve this?" Zalman wondered

aloud. "Why me?' He thought he could hear sirens in the distance. Was it true? Was the cavalry finally coming to his rescue? Was his legal life saved? Zalman listened again; now he was sure he could hear the shrill squeal of police cars coming closer! Yes! They were coming closer! Finally he could get out of this meeting! He was saved! "That's it, Kellar," he yelled at the producer. "Here come the cops! My guy called the cops, you hear me! Give up, man, it's all over for you!"

"The hell you say! They'll never take me alive!" Kellar yowled, waving the gun over his head. "This is my life! I'm not going down the tubes for this! Why is this happening to me!"

The sirens kept coming; they sounded like they were only a few streets away, now outside, now the noise was terrific and Zalman could hear a woman's voice screaming and a man screaming back at her and . . .

The only trouble was, they were next door. Zalman could tell, he could hear it. People next door were screaming at each other, a woman's voice spitting out harsh curses in Spanish. . . .

It was too much for Jerry Zalman to bear. "That's it!" he howled as he jumped up and over the couch and threw himself on top of Tom Kellar. "The gun is empty and I don't care anyway! I'm not taking it anymore, you hear me! Give up, Kellar, before I beat your head in!"

The two men were rolling around the floor and suddenly Kellar blasted off another shot, shattering the plate-glass sliding door, which crashed to the ground and made a tremendous noise as it smashed into a quadzillion pieces on the concrete patio. "Oh, shit," Zalman moaned, "I counted wrong!"

Inky went ki-yi-yi and took off across the garden, yowling miserably and making a terrible racket, and somehow, through it all, Zalman heard McCoy's booming voice shouting, "You see, you big dumb dork! I told you! Now do you believe me!"

Zalman glanced over Kellar's shoulder and saw McCoy and a pair of finely tailored Beverly Hills patrolmen standing on the patio. Both of the cops looked puzzled as they stared in through the ripped screen door at Zalman and Tom Kellar, who were still rolling around on the broken glass on the floor of the lanai, punching and kicking at each other.

"Ow-wow-wow!" Kellar hollered in pain as Zalman landed a good one on the back of his head.

"Get *offa* me, will you!" Zalman yelled as he whacked Kellar again.

The two cops looked at each other in astonishment. "Whaddayou think, Willie?" the younger cop asked the older one, frowning. "Looks dubious to me." He had his hat pushed back on his head and one hand firmly clamped on McCoy's arm.

"I dunno, Pete," Willie replied, shaking his head in disbelief. "Whadda *you* think?" He had his hand on the arm of an exceedingly unraveled Mexican woman in a white uniform who was chattering hysterically in a combo of Spanish and English. Her hair was loose around her shoulders and her dark eyes were flashing angrily at McCoy.

"*I told you!*" McCoy shouted at the cops, pointing at the two men rolling around on the floor. The woman lunged at him with extended claws and tore at his shirt. "Get away from me, lady!" he begged, trying to hide behind Pete. "Please, officer, you've got to believe me! I didn't do anything to her, I swear it!"

McCoy looked terrible. His hair was standing on end,

one eye looked like a Tahitian sunset, both his arms were covered with bloody scratches, and his shirt was shredded. "You guys gotta help me!" he begged.

The woman snarled at him and lashed out with her foot. "Dog!" she muttered as McCoy cringed and jumped back behind the cop again. "You will die for this!"

"Nooooo!!" Kellar screamed. "This is *not fair!* I refuse to accept this!"

"Get *offa* me, will you?" Zalman snapped. "No kidding, Kellar, I've had it with you!"

"Is something wrong, sir?" Pete the cop asked politely. "This gentleman here," he said, jerking a thumb at McCoy, "he said there was a problem in this house. Didn't believe him at first, but when we heard the shot and the breaking glass we figured we'd better look into his story. Somebody wanna tell me what's going on here?" His voice was soft and uncertain as he peered in through the screen.

"Get off!" Zalman howled. "I mean it, Kellar! Yeah, there's something wrong," he barked at the two cops. "This idiot's trying to kill me!"

"It's a lie!" Kellar howled. "We're rehearsing. . . ."

The two cops stared at each other. Willie, who had the lined good looks of a soap opera star, scratched his cheek and looked puzzled. "Gee, what show?" he asked Kellar. "I done some technical advice for cop shows back when Jack Webb was still alive," he explained to Pete. "He was a great man, Mr. Webb."

"Yeah, wasn't he?" Pete agreed. "He lectured at the academy when I was a rookie. Gave me his autograph, too. I thought he was a very impressive person. Had a real sense of his own inner integrity."

"That's it!" Zalman yelled, giving Kellar a knee in the

stomach. "I can't take it anymore! Kill me, go ahead, put me out of my misery. I can't go on!"

"Uhhhhhh!" went Kellar.

"C'mon, Zally," McCoy urged. "Don't be that way. . . ."

"My brothers are violent men," the woman purred. "My honor will be avenged."

"I mean it!" Zalman yelled. "I'm through! Life's too tough! I can't take it anymore. Get this dork *offa* me, will you, Dean, so I can go home and die in peace? He's gonna crush my rib cage here!"

The two cops looked at each other and Pete shrugged. "I dunno, Willie, whaddayou think?" he said again.

"I dunno, Pete. Let's just run 'em all in and the captain can sort it out when he comes on duty tonight," Willie said brightly. "That way, you and me'll be in the clear. Besides, tonight's my bowling league and I don't wanna work late. . . ."

"Jerry! Thank God I found you!" It was Earnest, standing at the door of the lanai. "What the hell are you doing on the floor? Kellar, get the hell off my son!"

"Drop dead," Kellar moaned. "He's trying to kill me!"

"Me! I'm not trying to kill you! *You're* trying to kill *me,*" Zalman snapped. "Dad!! What are you doing here! How did you find me?"

Earnest walked over and gave Kellar a pop behind the ear.

"Owwwww," the producer moaned. "You hurt me!"

"Drop dead yourself," Earnest said. "Easy, sonny. After you left the house, me and Lydia got to thinking—"

"Lydia can't think," Kellar snorted.

Earnest popped him again, harder. "Naughty, naughty," he said mildly. "Mustn't say mean things about a lady.

Yeah, we were worried about you, so we sat down and tried to figure out where you'd gone and here I am. Marty's dead, Caldwell's dead, and nobody knows where Bland is, so I thought I'd take a shot and come over here."

"How'd you find my house?" Kellar whined. "I'm a very private person! I even have an unlisted zip code!"

"Arnie Thrasher helped. He's a great guy, Jer," Earnest said. "You've underestimated him in the past. He got Kellar's address for me and here I am. In the nick of time, I'd say."

"Oh, God, will somebody get this guy *offa* me, please?" Zalman said. "Anything, I'll do anything. I've had enough!" he shrieked. "I'm a lawyer! I'm telling you, this man is a killer! I'm a lawyer and I oughta know!"

The two cops nodded at each other. "That's it," Willie said, shaking his head vehemently. "You guys are going in, all of you. Y'know, Pete, used to be, you didn't see this kind of thing in Beverly Hills. I'll get those two, Pete. You keep an eye on this pair," he said as he stepped into the room and unsnapped his handcuffs from the back of his belt. "When I started in as a rookie, about your age, this was a high-class town. That's why me and the wife moved here. Quiet. Good schools. Now, I dunno. Neighborhood's goin' to hell along with the rest of the city. I tell you that me and the wife are thinkin' about selling the building and moving up north next year?" he said as he flipped Kellar off Zalman and briskly clipped his hands together behind his back. "Maybe Pocatello. I got my twenty years in. Why should I put up with this kinda thing?"

Pete shook his head as he handcuffed McCoy and the Mexican woman together. As soon as she got next to McCoy she lashed out with her foot again, and this time she caught him a good one on the shin. "No, you didn't,"

Pete said. "I didn't know you owned that building. You got any vacant units?"

Willie shook his head. "Full up," he said. "We always are. It's the Beverly Hills address they like."

"Pocatello's supposed to be real pretty. Cold there, isn't it?' Pete asked.

"The weather's a problem," Willie said. "The wife's got arthritis."

"Owwww!" McCoy yelled at the woman. "That hurt! Lay offa me, will you? I didn't do anything to you!"

"You will die for this," she said darkly. "I have many brothers. . . ."

Willie unsnapped a second pair of cuffs and fumbled for Zalman's wrists. "This is too much," Zalman said. He put his head down on the carpet, closed his eyes, and inhaled a snootful of dust.

"You can't do this to me!" Kellar screamed, wriggling around on the floor like a beached turtle. "I'm in television!"

"Shut up," Zalman advised. "That's my advice to you as a lawyer, you murdering geek. Just shut up!"

"Okay," Pete said, brushing off his hands. "Now you two boys are going to get up off the floor and then we're all going to walk outside in one neat line like polite ladies and gentlemen, aren't we? And we're all going to get into the car, nice and easy. . . ."

"I'll call Lucille," Earnest said. "She'll know what to do."

"Great," Zalman moaned. "Just great. You know, I always wondered what a fate worse than death would be like," he mused as he lay on the floor of Tom Kellar's lanai with his hands cuffed behind his back, staring at the soles of Kellar's feet. "Now I know."

"I NEED A VACATION. THIS HAS BEEN THE WORST WEEK OF my life," Zalman told McCoy as they walked down the steps of the Beverly Hills Municipal Courthouse Building and out to Burton Way. "I mean, the worst! One hundred percent the worst!"

"Look at it this way, Jer," McCoy said sagely. "At least you weren't killed."

"No thanks to you, McCoy!"

"I made a mistake! One mistake!"

"You went in the wrong house, Dean! I'd call that a pretty big mistake, wouldn't you? I mean, there I was, risking life and limb trying to nail a vicious killer to the wall, and I expected you to come barging in the back door the minute I gave you the high sign. You forgot the high sign, Dean! Right? Worse than that, you were at the wrong house! You were next door getting beaten up by an enraged housekeeper. A big guy like you! It's embarrassing! Under the circumstances, I'd call that a big mistake, Dean!"

McCoy obviously felt unjustly maligned. "Look, Jer," he explained reasonably, "I run down between the two houses and all of a sudden there's this little maze thing back there, with hedges going in every direction? And to-piary stuff cut like weird animals? It was insane! So I had to make a decision right there on the spot. I didn't have time to cogitate, I didn't have time to make an informed, well-reasoned choice! I ran down the path that looked like it went to Kellar's joint, and I end up in the middle of Carmelita's herb garden back there! All laid out, like in brick planters? She's out there with a pair of scissors the size of Paul Bunyan's ax snipping parsley, sage, rosemary, and thyme, or whatever the hell it is this time of year, and humming 'Cielito Lindo'! So when she sees me she thinks I'm the mad rapist of Beverly Hills and takes off after me with the scissors yelling at me in Spanish! It was a nightmare!" McCoy shuddered.

"I coulda used her next door, Dean! On Kellar!" Zalman was disgruntled, hot, tired, and dirty. His jacket was destroyed, he had the beginnings of a swell migraine, he felt like he'd been mauled by a lion, and he'd spent the last three hours explaining to the Beverly Hills police why he and Tom Kellar had been rolling around on the floor trying to kill each other. Kellar continued to claim that they were rehearsing for a hot new reality-based sitcom he was breaking in for the Fox network's fall season, but even the Beverly Hills cops wouldn't buy that story.

Finally, Kellar was hauled off to have his head examined by a local shrink, but it wasn't until Captain Arnold Thrasher himself, in all his porky beauty, had vouched for him that Zalman was sprung. Thrasher! Thrasher! It was more than embarrassing. It was humiliating.

"Hi, honey!" Marie called, honking the horn of Zalman's Mercedes. "How was jail in Beverly Hills?"

"The spinach salad wasn't bad, but the mousse was terrible!" Zalman told her as he walked over to the curb. "I had to send it back." Rutherford stuck his head out of the rear window and began to bark. Earnest got out of the passenger side and ran up to Zalman and McCoy.

"Jerry! Am I glad to see you!" he said, slapping his son on the back. "I didn't want to miss you! Get out of jail okay, huh? I made a few calls. . . . You did a great job, Jer! I'm proud of you! And so is Lydia."

"Pookie!" Lydia called from the back seat of the car.

"We're going to miss our plane! Hi, Jerry, I'm glad they let you out of jail." She waved. "I just can't thank you enough for everything you did. You were wonderful. Are you sure you're all right?" she asked anxiously.

Rutherford continued to bark.

"Simply grand," Zalman said as she walked up to the car. "Shut up, Rutherford. Did I hear you say something about missing a plane? Who's going where?"

Earnest and Lydia looked at each other and smiled happily, their faces filled with the petal-soft bloom of new love in spring. "We're getting married," Earnest said proudly. "Got a plane to Vegas in an hour, gonna get hitched at last. I made a few calls, we got the bridal suite at the Desert Inn all set up. It's gonna be great," he said. "Then we're having a honeymoon for a week, then ba-bing! Back to Florida. Lydia's gonna look for a new partner to beef up the act, I'm gonna learn bridge. Sounds great, huh?"

"Congratulations, Dad," Zalman said as he and Earnest shook hands. "You too, Lydia. I hope you like being a Zalman. I swear I'll never call you Mom."

A car came screeching up to the curb. It was Bland's gigantic right-hand-drive Rolls, Lucille at the wheel. "Jerry! Everything's okay! He's back! You get out of jail all right? I made a few calls," she said as she abandoned the huge car, motor still running, and ran to her brother's side.

Phil Hanning was in the passenger seat, a twenty-four-karat smile on his handsome face. "Hi, Jer," he called, waving out the window. "How'd you like jail? I got great news!"

Zalman ignored him. "Who's back?" he asked as Lucille planted a big kiss on his cheek.

Rutherford continued to bark.

"Bland! Who else!" Lucille heaved a sigh of relief, wiping imaginary sweat from her forehead. "But listen to what Phil's got to say, will you? It's simply unbelievable!"

Hanning stuck his head out the car window. "Me and Isobel sold the Jack the Zipper franchise to some rich Arab investors," he said proudly. "I made a fortune, and I didn't even have to put up any dough! Is that great? There's gonna be a Jack the Zipper in every mall in the civilized world! These guys liked it so much they just bought the concept! I love selling concepts! I never realized you could sell concepts before, I thought you had to work for a living! Me and Isobel are so busy thinking up another one I don't think she's got the time to be your cleaning consultant anymore, Jer. Yeah," Hanning said dreamily, "I'm gonna sink it all into the Wild West Museum and make another fortune! Two fortunes! I'll have two fortunes!"

Lucille shrugged. "Can we call it dumb luck?" she whispered. "I'll try to skim some off the top and sink it into an apartment building, but it's gonna be tough," she said with a laugh. "What the hey, Jer, it's only money, right?"

"Congratulations, Phil," Zalman said, grinning. "Now that you're a rich man, you take me to lunch, okay? It'll be a first for you."

Rutherford was still barking.

"Great!" Hanning said. "I'd love it."

"So where was Bland all this time while you were tearing out your hair?" Zalman asked Lucille.

"He was up at Tassajara, that Zen meditation hot-tub joint near San Francisco? He was in a cosmic trance for three days and he claims he's had a vision of the true world path to peace. He says he's going to walk the length and breadth of the country wearing laurel leaves and a loincloth until peace breaks out! He's flipped, but completely! Oh, God, whadamygonna doooooo with him! He wants to have his tattoos lasered off! He says he's changed his life, his entire consciousness has been raised to the fifth chakra, whatever the hell that is, and now he's gonna fight, fight, fight for peace! He thinks he's some kind of spiritual soldier on the front lines of life! And the worst part is, he's got this goofy idea he doesn't want to be a musician anymore! It's worse than horrible! I'm killing myself first thing in the morning! Whaddamygonnnnadooooo with him! . . ."

"Relax, Lucille. As McCoy here would say, 'go with the flow,'" Zalman said, jerking a thumb at his hapless pal. "Call up that kid from *Rolling Stone* and tell him you got a hot story for him, a media breakthrough. You can call it 'Bland's Change of Heart,' 'Bland's Big Dream,' something like that. Social justice is very trendy these days, you'll make a fortune. Another fortune," he said, "since Phil's already made one for the day."

"Oooooooohhh, I like it!" Lucille said, her eyes glowing. "I like it mucho mucho! Jerry, you're a genius!"

"I know," Zalman said modestly. "But look, big news. Dad and Lydia are getting married. They're flying to Vegas in an hour."

"Forty-five minutes," Marie called. "Lucille, let's talk next week, we'll go shopping! Jerry, darling, get in the car, we gotta go!"

"Oh, how fabulous!" Lucille cried as she ran over to the car and kissed Lydia on the cheek. "Welcome to the family!" she said. "How do you like it so far?"

"Honey, get in the car!" Marie said. "We've got to get going or Earnest and Lydia'll miss their plane."

"Lucille, do something with that idiot McCoy," Zalman told his sister as he jumped into the Mercedes next to Marie. "Take him home and get Phil to throw a good feed into him. Then take him out back and drown him in the pool."

"Sure," Lucille cried as Marie peeled away from the curb. "Bye, guys! Good luck!"

Marie made it out to the airport in record time, weaving her way through the traffic on the San Diego South like she was at Indianapolis. "Oh, Jerry," she sighed as she squealed to a stop in front of American Airlines. "Thank heavens this is all over and we can relax!" she said as she jumped out of the car and ran around back to unlock the trunk. Rutherford saw an enemy cocker spaniel in a traveling kennel and began to bark furiously.

"Rutherford, I'm warning you," Zalman said. "You could be replaced by a ferret, pal."

"Lydia," Marie called as everyone got out of the car, "your scarf, don't forget your—here it is, dear," she said as she and Lydia embraced. "I'm sorry we haven't been able to spend any time together, have lunch or do anything fun, but maybe next trip, okay?"

"It's a date, Marie." Lydia smiled. "And thanks so much for everything, I can't tell you what a load it is off my—"

"Don't worry about a thing," Marie said. "It'll be perfectly fine."

"Good-bye, Jer," Earnest said as he hugged his son. "You're a great guy. I gotta say, I'm proud you're my son."

"Thanks, Dad," Zalman said as he and Earnest embraced again warmly. "I'm glad everything worked out. . . . Shut *up*, Rutherford!" Zalman bellowed as Lydia threw herself into his arms.

"Oh, Jerry, I'll just never be able to thank you enough! You saved my life. My mother thanks you, Ernie thanks you, I thank you—"

"It was nothing, Lydia," Zalman lied. "Piece of cake."

Earnest tipped the porter and he and Lydia ran into the terminal, waving and blowing kisses as they went.

Zalman got back in the car. "God, I'm so tired," he told

Marie as she pulled smoothly away from the terminal and out into the traffic. "I just want to go home and sleep for a week. Then, when I wake up, I think we'll take that trip to Hawaii we've been planning, huh, doll?" He leaned back against the seat. He felt himself falling asleep. "I'm gonna close my eyes, nap a minute or two, okay?" he asked Marie.

"Sure, darling," she said gently. "I'd love to go to Hawaii. After all that wedding nonsense, I need a vacation, too!"

Zalman fell asleep in a matter of seconds, and when he woke up, Marie was pulling the Mercedes into his driveway. As he got out of the car, he realized that he felt a lot better. As usual, a little nap had miraculous restorative powers, and Zalman knew he was on top again. Life was back to normal. His father was gone, Marie was home, tomorrow he'd go into the office and attack his overflowing desk. Once again, he felt like he was in control, the Alexander Haig of Beverly Hills.

He trotted toward the house, Marie and Rutherford right behind him, and stood in the golden glow of the mosquito light over the door, fumbling in his pockets for his keys.

"Oh, honey," Marie said. "By the way, there's something I meant to tell you on the way home, but you were asleep so I didn't have time. . . ."

Suspicion nibbled at the back of Zalman's neck. "For God's sake, Marie, don't tell me something I don't want to hear, okay? I'm a weak man, I've been through a lot, my heart can't stand the strain. . . ." he said as he slipped the key into the lock.

Zalman opened the front door, and as soon as he stepped inside he realized what Marie was going to tell him. The living room was a shambles. The drapes were hanging off the rods, ripped in a thousand places, lamps were knocked over, and there was a very, very bad smell in the air. "What the hell!" Zalman yelled angrily as the full extent of the damage to his newly redecorated living room hit him.

Suddenly, Sergeant Pepper came hurtling through the air and landed on top of Zalman. "I told Lydia I'd baby-sit him," Zalman heard Marie explain as he struggled with the monkey on his back. "But it's only until after the honeymoon," she went on. "I'm going to Federal Express him down to Lydia in a week or so! Just as soon as they get back to Florida! You don't mind, do you, Jerry darling?" she asked anxiously. "He's such a cute little woojums, and Rutherford simply adores him. . . ."

Zalman felt Sergeant Pepper's hot monkey breath panting in his ear as the viselike grip of his creepy little monkey paws tightened around his neck. *"Aarrggghhh!!!"* Jerry Zalman shrieked. *"Aarrggghhh!!!"*